For Angi

We The People

WE THE PEOPLE...

Preamble

January 20, 2001, 9:20 AM MST

Ben raised the well-used mug to his mouth for that first taste of morning coffee. Over the past twenty years, this ritual had changed little, except these days, the cup contained decaf, something his doctor had insisted on.

As the senior reporter for the *Rocky Mountain Post*, Ben had the privilege of choosing which stories he would cover. Standing here in the morning light, quietly drinking his coffee, he could picture the zoo-like atmosphere in Washington, DC today and knew without a doubt he had made the right choice. Life would be crazy enough here in Denver. Between the local reaction to today's inauguration of this millennium's first president and the one-month anniversary of the execution of Tim McVeigh, he would not be bored. With most of the editorial staff and four other reporters making the trip to the beltway, his chances for an early day were slim.

He stood in the paper's "wire room," a stuffy ten-by-ten all-glass enclosure filled with rows of noisy electronic gadgets. The three teletypes connected to UPl, AP and Reuters chugged out story after story from all over the world, a never-ending supply of war, death, and destruction. Tickers from the New York Stock Exchange and Chicago Commodities Market kept track of the country's economic pulse, four brand new fax machines, two of which were tied to Fax-Net, a worldwide fax distribution network. A dated shortwave radio for emergencies, plus a Pentium IV PC used to power the paper's web server, rounded out the collection. It was a strange assortment of old and new technology. Perhaps mirroring what modem newspapers had become.

Of course, there was still some delay in getting the words in print, but information from around the world was at their fingertips almost instantly, thousands of tiny wires running through the wall, little electronic reporters peering into all corners of the globe. Long gone were the days of endless hours on telephones, painfully prying information from anyone who could put together a sentence, provide a lead, or confirm a fact.

Small white scraps of paper littered the floor by his feet. They were the unimportant stories, torn away from the big news that sandwiched them. News castoffs, not meaningful enough to print, events that had shaped or destroyed peoples' lives, left on the floor to be swept away overnight and recycled into newspaper, so the process could begin again the next day.

Maybe it wasn't right, but to the rest of the world, an event wasn't significant until someone like Ben reported it. He had reported on thousands of stories over the years, a few important ones, but most were small human stories of life and death.

Ben hadn't avoided the big stories. On the contrary, for countless days and nights, he had waited in this very spot for "The Story." That once-in-a-lifetime event that shaped or changed the world. He'd watched as other reporters got their big break, lucky enough to have been in the right place at the right time. He believed it would have to be his turn someday. Something or someone had placed him here for a reason.

He had no way of knowing it, but Ben was about to be in the right place at the wrong time, come face-to-face with "his" story, and he would play a major part in how history would record it.

January 20, 2001. Even as Ben scribbled the date on his pad, he had to force himself to write 2000. After fifty years of writing nineteen-something, making the change still required some thought. He chuckled to himself at how little the world had changed with the turn of the century, as the violent changes predicted for the new millennium had not materialized.

Prophets, clerics, and skeptics alike planned for great change, floods, global warming, famine, computer meltdowns, and even the Second Coming. But the world continued largely unchanged. Plodding along like it had for millions of years, apparently unaware of man's calendar or superstitions.

Scanning the overnight copy, his experienced eye searched for the local hook. "Reporter lingo for a local angle to a national story," he said aloud, smiling as he recalled his wife's cute way of looking at him when he used this strange language. Repeating it "in English" for her had become a habit too hard for him to break.

Most of today's stories dealt with the big event about to take place in Washington DC, endless background and filler on the new president-elect, his humble upbringing and meteoric rise in national politics. It was pretty boring stuff to Ben, considering it had been covered repeatedly for the last two months. It wasn't extraordinary that so much ink had been used on last November's affair.

The 2000 Presidential election surprised even long-time politicos. The large gains by Republicans during 1996, and then the surprising losses of 1998 in both the Senate and the House, led most talking heads to conclude the public would undoubtedly have to be won over anew for Republicans to enter the White House in 2000.

The tactical mistake made by the party was their conviction that Vice President Gere would be the Democratic nominee. After Clayton's messy impeachment hearings in 1999, millions of Republican Party dollars were pumped into a well-scripted media blitz questioning Gere's involvement with various scandals in the Clayton administration and characterizing his environmental views as extreme. Their strategy worked well, and his public numbers fell swiftly. However, the backlash against their underhanded and expensive tactics became a liability for them as well.

No one, even the Democrats, envisioned that nearly overnight, a state senator from Michigan could become America's favorite son. Following his astonishing wins in the New Hampshire primary and Iowa caucus, Senator John F. Strugel gained national support and, more importantly, campaign dollars. The one-hundred-dollar cap imposed on all individual and business contributions by the 1999 Campaign Reform Act, something the Republicans had promised to the electorate in the 1998 campaign following the hearings by Senator Thompson in 1997, leveled the playing field in this election.

Ben covered the candidates as they made their Colorado swing, part of the exciting new super west primary involving eight states. Senator Strugel spent thirty minutes in Ben's office mapping out his plan for a new America. Throughout the interview, Ben was impressed by his ability to preserve eye contact and answer tough questions. He did not look or talk like a politician.

Large numbers of voters in Colorado and across America viewed Senator Strugel as a self-contained man with no ties to big business or PACs. Someone who could make the burdensome choices facing any mortal who takes the most thankless job in America. After three hard-fought votes on the floor of the Democratic Convention, Strugel was their nominee. Strugel immediately chose a popular southern Democratic Governor to fill the vice-presidential spot on the ticket, a move to help mend the wounds of that hard-fought primary and convention. It was a total non-beltway ticket, and the country was excited at the possibilities.

Last September, the *Rocky Mountain Post* endorsed John F. Strugel for president. He was elected in November with a tremendous electoral margin and garnered more than fifty percent of the popular vote in thirty-nine of the fifty states. It was the essence of fairy tales, and the country's mood was inspired.

However, his honeymoon with the voters would be condensed. The bloom came off the rose quickly. Word leaked out from the president-elect's camp regarding his first order of business, a complete pardon of former President Clayton. All three indictments from his grand jury testimony in 1998 would be dropped. Senator Strugel had refused to discuss the subject prior to the election, and most voters felt betrayed, a sick feeling forming in the pit of their stomachs, their great hope for a new kind of leader dashed in less than sixty days.

In 1974, when President Ford announced his pardon of President Nixon, he spoke at length about ending the country's long bout of suffering over

Watergate. Attempting to calm the political waters, the president-elect issued a statement impersonating Ford's sentiment.

"It's time for this great country to move forward. Let's concentrate our efforts and energy on the future, not the past. Nothing further would be served by this self-defacing political exercise."

Unlike the primary, Strugel was beginning to sound and act much like a politician, bowing to the pressure of the party, and the American people were not at all pleased with the sudden change. Reaction was swift from nearly all sectors of the country. Demonstrations, editorials, and calls for a new constitutional amendment to prevent presidential pardons saturated the news.

One of the most disturbing convulsions came from a Western Montana militia group headed by retired Army General Harvey Boyle. General Boyle started by renaming his group the American Revolutionary Army, commonly referred to as ARA.

Sporting his camouflage uniform, red beret, and flanked by half a dozen M-16 toting "Minute Militiamen," General Boyle was indeed a daunting figure. "The ARA will resist all attempts to ignore or rewrite the constitution with whatever means necessary. Freedom-loving Americans should unite and prepare for the coming struggle with tyranny. We do not want to wage a battle, but in 1776, our founding fathers did not want a revolution either. They were forced to fight a corrupt government as we are now," General Boyle proclaimed at his first and only press conference, held in front of a log building in rural Montana.

Most Americans paid little attention to Boyle. However, Ben's instincts told him to pay a lot of attention to the general and the ARA. Ben's FBI contacts told him the ARA was conducting paramilitary-style maneuvers all over America. Yet, the Bureau claimed to be hampered in their investigation by a ruling from the Supreme Court last June, striking down the Anti-Terrorism Bill of 1996 as unconstitutional. Something General Boyle lobbied hard for.

Ben's intuition was usually keen, and General Boyle made him uneasy. Ben planned to make the trip to Montana sometime soon to see for himself what the movement was all about.

Finally, a story with a local hook caught his attention. Whenever an event draws a majority of top federal government leaders to gather at one site, national security requires that at least one member remains in another locale. The fortunate cabinet member not attending today's inauguration was Secretary of Health and Human Services, Claire Louise Young. Secretary Young was home here in Denver, visiting her family and opening a new federally subsidized family health clinic in Lower Downtown Denver.

Ben made a note of the time and place. 10:05 a.m. MST at Sixteenth and Market, almost the exact time President-elect Strugel would be taking the oath of office in Washington. Ben would not waste his time watching the inaugural speech, keenly aware that the exact text printed in block letters from the UPI and AP wire services would be on his desk when he returned to his office.

Forty-five minutes later, Ben stood in the crisp Denver air waiting for Secretary Young to arrive. The temperature was twenty-four degrees, but the bright sunshine made the mid-winter Colorado air feel a lot warmer. Steam danced skyward from the paper cup in his hand filled with hot coffee. It tasted even better than it smelled. Purchased from a nearby street vendor, Ben was confident it wasn't decaf but also confident that his doctor didn't need to know.

The standard-issue black government limousine flanked by six Denver motorcycle cops made the turn from Market Street into the parking lot of the Lower Downtown Family Clinic. How motorcades with police escorts and no traffic were always ten minutes late was something Ben had never been able to understand. As the car door opened, a man wearing a small flesh-colored receiver in his ear and mirrored sunglasses exited first. Once satisfied with the lot's appearance and security, he motioned to the second agent waiting in the car, and Secretary Young stepped out.

Young had chosen the government over any kind of personal life and never married. Ben hadn't had the opportunity to meet her in person and was pleasantly surprised by her stunning presence. She was a tall and graceful Afro-American woman in her late forties with warm features and a lively gate. As she approached the small group of reporters gathered with Ben, she effortlessly slipped off her black gloves and tucked them into her coat.

"Good morning, ladies and gentlemen. Are you all here to see my last official act?" she asked.

In thirty minutes or so, they all knew she would be "Former" Secretary Young, swept out to make room for President Strugel's new Cabinet. The reporters responded with just the right amount of polite laughter. Ben had been hanging back in the crowd enjoying his coffee but now worked his way to the front of the group, a process made easier by the respect he had earned from his fellow reporters.

Pad ready, Ben began to ask his first question.

He never got the chance…

A dark flash behind the secretary caught his eye. Both agents were at a dead run toward her. Instinctually Ben looked around for the threat that caused them to act so suddenly, hoping to identify the source. He saw nothing.

His mind flashed to the videos of President Reagan, John F. Kennedy, and Lee Harvey Oswald being shot, all in super slow motion, frame by frame, frozen in time. Would people be watching his movements and actions for years to come? Questioning what he had done, what he hadn't? Would he be an eyewitness to murder?

Still, he saw no one else moving toward her. The first agent to reach Secretary Young took her by the arm and whispered something in her ear. Her face went flush, and she spun around, staggering toward the car.

It wasn't until then that Ben noticed the second agent pointing his MAC-10 at the crowd.

Denver police officers had drawn their guns and taken up positions between the reporters and the now idling limousine. Ben fought an urge to turn and run. Being in harm's way was for the young agile reporters, not someone like him. But there was nowhere to go and no time to get there.

Backing toward the car, the second agent jumped in after the secretary and quickly slammed the door. Sirens and squealing tires filled the early morning mountain air.

Stunned and totally confused, Ben turned quickly to his left and plowed straight into the barrel of a 12-gauge shotgun held tightly by his friend of more than ten years, Denver Police Sergeant Jim Arno. "Jim, do you know what the fuck is going on?" Ben barked, almost shouting.

"Jesus, Ben. It's Washington," he responded, his eyes wide and glazed over. Ben had never heard his friend's voice so shaky, and it chilled him to the bone.

"What about Washington? What?" Ben pleaded.

"It's gone. I mean…it's all gone." Jim's voice had lowered to a haunting whisper. "Shit. Listen, Ben. I gotta follow the motorcade. Do me a favor and go somewhere safe. I'll call you later." With that, Jim turned and disappeared into his squad car.

Ben stood staring after his friend, unable to formulate words to call out to him. He couldn't remember ever being so cold.

ARTICLE I

Denver, Colorado, January 20, 2001, 10:12 AM MST

Why today, of all days, had Ben not remembered to bring along his cell phone? It was bulky and not easy to carry, but at least he could call the office. The fear and questions swamping his usually well-organized mind numbed him to the rest of the world. The agonizing wait for the Regional Transportation Authority mall bus that would return him to his office seemed endless and unbearable. Transfixed, Ben looked straight past the faces of other commuters as they talked and laughed.

"What had Jim meant? 'It's all gone…'" Ben mumbled aloud.

"What's gone, pal?" asked a well-dressed man in his mid-thirties standing next to Ben. "What's gone?" the man repeated when he got no response from Ben.

"Uh, well, I don't know. It's just what Jim said, and, you know, I can't believe…" Ben's voice trailed off. He knew it couldn't possibly make sense to this curious bystander. Hell, who was he kidding? It didn't make any sense to him either.

The shuttle doors swooshed open, and Ben stumbled inside. He searched for a corner where he might be alone, hoping to quiet his mind until he could get more information. However, it didn't work. The questions came too fast, and his mind raced over the possibilities.

Where were they taking Secretary Young? To Washington? No, Washington was gone. Gone. What did that mean? Had the new president been assassinated? Jim said Washington was gone, but that couldn't be. He had to be wrong.

It was all a big overreaction. Ben had seen it too many times. A rumor starts, and someone goes overboard, pushing the panic button.

He would probably be back at the clinic this afternoon to finish what they had started this morning.

The fifteen-block bus ride seemed to last forever, each lurching start and stop, the endless wait as people slowly pushed on and off the shuttle, a huge contrast in quiet and the noise as the busy street spilled in through the open door. Ben's tension governor was close to the breaking point.

He unconsciously reached into his front shirt pocket for a cigarette. Almost eight years since he quit the nasty habit, but in times of stress like this, the instinct always returned. He found the package of spearmint gum that had replaced his urge for nicotine and placed a stick quickly into his mouth. When the doors to the bus finally opened at his stop, he stepped out and spit the gum into a nearby trashcan. Chewing it without removing the paper wasn't the best way to enjoy its flavor.

Relief washed over Ben that the morning rush hour had subsided, and he was alone in the elevator. The ride to his office on the twenty-third floor would be a quiet one.

He stared at his image reflecting back at him from the mirrored doors as they closed. Fifty-eight years had taken a toll on his features, but his hair remained full and the same natural brown matching his eyes. Thanks to his daily workout and a much better diet, he had trimmed fifteen pounds off his six-foot frame in the last year. The same fifteen he gained when he stopped smoking and started enjoying food again. Not that bad, he thought. Most people guessed he was in his late forties, and he was definitely in better shape than when he first arrived at the paper.

His memory of that first ride in this elevator almost twenty years before remained vivid in his mind. At thirty-eight, becoming a cub reporter was something his family and wife deemed "completely nuts." That, however, hadn't prevented them from becoming his biggest supporters.

With sweat running down his face and out of breath, Ben had been nearly ten minutes late for his ten o'clock interview with City Editor Don Bannon. At that time, Ben was scared out of his mind. Word of Bannon's gruff manner, and Ben's lack of experience, meant the likelihood of a short and painful interview lay ahead. Misgivings and common sense aside, he straightened his tie and stood tall in front of the doors as they opened.

It didn't look at all like he had imagined it so many times. The city room wasn't wide open, filled with old typewriters pounding away. Instead, small cubicles and computer terminals crammed the space as far as you could see.

It was early 1981, and Ronald Reagan had been president for just over two months. Denver was in the midst of a strong growth cycle, largely due to the oil and gas industry. An Arab oil embargo in the seventies meant wealth and prosperity for domestic oil production, and Denver was at the center of that frenzied activity. The paper was growing with the city, adding two new local reporters to the staff. Ben's journalism minor from Colorado State in the mid-sixties, combined with his Colorado roots, edged him through the preliminary stages of selection.

Now the decisive moment was at hand. The formal interview with Bannon. His stomach rumbled loudly, and Ben cursed at himself under his breath for not taking time to eat something for breakfast.

"Are you standing there taking up my air for a reason?" the voice belonging to Don Bannon boomed through Ben's ears. "Because you look lost as hell."

Ben was surprised Bannon's desk was right outside the elevator but discovered later that he liked to keep a close eye on the comings and goings of the staff. Rumor had it that Bannon could hear the door to the stairwell open from some one hundred feet away and would ride down the elevator to confront whoever was trying to slip away without his blessing.

Some people fit nicely into their stereotypes, and Bannon was the typical city editor. Early fifties, balding, thirty pounds overweight, a burning cigarette in the ashtray at any given time, and clothes you were sure he had slept in for at least a week.

Looking and feeling like a complete idiot, Ben thrust one hand out for Bannon to shake and the other holding his resume. "Uh, I'm Ben Blaser," he stammered.

"Blazer? I thought it was Blesser," Bannon said, frowning.

"No, sir. It's pronounced blazer like the truck." Ben had become accustomed to people mispronouncing his name.

Bannon smiled almost uncomfortably. "Whatever. We can always change that." Completely ignoring Ben's offered hand, Bannon ripped the resume out of Ben's hand.

"Sit down. I don't have all day." Bannon's gruff voice demanded compliance, and Ben sank into the straight back chair facing Bannon's desk.

Ben watched for any sign from this hardened news veteran's face, but he gave nothing away. After several agonizing minutes of silent reading and unpleasant facial expressions, Bannon looked up. "So, this would be your first job at a newspaper?"

"Yes, sir," Ben responded promptly, attempting to hide his fear that the worst was about to happen.

"Good. Then I won't have to break you of any bad habits." Bannon leaned over the side of the desk to throw Ben's resume in the overflowing trash. "Stop and see Ellen in personnel downstairs. You start tomorrow night, ten sharp. Oh, and by the way, you've already had your one time to be late. If it happens again, I'll have your ass back in the employment line before you can spit."

Not totally confident he had heard him correctly, Ben struggled to his feet. "Thanks," he said in an abnormally squeaky voice.

Bannon, who was already on the telephone swearing loudly at someone, once again ignored Ben's attempt at a handshake.

As Ben left Bannon's office that day, he wondered what he had gotten himself into, working for this tyrant. But over the years, he and Don had become close friends. Both of their sons now worked for the *Chicago Evening News*, a great newspaper. Ben's only regret was that Don hadn't lived to see it. He died of a massive heart attack five years ago, sitting in his chair at the paper, just two weeks before his retirement party. Ben still missed him every day.

The lurch of the elevator stopping on the twenty-third floor brought Ben back to reality, and he stepped quickly off into the city room. His eyes scanned hastily for signs of activity or a familiar face. He tried not to think of the fate of his colleagues in Washington or whether he would ever see them again. All the cubicles were dark, with only the sounds of ringing telephones and the muffled voices from a television in the back conference room breaking the silence.

"Where the hell is everyone?"

Ben attempted to pass by the door to the wire room, but instinct drew him inside. Nearly all the teletype terminals were completely silent, it was something he hadn't heard before, and large goose bumps rose on the back of his neck. Out of habit, he checked UPI first.

The last entry read…

FLASH…FLASH…FLASH... WASHINGTON DC 9:58 AM EST, AN EXPLOSION HAS LEVELED WASHINGTON DC. MOST, INCLUDING PRESIDENT-ELECT, FEARED DEAD.

WASHINGTON DC - INITIAL REPORTS INDICATE COMPLETE DESTRUCTION OF THE WHITE HOUSE, PENTAGON AND CAPITOL HILL.

SOURCES SPECULATE MOST, IF NOT ALL, ATTENDING THE PRESIDENTIAL INAUGURATION WERE KILLED. THE EXPLOSION WAS REPORTED AS A NUC ... end transmission ... connection lost… 08:06 MST.

Ben read it three times. The words on the paper remained the same, and still, it didn't seem real. How could it be?

He had been working the day of the Oklahoma City bombing and recalled the disbelief as he read the copy.

However, that was a building. One building. This was an entire city. The nation's capital.

He felt sick to his stomach.

"Where's the rest of the story? Why isn't New York transmitting anymore?" Before Ben could think of an answer, he suddenly realized the room was no longer quiet. Frantic, he searched for the source of the noise. It was an incoming fax from Faxnet services.

Ben thought about just leaving the room, sensing he was unable to digest more vile news, but somehow his feet moved one in front of the other until he had crossed the room. He stood for a moment staring blankly at the red alert light flashing on the machine.

Holding his breath, he reached down and plucked out the first page, and began to read.

FOR IMMEDIATE RELEASE

TO ALL CITIZENS OF THE UNITED FREE STATES OF AMERICA

We, the people, in order to form a more perfect government, have, at exactly 12:00 PM EST, taken such action as to ensure the return to our original constitutional government. Criminal government leaders have been eliminated from our landscape. Atomic explosive devices have been detonated in Washington DC, New York City, Chicago, Los Angeles, and Denver.

Destruction of these cities was necessary to facilitate a breakdown of the corrupt financial and media industries. With the help of the United Nations, these traitors have attempted to implement a one-world government upon an unsuspecting American population.

The American Revolutionary Army regrets the loss of innocent lives due to this action. However, returning to a constitutional-based government is imperative if we are to save our country before it is too late.

Therefore, be it ordered that:

The current federal government is hereby disbanded. All state militias should take up arms and resist any attempt to reestablish a federal presence. State conventions will be called within six months to determine what powers (if any) will be restored to a new smaller federal authority.

Members of the federal armies will immediately turn over control of all weapons and facilities to the closest state militia commander.

American naval forces at sea will port at once. Military personnel stationed outside the borders of the United Free States are recalled and will stand down upon their return.

State martial law is in effect. Any treasonous act against the constitution of the United Free States or sovereign state constitutions will be dealt with immediately and harshly.

National defense will be the sole responsibility of the ARA. General Harvey Boyle will serve as Interim Commander in Chief until a new president is elected.

Communications with the ARA will be via shortwave radio only. Any attempt to invade, overrun, or destroy ARA headquarters will result in detonation of additional strategic weapons located in several large cities. All state militia commanders will report today by 1500 hours MST their readiness condition and manpower to General Boyle.

Arrest warrants from the Peoples Common Law Court, signed by Acting Chief Justice Alvin T. Bradley (former supreme court justice), shall be issued for surviving members of Congress or former high-level federal employees for their crimes against the American people. The old federal court system sustains no current rule of law, and no citizen is obliged to answer or appear in their court. All federal judges are hereby dismissed.

Federal penitentiaries will be vacated immediately. FBI, CIA, DEA, ATF, and the Department of Justice, are ordered to stop all "proceedings or investigations." No files or records will be altered or destroyed. The contents of these files will be published in full. As of today, the evil secrecy and lying by our government ends.

All federal oversight of commerce and industry will cease at once. Federal monetary notes will be seized and destroyed. The United Free States of America's gold standard is hereby re-instated. No financial transaction shall occur with any other country or business located outside the territorial borders of the United Free States. No federal taxes shall be collected or dispersed.

All foreign nationals, foreign troops, or resident aliens (legal or illegal) have twenty-four hours to leave the United Free States or face arrest. Persons meeting the previous description may not remove gold or liquid assets from the United Free States. Persons attempting entry into the United Free States, who are not current citizens, will be arrested or shot. The borders of the United Free States will no longer be overrun by people bent on the destruction of a free and prosperous America.

Airline flights bound for destinations outside the United Free States shall be unlimited. Flights inbound for the United Free States territory will be limited to returning American citizens and gold returned from illegally held sources.

American ambassadors are recalled to the United Free States and dismissed from their duties. Treaties and agreements with foreign governments no longer exist and should be considered null and void.

A peaceful transition back to a true, constitutional government has always been the goal of the ARA. However, we are prepared to take any action necessary to preserve our great country. Let no one doubt our resolve or ability.

God bless America and let freedom flourish.

General Harvey Boyle
Commander in Chief

American Revolutionary Army
The United Free States of America

It had been twelve years since Ben had cried. That was right after the funeral services for his wife and daughter, who were tragically killed in an auto accident. As his eyes returned to the pages in his hand, great sobs filled his chest.

"Oh God, I wish I could join them now."

ARTICLE II

North Carolina, January 20, 2001, 4:07 PM EST

The North Carolina Coastline zipped past beneath them. An almost deafening roar came from the twin jet engines that powered the Center for Disease Control's new Bell Ranger 9000 to speeds nearing two hundred knots. Following a few insane hours, Dr. Michael Jenkins finally had some time to size up his fellow passengers.

Next to him, right behind the pilot, sat Sally Thorpe, Special Agent in Charge with the FBI's Atlanta office. Sally was a longtime friend, and her strong vocal support of Mike with his CDC brass hadn't hurt his meteoric career path. Sally's rise in the ranks of the FBI was legendary. Her role in hunting down the seven co-conspirators involved with the Oklahoma City Bombing sent her stock soaring.

It was ironic, he mused, that she seemed to care so little for her appearance. Sally could have been beautiful with just a little effort. Her coal black hair, cut brutally short, combined with a disdain for even the most basic makeup, greatly pronounced the dark circles beneath her eyes. Even more noticeable was her contempt for dressing the part. The black loose-fitting slacks, and a cheap gray jacket, made her look more like a department store security guard than one of America's best cops.

Even under normal circumstances, Sally wasn't very cheerful. Today's events insured that she was downright gloomy. But, heading into this hell beyond imagination, Mike knew he would need the tough, smart woman hiding behind those mirrored glasses.

Directly behind Sally, sitting with his face buried in a technical journal, was Billy Forest of the Bureau of Alcohol, Tobacco, and Firearms. Mike hadn't met him before today and knew little of his work. He did know, however, that Billy was stationed in Houston and had participated in the original assault on the compound in Waco. His limp from a Branch

Davidian's bullet was barely noticeable, but Mike sensed that Billy didn't care if anyone did. A large burly man of forty-seven or forty-eight, his blond hair was cut within a quarter-inch of his scalp.

Billy Forest would never inspire the stereotypical picture of a bomb nerd. Hell, Mike wasn't even aware before today that the BATF had nuclear specialists on staff. But today, Billy might get an opportunity to redeem an agency in meltdown since the mid-nineties.

The fourth and final member sat next to Billy, and behind Mike, Alex "Bo" Hampton rested against the bulkhead, his eyes closed. Bo retired from the Atomic Energy Commission almost twenty years ago. At eighty-two, he could have passed for sixty. Towering almost six feet seven inches tall, with leathered features and a full head of bright silver hair Bo still possessed a commanding presence. Part of the original Manhattan Project, his papers on radiation sickness where still required reading, and his descriptions of the destruction in Nagasaki and Hiroshima, placed a human face on otherwise cold statistics. He was the only passenger with any real idea of what may lie ahead in the smoky darkness.

Mike was Executive Director at the CDC in Atlanta, promoted just two short weeks ago. Only thirty-eight, most thought him far too young for the post. He was determined to prove them wrong.

All through high school and college, Mike had been throwing off the curve. Pushed hard by his father, a successful lawyer, Mike had become a chronic overachiever in every aspect of his life. Ordinary looking and not possessing a physical presence that would inspire those around him, Mike had to rely on his intellect to get him where he wanted to go. Nevertheless, balancing a high-stress job, his wife and a new baby proved difficult, even for him.

A large pile of untouched papers collected dust on his desk, causing constant friction with the powers to be. His lab and office staff were top-notch and did what they could to ease the stress during transition. Unfortunately, Mike had little patience for bureaucracy. Many times, he bumped heads with "the Washington idiots." If only he had known what was going to happen today, maybe he would have tried harder to understand their concerns.

Mike tried to rest for a minute, now more comfortable knowing that the group possessed the knowledge and experience to complete their mission.

A few hours after the tragedy unfolded, Sally called him, asking if he could put together a group to go in to assess the damage and casualties. She faxed Mike a list of supplies and people who might be helpful. Although he was a bit confused by her coming to him for help, considering the resources she had, he couldn't say no. However, facing the devastation they were flying into, he was unsure how much help they could possibly be.

Billowing smoke, backlit by an orange glow from the raging fires in Washington, was already visible on the horizon. Constant course corrections to avoid likely radioactive clouds were beginning to take a toll on Mike's nerves and his stomach. Although he was unsure why they would need an escort, the two F-18 jets, courtesy of the Marine Corps, flying in front of them did make him a bit more comfortable.

"Here, put this on," Bo said, passing Mike a clip-on lapel radiation indicator. Mike attached it to the black CDC windbreaker, trying not to think of the dreadful implications of it turning bright red.

The pilot turned and motioned for them to put on the radio headsets dangling by each of their seats. "We'll have to turn inland now. It's way too hot out here," his firm and reassuring voice crackled in their ears.

"Any word yet on which direction the Chicago cloud is headed?" Bo asked quietly.

"Not yet, but they tell me a storm front is moving toward the East Coast," the pilot responded.

"Well, that may be good news and bad news," Bo replied, almost to himself.

"How so?" Sally asked, turning slightly to look at him.

"It's just that storms can help some areas and be problematic for others. Rain passing through a radioactive cloud causes the particles to condense, making them fall to the ground sooner. That reduces the amount of radiation left in the cloud traveling downwind, sparing some areas of contamination. However, the areas under the cloud will receive a much higher dose so, long term mortality rates in those areas will likely increase two or three-fold." Pausing for a minute and pointing toward the east, he continued. "Best case scenario for the coastal areas would be strong easterly winds, blowing the cloud out to sea." Bo didn't have to struggle for the information. Sixty years of experience flowed off his tongue. Without even a hint of emotion, he added, "Guess that's not so great if you're a fish."

Mike was thankful Bo had made the trip and grinned at him.

Billy had stopped reading now. "What about the Denver and LA clouds?" he asked.

"Yeah, whole different story," Bo said, sitting more erect in his seat. "Trouble with those bad boys is the wind will likely spread death and cancer over the southwestern states from LA and the Heartland and Midwest from Denver." His eyes indicated that traumatic memories from many years ago had been rekindled, racing back to the forefront of his mind.

Soon they all would have similar memories to bury.

"There isn't confirmation on the Denver bomb," Sally added after a few moments of silence. "The word I got is we have contact with our agents there. So, it seems it didn't go off. Not yet, anyway."

"Oh, that's good news," Billy said. "I hadn't heard that."

"Where are we going to sit this thing down?" Sally asked the pilot.

"I wish I knew, Agent Thorpe. Details about what's left down there are sketchy at best." Although he wasn't a military pilot, he tried to sound calm and reassuring. That task was made more difficult by not having a clear route or firm destination.

"Why can't we reach anyone on the damned radios?" Sally protested. She was beginning to sound irritated by the lack of order and a firm chain of command. Flying blind without a defined plan wasn't even remotely her style.

"EMP," Billy said, his tone flat like everyone should know what it meant.

"Look genius, I know I'm the only non-scientist here—" Sally began, her tone taught, and her forehead wrinkled "—however, I would appreciate, just once, an answer in English. What the fuck is EMP?"

Billy looked up from his manual, his face starting to redden. After deliberately clearing his throat, he glared straight at Sally, his eyes riveted to the back of Sally's now turned-away head. "Electro-Magnetic Pulse. As a result of the energy released by a nuclear device, electrons in the nearby atmosphere can be disturbed. The resulting electromagnetic field passing through electrical devices can, if close enough, destroy electric circuits or, at the least, affect any number of them, including car batteries, radars, radios, computers and ignitions. The extent of the effect depends on the height from which the nuclear device was detonated. Based on the data I have, it's safe to assume this was a ground or close-to-ground burst. That would limit the range of the EMP greatly." After a short pause, he added, "Clear fucking enough?"

At that moment, Mike knew Billy had the balls and the will to go toe to toe with her. However, he hoped they wouldn't butt heads often. There were way too many tough hours ahead to be a splintered group already.

Thankfully, Sally, knowing she had overreacted, just nodded.

Mike understood her and made a mental note to tell Billy that her lack of response was as close as she would ever get to saying she was sorry.

Billy resumed reading. All onboard had discovered two things about him. First, his fuse appeared to be very short, and more importantly, he understood these bombs. How they worked and what they were capable of.

Slipping off his headset, Mike leaned closer to Sally. "You worried about Quantico?"

Jeff, Sally's ex-husband, was an instructor at the FBI's training facility located at Quantico, Virginia, just thirty-five miles from Washington. Though their marriage hadn't worked out, they remained close friends, and Mike knew he was the only man she ever really loved.

"Yeah, stupid bastard better not have gotten himself killed," she said, trying to force a smile.

Regretting he had brought up a subject so close to her heart, Mike attempted to change course. "Who are you reporting to?"

"That's the question of the day, isn't it? General thoughts are that all of the regional heads were in DC today. Right now, I'm the master of my own domain." Sally must have been uncomfortable with the possibilities her statement implied and quickly added, "Of course, I've been in touch with other special agents in Dallas. We're trying to coordinate our efforts the best we can." Having a gruff blunt personality meant she had to be good at damage control.

"If Denver is still there, it must be a hopping place," Mike said as he winked at her. It was his way of telling her the qualifier hadn't been needed.

"Understatement of the year. No one is sure if the bomb just didn't go off or if the ARA wanted everybody and his dog in Denver to be looking for one. Great way to keep all our best bomb guys busy and out of their way."

"Don't you mean some of *our* best bomb guys?" Obviously, Billy had been listening and now wore a large grin across his face.

Sally apparently couldn't stop the frown from leaving her face. "Yes. Yes, a few of the no talent, nothing better to do, bomb guys." She laughed and flipped a hand in the air. "It goes without saying the best bomb guy would be assigned to protect me."

They all chuckled, relieving the tension between them.

The humor was short-lived, however.

Suddenly and without warning, the chopper veered sharply to the left, forcing everyone to stiffen as they were pushed nearly out of their seats. "We've got incoming," the pilot shouted, then responded to radio traffic they couldn't hear, "Roger F-18, dropping to five hundred feet."

The radio crackled with conversation. A Surface to Air Missile had narrowly missed bringing down the Ranger. Only swift countermeasures by the Marine F-18s saved their lives.

"They must have overrun a military base and gotten their hands on some missiles," Mike assumed aloud.

"Not necessarily," Sally growled. "SAMs are easier to buy than crack."

"SAM? What the hell is a SAM?" Mike asked.

"Surface to Air Missile, Mike. Handheld, probably. Between the numbers we sold to third-world countries, and the number they make on their own, there might be enough down below to shoot everyone out of the sky." Obviously, Sally wasn't a fan of selling arms to anyone who could afford it and the disdain was embedded in her voice.

"Hey. Great news," the pilot broke in. "The Marines just took out the SAM site. A brick warehouse just outside of Richmond."

Mike took in the pilot's words but didn't feel the joy he expressed. Mike had been too focused on dealing with the effects of the explosions and giving aid to the survivors. Now visions of Americans launching missiles at American aircraft and Marine planes destroying buildings in Virginia filled his head. What was this madness?

"Hey Doc," the pilot called, catching Mike's attention. There's a mall parking lot down below. What do you think?"

Sensing the encounter with the SAM and Sally's views on the likelihood of many more waiting had hastened the pilot's desire to get his bird out of the sky sooner rather than later. Mike asked, "What's our position?"

"About forty or fifty miles southwest of Washington. Or what's left of it anyway."

Mike looked around at the others to see if they would protest or interject, but they sat in silence. It appeared the CDC chopper was Mike's to control. "Okay. Go ahead and set her down."

Mike thanked the Marines for the escort and asked them to call back to Atlanta, noting their approximate position. In addition, he asked for the required ground forces to protect the chopper until their return. He didn't want to try and compute the odds that they would actually be able to get back in one piece.

It had been just under six hours since the blast, and the sunlight was beginning to fade in the midwinter sky. Mike noticed two sunsets, one in the west as dwindling sunshine passed through the dust particles, turning them incredible shades of red and orange, and one in the east a distinct yellow-tinged glow from the fires in DC. Under most circumstances, it would have been breathtaking. As soon as the chopper touched down, Mike reached for the door handle. A large firm hand on his shoulder stopped him cold.

"How about you let me jump out and take some quick readings first?" Bo's question was clearly rhetorical. He wasn't a man to be questioned, and Mike nodded in agreement.

As Bo slipped quickly from his seat, those left inside couldn't help but admire his agility. They watched him carefully unpack a series of black hard side cases. Like he had done it a thousand times, he placed several electronic meters on the ground encircling him. He lifted one after another with deliberation, calibrating, measuring and writing in a small notepad. Twenty minutes passed as he computed the possible exposure risks. For some odd reason, no one spoke as they waited. It was amazing watching this man go about his work, every movement planned, and no wasted or unproductive actions, his life unimportant and at risk to ensure the safety of the group.

Finished, he opened Mike's door. "Sorry it took so long. I wanted to calibrate the equipment before we got started. Come on out. It's fairly safe, running about five RADs per hour now, and that should go down quickly unless we get a wind shift."

Mike nodded at Bo like the odd numbers made perfect sense to him and turned his attention to transportation. He immediately knew who to ask to solve the problem. "Sally, can you get us some wheels? Something big enough to carry the equipment and rugged enough to go cross country if we need to?" He knew she always loved a challenge.

"You bet your ass, Doc. Give me thirty minutes, maybe less." With that, she jumped quickly out of the chopper and strode briskly toward the shopping mall shadowed behind them.

They had been on the ground unpacking the chopper for almost thirty minutes, and Mike hadn't even thought to check the area surrounding them. A chill ran down his spine. What about ARA ground forces? Had they heard the chopper land? He looked around at the darkness surrounding them. "Billy, are you armed?"

"Just this little 45 auto on me." Billy opened his jacket so Mike could see his shoulder holster and sidearm. "But the boss did send a couple of fully auto M-16s in my gear," he said, flashing a quick, sly smirk.

Mike liked him more every minute. "Should we get them out?"

"Yeah, not a bad idea. I'll find them," Billy responded, already digging in the baggage area for the weapons.

There didn't appear to be any substantial blast damage in the area, and it was somewhat reassuring to Mike. "Hey, Billy, what's your guess on the damage? How close can we get?"

Billy stopped digging in the chopper for a brief moment and looked into the sky as he pondered the question. "Hard to say. We think from the limited reports we have that it was a ground burst. That means the terrain should have contained some of the blast wave and kept it from spreading out. The shock wave gets broken up and absorbed by the hills and buildings. Close in stuff, say five to ten, maybe even fifteen miles will be too hot to risk exposure for a long time. Depending on the size of our balls and these little death badges," he said, pointing to his lapel radiation indicator, "I would guess twenty to twenty-five miles from ground zero. It won't be pretty. Radiation, flag fires, and burn victims. The casualties will be heavy and gruesome."

The picture Billy painted had Mike wondering if they shouldn't load up and get the hell out right now. Bo had finished unloading his gear, and Mike decided to pick his brain for more information. "Good to have you along, Mr. Hampton. I was curious. Five RADs. Is that about what you expected?"

''Please, Mike, call me Bo," he said softly as he stepped closer. "No, not really. To be this low inside sixty miles after only six hours indicates to me that we got lucky with the winds. My best guess is the winds took most of the fallout out to sea."

"That's great." Mike was thrilled with this first bit of good news. He allowed the tense lines on his face to relax as he began checking the supplies packed by his staff. Bo was the radiation sickness expert, but it would be up to him when the time came for medical treatment.

He opened the large green trunk stenciled, PROPERTY OF THE CENTER FOR DISEASE CONTROL, ATLANTA, GA. On top of the supplies lay a handwritten note from his staff.

Dear Doc,

Hope your vacation is going well. Seems to us you picked a strange time for a sightseeing trip to Washington. Please send us back a postcard (non-radioactive, please). We were going to say that we wish we were there with you, but the truth is we don't.

Love

You're Staff

P.S. Our prayers are with you. Be safe and hurry back.

Mike fought back a large lump in his throat. He wasn't sure if any of his party would understand their humor. He folded the note and placed it in his pocket. It would be something he would keep.

Checking the contents, he found IVs, cysteamine, potassium, iodine, antibiotics, medication for nausea and vomiting, and various sizes of Telfa pads, tape and bandages. There would be a need for many more supplies like these. Maybe a hospital or military base could be found intact.

Suddenly bright headlights flooded their location, and for a terrifying instant, the group froze in place.

Sally's voice, for the first time today, sounded upbeat as she bounded out of the driver's seat. "Best I could do on such short notice." She had acquired, and no one wanted to know how, a bright red 1999 Ford Explorer.

The group piled in the vehicle, choosing their seats just as they sat in the chopper—Sally and Mike in front and Billy and Bo in the back. Sally removed her jacket and took the wheel. As Mike suspected, she was carrying a side arm tucked away in its holster. A standard bureau issue 9 MM Berretta. To make them more accessible, Billy had retrieved the M-16s and placed them on the floor of the backseat. With all their gear now loaded, they set out for Washington.

"Anybody know where the hell we are?" Mike asked. For some unknown reason, he had taken on the leadership role. He had hoped that, eventually, Sally would step to the front. There was certainly no doubt she had more experience at this kind of thing than he did. But so far, she appeared to be content to let Mike direct them. Maybe if they had flown in one of her choppers? Well, no matter. The dye had been cast.

"Falmouth, Virginia," Sally replied. "Just under fifty miles from DC. We need to locate US 1 and take that to I-95." It seemed she had been busier than he thought during her brief absence.

"Going to be tough with the electricity out," Billy added.

Mike had been so busy getting organized that he hadn't really noticed the sun had set. Every building was dark, and the streetlights were too. Except for the unnatural glow on the horizon, their headlights and an occasional emergency light, candles, or flashlight provided the only illumination. At least there wasn't any traffic on the streets. Thankfully, most of the residents—those who survived—had fled west shortly after the blast.

Following a few wrong turns, the Explorer found its way onto US 1. It was more than a little unsettling, driving down this dark stretch of highway with little conversation, the light from the fires ahead growing steadily in the windshield.

Three miles later, just before reaching the I-95 on-ramp, they came across two police cars sitting at forty-five-degree angles, their lights flashing, allowing only one lane of traffic to pass between them.

Mike was relieved to see a police presence. "I guess we aren't the only ones working tonight."

His mood changed quickly as the distinct sound of Billy chambering a round into the M-16 filtered from the back seat. As Mike turned to look at him, he saw Sally slip her gun from her holster and slide it under her right thigh.

"What the hell are you two doing?" Mike whispered, the concern and confusion in his voice clear.

"An ounce of prevention, you know?" Billy replied, now intensely staring at the scene outside his window.

Lowering the driver's window, Sally pulled slowly forward between the two cars.

"Where in the hell do you think you're going?" the sheriff's deputy asked, moving close to the driver's side door. Perhaps not viewing her as a threat, he looked straight past Sally to Billy in the back seat. With his hand intimidatingly resting on his weapon, the deputy waited for someone to answer.

"DC, Officer." Sally's response was short but respectful.

"What the hell for?" There wasn't any shred of respect in the tone of the officer's follow-up question.

"Humanitarian relief." Sally was no rookie. Sizing up the situation, she doled out information in small, measured doses.

Mike strained to see the deputy standing on his side of the car, but the man remained in the shadows.

"Who do you work for?" the officer growled while pointing at Mike.

"A private foundation," Mike stated. He wasn't sure why he lied but sensed, based on Sally's response, it was the right thing to do.

"That's so much horseshit. You're Feds, all of you. I can smell you assholes a mile away." Mike winced at the aggression shown by the officer. "You know that Commander Boyle has declared state martial law, and you hotshots are out of a job, right?"

Sally didn't respond to the taunt, probably hoping the situation might defuse itself. "Sir, we are just hoping to be of some assistance. Many people must be injured, and they need our help. May we pass, please?" Sally asked, keeping her tone non-threatening and even.

"Look, sister, those idiots up there in Washington got just what they deserved. Good book says you reap what you sow. You national boys been pushing us local boys around for a long time, driving around in some fancy car that my tax money bought, flashing your cards filled with fancy letters and titles. Bet you got a degree from some snooty liberal college up north. Well, honey, that crap don't mean snot to me. Maybe you should call your boss in Washington and tell him I've been rude. Tell him not to send any more of my own money back to me. Nah, let's just tell him to kiss my patriot ass. Oh, wait. You can't do that because Washington isn't there anymore. Too damn bad." The officer's face was bright red now as he nearly shouted the last sentence.

Taking a step back, he pulled his gun from its holster and growled. "Now turn off the engine, and get out of the car."

"Get us the fuck out of here," Billy whispered from the back.

Mike was thrown back in his seat as Sally suddenly smashed the accelerator to the floor. Speeding away with the crackle of gunfire behind them, Mike ducked down, making himself as small as possible near the floor. At least one of the bullets found its mark, shattering the rear window with a loud pop and sending small cubes of glass flying throughout the cab. Mike was sure they would roll over as Sally almost lost control, taking the sharply banked interstate ramp at over sixty-five miles per hour.

A mile or so down the interstate, Mike forced himself to breathe again. Thankfully, Boyle's homegrown Storm Troopers had no interest in chasing them into the bomb's blast zone. "Can you believe those fucking idiots?" Mike tried to put some toughness into his voice, not allowing anyone to see how much he trembled. In fact, his hands were shaking so badly he had trouble picking up the flashlight rolling around on the floor with the shattered glass at his feet.

Glancing over at Sally and seeing the expression on her face, he gathered she, too, was angry and a bit shaken. "It won't be our last run-in with idiots," she barked. "Damn, I hope some of the Marines at Quantico survived. Jeff told me a lot of the buildings were fortified because it was clear Washington would be a main target of the Russians, so it's possible. And we're going to need some help."

Mike stared forward. "Yeah, we'll definitely need hel—"

"Shit!" Billy screamed, cutting Mike off mid-sentence. "Oh God, no. Christ, he's hit. The dumb bastards shot Bo."

"Is it bad?" Mike asked in a panic as he wheeled around in his seat to shine his shaking flashlight on Bo, whose tan face was ashen, and there was no movement from his lanky frame.

"Looks bad," Billy replied as he searched for a pulse, blood from Bo's chest wound covering his hands. Unable to find one, Billy sunk back in his seat, his head hanging down. "He's had it. Dammit. Why didn't I shoot that stupid redneck? I should have protected Bo, seen it coming and done something." Billy's voice trailed off, and the cab of their vehicle became silent.

After a long minute, Mike switched the flashlight off.

Alex "Bo" Hampton, humanitarian and survivor of nuclear testing, radiation, World War II, Korea, and the cold war, lay dead, shot in the back by a Virginia deputy sheriff. The madness seemed to have no end.

ARTICLE III

Denver, Colorado, January 20, 2001, 11:25 AM MST

Ben stood in the shower, hot water pulsating against the back of his neck. Since his childhood, this had helped him relax and get warm. Winter in Northwest Colorado was brutal, the snow arriving in November and continually showing up time and again until May. At times, temperatures plunged to thirty or forty degrees below zero. Standing here now made him feel safe, warm and more normal.

After toweling off in front of his locker, he sat down on the wooden bench, his head buried in his hands. The Bannon Health Club had become his home away from home. Built on the twentieth floor four years ago in Don's honor, the paper hoped to promote a healthier lifestyle and workforce.

Thirty minutes of sobbing had taken a toll on Ben, leaving him stressed, exhausted and washed out. As he dressed, his son's face flashed through his mind. Although physically there was no resemblance—his son was six feet two inches tall, with well-defined muscles and features, none of his father's vices so detrimental to good health—Chris was like Ben in many other ways. His boy was loyal and honest, and he loved the newspaper business and flourished under pressure. The Chicago job was too good to pass up, and Chris had to find his own identity separate from Ben. However, he was the only immediate family Ben had remaining, and life had been lonely since Chris moved away.

Many years of experience told Ben not to assume the worst, but an atomic bomb had exploded in Chicago, so holding out hope wasn't easy. Maybe Chris was out of town on assignment. Maybe his building survived the blast, and maybe… It was useless to speculate. Ben owed it to himself and Don to discover the fate of their sons.

"Telephone call for Ben Bleser, Ben Bleser, pick up line six, please," a voice crackled from the overhead speakers.

The hair on the back of Ben's neck stood straight up. He was afraid to answer, afraid not to even know if it was bad news, he could go back into the shower.

He slowly made his way toward the telephone, pressing the blinking red light under line six. "This is Ben Bleser."

"Hi Ben, it's Jim. Sorry about being so abrupt this morning." Sargent Jim Arno's voice sounded much better, strong and soothing, a big change from this morning's encounter in the street. "I Heard about Chicago. I'm really sorry. I've got two nephews on the force there."

Ben fought the emotions rising in his chest. "Good to hear your voice, Jim. It's been a tough morning for everyone."

"What's your plan?"

"Don't know yet. Thought maybe I'd head back to... Well...you know, look around?" Ben stumbled for the words. A long pause followed. "Jim, you there?"

"Yeah, I'm here. Uh... I have a proposition or maybe a request from the president." Jim sounded uncomfortable with the words he had just spoken.

"The president? Jesus Christ, are you telling me Strugel survived the blast?" Ben now stood erect and tense.

"God, no. You don't understand. The new president, President Young." Now Jim sounded almost excited.

Ben sat down hard on the bench. "Secretary Young?" he asked in disbelief.

"Forty-five minutes after you saw her this morning, she took the oath of office. It's President Young now."

Ben now fully understood the look on her face this morning as the agent whispered in her ear. "What does she want from me?"

"As you might imagine, it's important for the country to know someone other than Harvey 'asshole' Boyle is in charge. The Secret Service contacted my department asking if we knew someone trustworthy in the press. Ben, I told them you're that someone. I hope you're okay with that." Much had happened to the world in the last few hours, and Jim seemed to struggle with the new role he had been handed.

A few short minutes ago, Ben was sure about heading to Chicago to find Chris. But now? For so many years, he had made choices between his family and work. The night his wife and daughter were killed, he should have been driving the car but had been called in to cover an airline strike. She was never good at night driving, and he always wondered if they would be alive if he had been there. He missed his mother's funeral too, volunteering to cover a Colorado Reserve Unit in Iraq, activated during Desert Storm. The news of her passing didn't reach him until the day of the funeral. His two uncles hadn't spoken to him since.

"Ben, what should I tell them?" Apparently, Jim wasn't pleased with the silence on his end of the receiver, and he pressed for an answer. "Ben? Christ, Ben, answer me."

Ben knew saying no to the president at a time like this wasn't a good idea and relented. "Okay, okay, I'll do it. But I want some help with my son. I need to know about Chris. I mean it, Jim. I need to feel right about this, or you can all kiss my ass."

"I'm sure that won't be a problem. Helping you with Chris, I mean. I refuse to kiss your ass." Jim chuckled lightly. "I'll pick you up in thirty minutes." He hung up without saying goodbye or giving Ben a chance to change his mind.

Ben returned to the twenty-third floor and gathered his notebook, tape recorder and cell phone. After talking over his plans with the editorial staff and getting their blessing, he went down to the street to wait for Jim.

Broadway was bustling with activity, and Ben watched as people ran to the bus terminal across the street. Word of the day's events was spreading quickly. *Controlled panic*, he thought to himself. And who could blame them? No one knew what was going to happen. Traffic out of the city was at a standstill, all the banks were closed, fearing a run, and supermarkets were swamped with frantic shoppers. People downtown scurried to the suburbs to be with their families and protect their homes as rumors of an unexploded device in one of the skyscrapers quickened their pace.

He knew the country would never be the same, safety had been an illusion, and it was gone now. A huge crack had opened in America, each side thinking the other was evil, and ordinary people were caught in the middle. Young children, helpless older Americans, strong men, it made no difference to a bomb. It didn't matter in Oklahoma City, and it didn't matter now. Maybe the profits and clerics had been right about the end of the world, and General Boyle was just a year late. Thinking about it made the cold January air seeping in through the front of his jacket even colder.

"Where the hell is he?" Ben grumbled, pulling the collar of his lightweight coat closer around him.

He expected Jim to pick him up in his squad car, so Ben certainly wasn't prepared for the procession racing quickly down the street toward him. A large black limousine flying dual American Flags flanked by two Denver police cars and four motorcycle cops, all running lights and sirens, pulled to the curb directly in front of him. Two plainclothes agents, brandishing automatic weapons, jumped from the limo.

"Mr. Bleser?" the first one out asked. Ben nodded. "Sir, please get in quickly." Ben complied, entering the waiting car with the two men following him into the back. "Thank you, sir. We'll be there in a few minutes," were the only words spoken during the seven-block ride to the Federal Building.

Two half-tracks and a squad of combat-ready soldiers from Fort Carson stood guard around the Federal Building, with multiple strands of barbed wire strung out around the entire perimeter. It was like entering an American Embassy abroad while under siege.

By now, Ben's mind had become numb. Shutting down his emotions was the only way to deal with this dream-like day. The reporter in him had taken over. Jim had no doubt counted on that when he'd called Ben.

After careful inspection of the limo by security agents and soldiers, the vehicle squealed its tires and entered the underground parking area. Following countless turns snaking through the garage, the limo barely clearing the walls, it came to an abrupt stop.

Ben was relieved to see Jim's familiar figure standing in front of the elevator doors. "Come on out. She's waiting for you," Jim said as the car door opened.

Ben grumbled as he exited the limo, "What happened to 'Hello, Ben.' 'Nice to see you, Ben.' 'Would you like a cup of coffee, Ben'?"

Jim laughed, his round face slightly reddened. "Sorry, buddy. Hello, Ben. Nice to see you, Ben. We don't have time for coffee, Ben. Now can we go?"

Ben made a sincere effort to look amused and placed his arm on Jim's shoulder as they made their way to the elevator. "Where are we going, smart ass?"

"Straight down about two hundred feet below ground."

"A bunker?" Ben asked, his tone quickly rising.

"More like a fortified command post. Everything needed is down there. Are you claustrophobic?" Jim asked as they entered the elevator.

"I guess we'll find out, won't we?"

He didn't see her at first, a tall woman wearing all black, but now, with her sidearm pointing directly at him, the Secret Service agent quickly became Ben's focal point.

"ID," she barked, her voice sharply in contrast with her appearance. "Slowly," she added while staring intently at Ben.

"Yes, of course." Ben tried to sound calm as he slowly reached into his front jacket pocket for his press card and driver's license.

From over his right shoulder, another agent took the documents from his outstretched hand and walked away. Muffled sounds of two-way radios echoed off the concrete walls. Ben didn't know what to make of this stunning woman holding a gun on him. Natural blonde hair—if he judged correctly—cut "Agency" style, a tailored black jacket with a white blouse, and long sleek legs extending down miles from her skirt. She was at least twenty years his junior, two inches taller, and wore no ring on her left hand. It had been a long time since a woman had stirred his interest like this. Ben wondered about what terrible timing he had. If she didn't shoot him first, he would like to get to know her better.

"Roger...out." Ben heard the footsteps as the agent approached from behind. "He's okay. Sir, please step forward and place your hands on the wall." Although the words were polite, it was a command, not a request. Ben complied quickly and quietly. Glancing over his shoulder, he saw Jim standing in the corner of the elevator, unfazed by the proceedings. The bastard could have warned him. The male agent searched Ben carefully, checking his cell phone but only keeping his tape recorder.

"Clean," the agent announced. With the inspection complete, the woman holstered her weapon and approached.

"Agent Ashley Prescott, Mr. Bleser. Pleasure to meet you. Sorry about the precautions, but I'm sure you understand." Her voice had changed, now more pleasant, almost sexy.

Ben reached out and grasped her hand. "Of course. Of course, no problem."

"From now on, you're my responsibility. We've code named you Notebook."

Ben enjoyed her warm smile but blushed, suddenly aware of her attempt to free her hand from his. "Thank you, Ashley." He smiled in return as he released his grip. The elevator was now moving swiftly downward.

Jim leaned closer to Ben, whispering, "Easy, big fella, she's armed."

Had he been that obvious? Maybe she hadn't noticed.

Ashley spoke softly into her wrist microphone, "Spider here. Notebook has arrived, and we're on the move to your location."

"So, you're Spider. Why do they call you that?"

"Well, sir, I think it's because I always kill then ingest my lovers," she quipped, a sly grin flashing across her face.

Apparently, she had noticed. Now fully embarrassed, Ben understood a sidearm was not the only weapon she possessed.

The elevator doors opened, and another agent stationed in the dimly lit concrete corridor greeted them. "Notebook?"

"Yes, sir. So they tell me anyway." Ben wasn't yet comfortable with his new handle.

"This way. The President is expecting you." The latest agent to make his acquaintance turned, walking toward the steel door at the end of the hall.

"Catch you later, Ben," Jim yelled.

Ben turned just in time to see the elevator doors close, his friend still inside. "Isn't he coming with us?" Ben asked Ashley.

"No, sorry. Essential personnel only down here. We have a limited amount of space and supplies. Right now, including yourself and security, we've got thirty-seven bodies." Ashley seemed more relaxed in the safety of the bunker. "I'm afraid you won't get your tape recorder back. No one is allowed to record or film down here. We would have taken your cell phone if it worked below, but it won't. Too much concrete."

She continued, talking softly enough not to be overheard by the other agent. "The president spoke to me earlier, and she's concerned about balancing national security and command-level intelligence with letting the public know what her plans are. She thought an outside reporter would be more credible than press releases from the bunker. However, she has asked me to impress upon you the importance of keeping strategic and tactical information within these walls."

They had stopped walking now, about twenty feet short of the entry door. Ashley leaned close to Ben, and her perfume filled his nose. Knowing what was at stake, he forced himself to concentrate on her words. "We're not going to censure you, but..." She paused, looked at the floor, then back at him. "I hope you take this the right way. If we feel you intend to jeopardize national security, I will kill you."

Looking into her soft blue eyes, Ben wondered if events warranted if they might be the last thing he ever saw. "Fair enough. I'm aware you don't need a reporter down here to disseminate information. I'll discuss with you any information I intend to use." He reached out, gently touching her arm. "Would you really...kill me?"

Turning toward the doorway, she said, "Remember the spider?"

Ben couldn't see her face but hoped she was smiling.

With bright blue carpeted floors and white drapes hanging on the walls, the inside of the compound was much brighter and more spacious than he had expected. The large Marine stationed at the front desk handed Ben a plastic-coated ID card complete with a neck chain. Ben's DMV picture stared back at him. "Don't lose this, sir. You'll need it for access past this point." Ben nodded, and the Marine asked, "Anything special we should know about you, medication, medical condition, special diet, or religious services?"

"I don't think so, though my doctor does think caffeine should be illegal," Ben quipped.

"Got it. Oh, and, sir, there is absolutely no smoking," the Marine added.

"Damn. And I was seriously considering taking it up again." Ben smiled. The Marine did not.

Ashley wrapped a hand around Ben's arm, directing him toward another doorway. "Hold your card up like this," she instructed as they reached the clear glass barrier. Ashley placed her card flat against the image reader mounted on the wall, glowing red scanners traced across its surface, and a few seconds later, the door swooshed open. It closed just as quickly after she passed through. Ben repeated the process and joined her on the other side.

"Next stop, the not-so-oval office." Ben appreciated her attempt to lighten the mood and calm his nerves. "In here." Ashley motioned him into a large conference room already bustling with activity. From behind the open door, President Young stepped in front of him.

He expected her to look older and worn out, but the same warm features that so impressed him this morning were intact. She smiled and extended her hand. "Mr. Bleser, glad you could join us. Didn't I see you this morning?"

Ben was impressed with her recall. "Yes, Madam President. It's been quite a day."

"Not over yet," she said, already walking away. "Okay, ladies and gentlemen, before we get started, I would like to introduce Ben—it is Ben, isn't it?" She glanced over at Ben, now seated at the other end of a large white pine table. He nodded. "Yes, Ben Bleser of the *Rocky Mountain Post*. He's going to help us get out the word. Anything you would say to me can be said in front of him. Because we had to scramble to assemble this group, and some of you may not know each other, I have asked my chief of staff to introduce herself, and then we'll go around the table. Bobbie, please go ahead and start." With that, the new president sat down at the head of the table.

Smallish in stature and looking every bit a bureaucrat, Bobbie was about fifty years old and wore a conservative hairstyle and dress. Lifting the large notebook on her lap, she popped to her feet.

"Thank you, Madam President." Sounding as if she had said it a thousand times, Bobbie adjusted her dark-rimmed glasses and continued. "I'm Bobbie Stenson, Chief of Staff." All business, she promptly took her seat and nodded to the person on her right.

"Hello. I'm Dr. Sidney Green, Acting National Security Advisor. I spent eight years at the Department of Defense and, until a couple of hours ago, was retired." A slight smile crossed his well-tanned face. In his late fifties, well-fit and casually dressed, Ben was sure Dr. Green had come straight from the golf course or tennis court.

Spent eight years with the DOD, Ben scribbled. He had been around long enough to know a generic description like that usually meant military intelligence.

A well-dressed young black woman in her late twenties spoke next. "Dedra Jones, Press Secretary." Ben had seen her this morning with then Secretary Young. Dedra had taken a huge step up in just a few short hours and was not yet sure of herself, judging by the nervous wobble in her voice. Ben had no doubt that before this was over, she would be a hardened veteran.

Ben recognized the next man before his turn arrived. "General Terence Clifton, Acting Head of the Joint Chiefs," he boomed. General Clifton retired to Aspen last year, a three-star tyrant with forty years of experience. Attired in full dress uniform, military crew cut, and his barrel-shaped chest covered with a rainbow of campaign ribbons, he was an impressive sight. Many men and women towered over his five-foot-six-inch frame, but raw power was a great equalizer. Rumor had it a special chair had been constructed for him in the Pentagon, making him appear to be much taller.

An enormous Native-American man rose to his feet. "Larry Raincloud Franklin, Former Senator from Arizona, Acting Secretary of Defense."

"Dr. Ilene Alexander, Professor of Economics at Colorado University, Acting Special Advisor on Domestic Economics." Dr. Alexander appeared frail, her auburn hair having long ago lost its natural color and experience and wisdom written in the lines of her face.

"Marie Zambrano," announced an olive-skinned woman of around forty-five, in a distinct Hispanic accent. "Former Undersecretary of

Transportation, now Acting Secretary of Transportation."

"Herman Bostow, Chief Justice Sixth Circuit Court of Appeals, Acting Attorney General."

Ben had interviewed "Hard Right" Bostow several times. Only forty-eight—if Ben remembered correctly—Bostow had been on the fast track toward the Supreme Court for years. His decisions on Constitutional Law had never been overturned. Average looking with bad skin, bad teeth, and almost no hair remaining, Bostow was still a bachelor.

The final two people at the table were familiar to Ben and most people in Colorado. "James Morrison, former Colorado State Treasurer, Acting Secretary of the Treasury." Standing only five feet tall and weighing nearly two hundred pounds, he cut a strange figure walking the halls of the State Capitol. Elected five times by Colorado voters, Morrison had turned down the requests of two presidents to move up to the federal level. Apparently, he had little luck with that answer to President Young.

Unlike James Morrison, the current Governor of Colorado was a handsome man of fifty-two, sharply dressed in a dark blue Armani suit, not a hair out of place. He sat leaning back from the table, legs and arms crossed. Bringing himself more upright as his turn to introduce himself arrived, the governor spoke confidently. "Governor Guy Robbins, Acting Representative for The National Association of Governors."

Ben had been taking notes as each member spoke. Next to Robbins' name, Ben jotted, *why did he cancel DC trip?*

Ben couldn't help being impressed by this cabinet. Despite the time frame in which it had been assembled, it included a great mix of experience and youth.

Before President Young could speak again, General Clifton leaned forward. "Excuse me, Madam President, but may I have just a moment before we start?"

"Of course, General, go ahead." Obviously unsure of his motives, the president's eyes darted toward Bobbie.

"Thank you. I would just like this opportunity, in front of everyone, to renew a few of my concerns. First of all, we should not be here. The threat of some unexploded atomic device is a risk we should not take. I must repeat my opinion that this body belongs in a more secure location. I would suggest Cheyenne Mountain or the Omaha Command Headquarters." He paused, his gaze scanning the other occupants of the room, Ben assumed, checking for any reaction. "Second, I cannot condone the press having access to sensitive military data. It is an outrage, and he should leave at once." The general's index finger pointed straight at Ben. "Madam President, with all due respect, I demand that he not be a part of this meeting."

Ben wasn't surprised by the general's viewpoint. Throughout most of his military career, the press had not been kind, dubbing him "Terry the Tyrant." Largely his own doing, Clifton expressed early and often his mistrust of the media. Ben expected President Young to lightly deflect the assault, but as he turned his attention to the newly appointed president, Ben got the impression he was about to witness a new side of her.

"General Clifton, as you are well aware from our previous conversation," she began, her voice low and deliberate, "I will not run from these murderous bastards. They have destroyed whole cities, taken many thousands of innocent lives, and crumbled monuments built to honor our dead. This son-of-a-bitch Boyle is a mass murdering terrorist disguised as a patriot. I will not give him or his followers the satisfaction of turning tail and running, not from my hometown, not today, not tomorrow, or ever." Her hands now clenched tightly into fists, and her breathing rapid, she paused.

Following a brief repose, she appeared to collect herself before continuing. "As for Mr. Bleser, he stays. He has agreed to withhold any sensitive data." Ben found himself unconsciously nodding in agreement. "You know, General, the people out there are scared and confused. They need to know what we're doing to help them, who we are, and why they should stay and fight with us."

She paused and stared right at the general. "Oh, and Terry, don't ever try to bull rush me again. Is that clear?"

If there had been any doubt in Ben's mind concerning President Young's ability to lead the country, it was gone.

General Clifton opened the agenda in front of him. Though he said nothing, Ben felt this battle was far from over.

President Young's composure had returned. "Okay, let's get started. Everyone should have an agenda in front of them."

Ben opened the dark blue folder sitting in front of him on the table.

Emergency Cabinet Meeting

January 20, 2001

1. National Security

    a. Defense Status

    b. Foreign Reaction

    c. Plan of Action

2. Rescue Operations

    a. Damage Estimates

    b. FEMA

    c. Radiation

    d. Plan of Action

3. ARA

    a. Background

    b. Strategic Weapons

    c. Troop Strength

    d. Plan of Action

4. Other

    a. Transportation

    b. Economy

Ben was starting to understand the scope of the problems that faced the nation and its new president.

"Secretary Franklin, would you please start?" the president asked.

Larry "Raincloud" Franklin could easily dominate a room. His enormous frame and distinct Native American features, and a two-foot gray ponytail hanging down his back brought back visions of proud people taming a vast continent. With twelve years on the House Defense Committee and twelve years' service on the Senate Intelligence Oversight Committee, he knew the military well.

"Strategically, we're at Def Con Two, just one step below all-out war. SAC—that's Strategic Air Command for anyone here who isn't familiar—is in the air twenty-four-seven. Omaha is online and on alert. SAC automatically went to Def Con Two upon confirming nuclear activity. Of course, they assumed the source was external."

Franklin paused as if waiting for questions. When none came, he nodded and continued. "I hasten to mention this, but for about six and one half long minutes today, we were at Def Con One. We were technically at war, the birds were warming in the silos, and the subs had been sent their first set of flash launch codes."

Ben couldn't believe his ears. Boyle had almost unleashed full nuclear war on the entire planet. How quickly these events could spiral out of control. Why wasn't everybody at the table up screaming and crying? Taking a deep breath, he focused back on the conversation.

Franklin continued. "SAC believed all the civilian authorities had been taken out and, in that scenario, they had orders to launch a full-scale retaliatory strike. Thankfully, no one knew who to target. There hadn't been any launch detection from ICBMs or any tactical submarine action. When the service reached them with word that you were safe, Madam

President, they stepped back to Def Con Two and waited. There was a brief discussion about hitting the Russians and the Chinese hard before they decided to take advantage of the situation and hit us, but cooler and wiser heads prevailed."

"Jesus Christ." President Young shook her head and dropped her chin to meet her chest.

Franklin raised an eyebrow and continued. "Our most recent satellite images indicate some movement by Russian naval forces, and the Chinese have moved a few ships toward Taiwan and South Korea. However, both acts appear to be largely defensive in nature."

After another noticeable pause, he added, "The general and I would prefer dropping to Def Con Three. It's less volatile than two. People relax a bit and don't make stupid mistakes." His presentation of the facts was concise and to the point.

Ben thought Franklin was done and transferred his gaze to General Clifton, expecting him to speak up next. But then, Secretary Franklin went on.

"We've contacted NATO and filled them in. They offered troops and humanitarian relief. Canada is concerned about a flood of Americans trying to escape the fighting and radiation from the Northwest and Northeast. Their situation is worsened by the fact that they lost their prime minister because she had made the trip to DC. Also, Mexico is moving troops up near the border. They're worried about an invasion from the group known as Americans for a Free Texas, who have been talking about that for the last two years. Mexico feels they could take this opportunity to become aggressive. There are a few scattered cases of troops leaving their posts, but it doesn't look like a major concern. To the best of our knowledge, no major weapons, strategic or conventional, have been lost to the enemy. I would conclude that no outside force is a threat at this time."

"Any questions or comments, Sid?" President Young asked as she completed her notes.

"Just that we need to be aware of smaller terrorist groups who might see this as an opportunity to infiltrate. You know, while we're distracted with the internal stuff? I have a briefing scheduled tonight with the senior CIA man we could locate. He's due in at ten thirty tonight. Should have more for you at midnight, maybe a little later." Larry, what about the Middle East?"

Ben made a note. *Sid is definitely from the intelligence community.*

"No word yet. The ambassador is speaking via a conference call with a group of leaders now," Larry replied. "General, anything to add?" Larry knew how to play to the general from his years on the hill.

"Yes. Thank you," Clifton said, sifting several papers in front of him. "I've made thirteen recommendations for emergency field promotions to fill posts left vacant by the losses in DC. Most branches lost their top people, and we need to fill them soon. Their names and jackets are included in the red folder in front of you, Madam President. I might add the military will hold together, and the world still fears our might. But a show of force somewhere may be necessary to reaffirm it. Help them understand that someone is still in charge and watching the back porch." With his ego in check, the general had a down-to-earth style and treated the president with respect and intelligence.

"Thank you, General. I'll sign those orders following our meeting." President Young looked down at her notes. "Okay, step back to Def Con Three for now. Send out a communique to all our commanders overseas. Any provocation by foreign forces should be met quickly with an equal response. However, they do not have nuclear clearance. I must always approve that step. Always. I also want them to be careful with the Russians and Chinese. Let's not start anything that might go global."

The president sat back in her seat with an audible sigh. "General, please don't let them get in over their heads either. Getting our boys shot in Bosnia is not the kind of message we're looking for. Contact Canada and Mexico. Remind them we have been there many times when they needed our help. Assure them we will take whatever steps possible to prevent an overrun of their borders. However, make damned sure they understand that unless armed forces cross into their countries, we expect no bloodshed or mistreatment of American citizens, and we would be prepared to move in troops to ensure that if necessary. Also, pass on our regrets over the loss of Prime Minister Tremioux. She was quite a woman. Did I leave anything out?"

"NATO," Bobbie gently reminded her.

"Yes, NATO. We'll take all the humanitarian relief we can get, but no troops. That is the last thing we need now, foreign troops running around in American cities. Larry, if there are any here now, training, let's get them home right away. Is that it then?"

Ben marveled at her swift grasp of the situation and decisive action. She had definitely paid close attention during her many Cabinet meetings and learned fast.

The table was quiet, and she moved on. "Let's go to the second item. General, if you would, please."

General Clifton cleared his throat. "I'm afraid it looks bad. What little we can see through the smoke on the satellite photos points to near-complete devastation in and around the Washington area. DC proper has been leveled. Our best guess is a twenty-megaton device. We think ground zero was somewhere near Rock Creek Park. Ten miles or so north of the White House. Probably a ground burst. Arlington and Alexandria were also nearly destroyed. Although we can see some remnants of the Pentagon. We can assume one hundred percent casualties for about eight to ten miles in every direction from ground zero, eighty percent for another five to six, and about forty to fifty percent in the next six or seven. That's approximately a nineteen-to-twenty-three-mile radius, just from the initial blast effects. The death toll is staggering. Somewhere between one and a half to two million."

The general looked down, pretending to straighten his papers, but even this rigid war veteran fought to keep his emotions in check. Everyone at the table was silent except for Dedra, who cried quietly.

"Okay, folks. Let's try to get through this. We all lost friends today, but the American people need our strength and action now. I, for one, plan to have a good long cry when this is over." Claire Young had been president for just over eight hours, and she already knew when to speak and what to say. "General, please continue."

"I'm afraid it doesn't get any better. New York's bomb was detonated in Manhattan, probably in one of the scrapers. Chances are it was also a twenty, but the additional height made it more effective." He paused again. "Between three and five million lives lost. Chicago suffered a similar bomb. However, with the lake so close and the way it sprawls to the north and south, our hope is those numbers are half of New York's, maybe even less."

Ben placed his head in his hands. "Maybe Chris made it."

Obviously hesitant to continue, General Clifton shifted in his seat. "Los Angeles. My God. Initial reports are that a plane, most likely a de-commissioned A10, was being tracked by San Diego Air Traffic Control. It passed over LA at a high-altitude minutes before the blast and dropped what we believe was a fifty-megaton device over downtown. It detonated at about two thousand feet above ground, which is the optimum destructive height. The blast was seen and felt clearly in Las Vegas, and the damage was immense." His voice lowered dramatically, so quiet now it was barely audible. "My people tell me the number of dead there may go as high as nine million. I pray they're wrong. All told, somewhere around twelve to sixteen million dead today. I hasten to add, if my people are right, twice that number will die of disease and radiation sickness before this is over. That's another twenty to twenty-five million."

Everyone in the room looked to be as much in shock as Ben felt. America's population had decreased by five percent in the blink of an eye, and another ten percent may still die. No matter the need for strength and action, it was too much, and the president knew it.

"Let's take ten minutes for a cup of coffee," she suggested, her voice that of a mother trying to calm her family.

Before Ben could rise from his chair, Larry gently clutched his arm. "I couldn't help but overhear. You have somebody in Chicago?"

"My son, Chris," Ben said, fighting back emotion.

"Give my aide some information about him. We'll see what we can find out." Larry gave Ben's arm a quick squeeze and left the table.

"Thanks," Ben replied, now talking to Larry's back. Crying for the second time today, Ben scribbled on the large yellow pad in front of him all the information about his son and Don's son too.

ARTICLE IV

Western Montana, January 20, 2001, 3:07 PM MST

"So, what the hell happened, Major? This was your operation, your responsibility. Tell me again why the Denver bomb didn't go off."

Even through the heavy closet door, Jamie recognized General Boyle's voice. Passed over for his second star three times, General Harvey Boyle had always lived on the edge of the military right. Convinced all civilian leaders got elected only to line their pockets and ruin the life of the common soldier and American, he had no use for friends on the hill. Too often, those in and out of uniform viewed him as the voice of the militia and the Christian right. Many friends and foes alike had tried to convince him to "play ball" but to no avail. Finally, after thirty-two years and a public shouting match with one of the joint chiefs, General Boyle decided to retire. No one attempted to stop him.

If his message hadn't resonated with those in power, it had struck a chord with many of the common foot soldiers and some patriot groups. He was invited to spearhead a group known as the "Sons of the Patriots" in Michigan. It was during that period that he received a cryptic letter from a captain watching over the destruction of the nuclear arsenal in North Dakota. The general, the patriot movement, and the country would never be the same.

Jamie's heart beat so hard that she found it difficult to breathe. The consequences of her being discovered here would be swift and painful, but she had to hear this conversation—had to know for sure. Before she acted.

She had arrived at the camp even before the general, two years ago next week. Her intensive training had honed her body and mind but taken a visible toll on her soft features. Other than the general, the men in camp didn't even look at her as a woman any longer. She was a soldier no more, no less. Hell, she couldn't even remember the last time her long red hair had been worn down. Even her bra and panties had been replaced with sleeveless undershirts and boxers. An attempt to look more like a man. After all, she would be expected to fight like one.

Not so long ago, finding an eyeliner that didn't clash with her green eyes could take up an entire afternoon. Now night vision and urban warfare training filled her days.

The excitement she felt the day General Boyle arrived was almost spiritual, close to an out-of-body experience. He would change the course of their struggle, make them a force for change, and change was needed. Jamie had been convinced of that ever since that terrible day her husband received a mandatory twenty-five-year sentence in federal prison. That was over four years ago.

It was so unfair, a system rigged against him, the outcome already known. Ken was a victim in the war against drugs, the unwitting passenger in a friend's car carrying two pounds of crack cocaine concealed in the frame. An ordinary fifteen-minute ride that would change his life and hers forever. Prosecutors had offered him a deal if he talked, but what could he tell them? He didn't know anything. Convinced he was holding out on them, they hit him hard, giving no mercy and no deal.

It shattered her life. What would she do now? Go back to dancing? She had quit her job as an exotic dancer when Ken found work at the General Motors plant in Kansas City, but her body wasn't what it was five years before. Besides, Ken would never agree to that.

Broke and depressed, Jamie moved in with her brother in Deer Path, Colorado, not far from the prison in Denver where Ken was being held.

Her brother was a member of the Colorado Militia, and she began attending the weekly militia meetings with him. What else was there to do in Deer Path? When not at the meetings, she listened to a local AM radio station that was a part of the freedom movement and provided the real news for those willing to listen.

As the months passed, Jamie began to learn the depth of corruption and deceit practiced by the American government. A cover-up of FBI involvement in the Oklahoma City bombing, CIA drug running, the Tri-Lateral Commission, and murders committed by people close to the president himself. It was terrifying and caused her many sleepless nights.

Meanwhile, just days after her arrival in Deer Path, she started hearing about a compound in the northwest where several of the local patriots had visited for a time and raved about the feeling of belonging there. Tucked away in remote Montana, it beckoned to freedom-loving Americans prepared to join in the battle against the draft dodging, pot smoking, womanizing, no good coward, Heir Clayton. Some thought him the Anti-Christ bent on world domination, while others saw Clayton as just another in a long line of crooks.

It was said that in Montana, you could live free and get ready to fight the coming war for true independence. So, with Jamie's increasing concern over recent government actions, and the two-year stay with her brother wearing thin, she packed up a few things and headed for the camp. She was welcomed by dozens of like-thinking Patriots, as devoted, if not more than her, to freeing the citizens of the United States from the new world order. Here she could take the next step past talking and protesting. Here they would change the world forever.

The training was intense and effective. Life felt right, and before long, she would be a part of history, a new, truly free America.

The general's arrival enriched the spirit of the entire camp. He moved Jamie, in particular, and in a short time, they became close. Maybe too close, for after only two months, she moved into his cabin, and their relationship moved beyond friendship. She had missed the touch of a man, and making love to such a powerful one was the ultimate aphrodisiac. Lying together, their bodies sweaty and spent, she gazed into his eyes as he spoke of a world free from tyranny. She even stood at his side while he presided over the memorial service for Tim McVeigh, a hero sacrificed by the federal government to hide its own involvement.

Jamie had been on top of the world. That is until recently when she started noticing changes in the general. Jealousy and possessiveness had become commonplace. Enraged one day because she ate lunch with a staff sergeant, Harvey locked her in their cabin until dark. Then, last week, she stumbled across the most recent letters she had written to Ken in prison, opened and never mailed in Harvey's top desk drawer. Jamie moved back to the women's barracks that day.

Now she was forced to sneak back in and hide in the closet, spying on him like a traitor. It was the only way to find out if the horrible rumors were true. Did the general start the war he so desired to fight? Did he kill millions of innocent people without warning? Was Denver an unfulfilled target of his rage? She put her ear closer to the door to hear every word.

"You know damn well I will not tolerate incompetence. Who is responsible?" General Boyle's voice boomed against the door. From the sound of it, Major Hollis, Boyle's right-hand man, was struggling to deflect his anger.

"General, it was not our people. They were ready. It should have gone off."

"Then what happened?" Boyle snapped back to him.

"We were double-crossed, I believe," Hollis said so softly Jamie could barely make it out.

"By who? I want names."

Major Hollis lowered his voice, and Jamie strained even harder to hear. "The governor. He canceled his trip to DC. We had a great cover story for him. His plane was to have some minor equipment problems and be delayed in Kansas City, but he never got on. Robbins wouldn't have stayed in Denver unless he knew that bomb wasn't going to go off."

"What did he have to gain?" Boyle shouted. "I offered him the regional presidency, the whole goddamned Western United States. He could have been one of the four most powerful men in The United States. Now he's a dead man."

"Do you want the truth?"

"Of course I do."

"I think the calculating bastard figured we weren't going to be able to pull this off and decided to take his chances with the other side. Play it safe." Jamie recoiled from the door as the general nervously paced past it, his shadow breaking the beam of light flowing beneath the door.

"How much does he know? Can he hurt us?"

It was quiet for a few seconds before Hollis responded. "Nothing useful, and I wouldn't worry too much. He can't give us up without implicating himself, and that fucking coward will never do that."

Jamie could almost visualize Harvey through the door, standing erect, hands firmly on his hips, dressed in field fatigues, his steel gray eyes narrow and intense. Vain about his graying hair, he shaved his head every morning. Many days before dawn, Jamie watched his shining head bob up and down beside the bed—his fifty push-ups and one hundred sit-ups were never missed. His passion for being young again, which so intrigued her in the beginning, was now sad and pathetic.

"Major," Boyle said slowly, "we discussed why this was so important to me. It's absolutely vital that Denver be destroyed. As long as that useless drug smuggler is alive, Jamie will belong to him. The bomb must be rearmed and detonated before Robbins decides to lead them to it. I don't give a shit how you do it. Just get it done. If by some chance Robbins isn't there when it happens, find him and kill him. Send Wally if you have to."

"I understand, General, but I'll need the authorization codes." Hollis was a soldier, a follower, and Jamie knew, right or wrong, he would carry out the general's order. Ken and a lot of other innocent people were going to die if she didn't stop him.

"No one sees them but you and the operator. Check over there in the closet, top shelf. Here is the key."

Jamie's heart stopped. She was about to die. She had chosen the closet because it was locked, and she knew where Harvey had hidden the spare key. Quickly she moved to the far corner of the small enclosure burying herself behind the general's full-length dress coat. It seemed to take forever for the major to unlock the door, and for a moment, Jamie was afraid Harvey might tell him to use the spare. After a few more clicks, the closet door opened, and Jamie held her breath. Major Hollis partially entered the closet, his nose and cap brim visible from her vantage point. Any sound now, the slightest movement, and she would be discovered.

Could he feel her presence behind the coat? Smell her deodorant or toothpaste? Hear her heartbeat as it tried to rip through her chest, banging like a bass drum in her own ears?

His head turned slightly toward her end of the small closet. Jamie closed her hand around the stock of her 9 MM tucked in the waistband of her fatigues. She didn't want to kill Hollis, but she knew he would kill her if she was detected.

Thankfully, he found the book containing the codes without more effort and soon closed and relocked the door. She was sure that everyone in camp could hear the audible sigh escaping from her mouth as it went dark again. However, the door remained secure, and Jamie eased the grip on her gun.

"Major," Harvey snapped. "Before you go to the communications shack, muster the troops in the main hut. I want to brief them on tomorrow's ground assault."

"Yes, sir," Hollis said, his voice trailing off into the night.

Jamie heard the cabin door close as the major left.

She knew it was cold out tonight and prayed the general would not want his dress coat for the rally.

ARTICLE V

Denver, Colorado, January 20, 2001, 1:58 PM MST

Fifteen minutes later, the meeting resumed. As the first one seated in the room, Ben stood as the others arrived, taking in the grim and already tired expressions on their faces. Ben too was feeling the weight of the day on his mood. Not only had he spent ten minutes explaining to Larry's aide the details of Chris's life, but he also had two urgent phone messages from the editor asking for copy. He had no way of knowing how soon or how much he would be allowed to tell them.

President Young opened her folder and turned to the new Secretary of Transportation. "Marie, I know this isn't a normal function of transportation, but I'm going to ask you to ride herd on FEMA." President Young began. "My first concern is mobilizing a relief effort without endangering the rescuers. I'm told there will be many fires and unsafe structures, but you can see those hazards. Radiation is our major hurdle. You can't see it or taste it. It just kills you. You might last a couple of days or weeks or get cancer in twenty years. I've been thinking, could we use people already in the area? Minimize the risk to others?"

"Do we have a radiation expert we can tap?" Marie asked.

"My staff tells me Alex Hampton I think they call him Bo—is already scheduled to make a trip to Washington with a small group from Atlanta. Bobbie has a call into the Nuclear Regulatory Commission in Northern California for an alternative."

"I'm no expert," General Clifton interjected, "however, I do know radiation has a cumulative effect, and leaving people inside a hot zone is problematic. It would be necessary to inform them of the dangers of staying. Maybe rotating groups in and out to minimize their exposure time might be safer."

"You may have something there, General. Bobbie, get me someone from the NRC. I'll not fly blind on this issue." The president paused a moment, looking down at her folder again. "Let's come back to this later. Governor, do we know how many of your colleagues were in DC?" she asked as Bobbie slipped quietly from the room.

"I had my staff look over news accounts and press releases. Our records indicate twelve to fifteen. Since this morning, I've talked personally to six governors of western states."

"I would appreciate your help in contacting all of them and bringing them up to speed."

"I'd be glad to. Even if you are a Democrat," the governor quipped.

Judging by a quick scan of the occupants of the room, and particularly, the expression on the president's face, Ben gathered the governor's attempt at humor bombed terribly. Mentioning partisan politics at a time like this showed little class.

President Young kept her head down, obviously fuming. Through tightly clenched teeth, she replied, "Thank you."

Apparently unaware of his error in judgment, the governor added, "You need to be careful not to offend any of the local authorities. Include them in your plans. This is not just a federal problem, and you can't just waltz in and take over."

Ben got the distinct impression President Young could hold her tongue no longer even before she spoke. He could see it in her eyes and the stiff set of her jaw. "Governor, do you have a problem with anything we've discussed here? Have we stepped on your toes? Gone beyond our constitutional authority?"

Robbins fumbled for answers to her questions. "Well, no, of course not."

"I said from the beginning everyone would have to work together. That's why you're here and why Mr. Bleser is here," Young snapped. "Did you speak with the Governor of California?"

"No, I did not," Governor Robbins replied, seemingly still defiant.

"How about the Governor of Illinois?"

"No."

"New York?"

"Nope."

"Maryland?" she asked, now staring directly at him. No response came from the governor. "Why don't you call them and see if they're concerned about being offended or if they want our help. Please let me know if they don't because we have more than enough to do."

For the second time in less than an hour, a challenge to the president's authority went down hard.

Having said enough, apparently, the president shifted in her seat and moved on with her agenda. "I don't think we have enough information to formulate a plan yet. After we receive more radiation data and hear from the governors involved, we can put something together. General, please tell me about the ARA."

"My FBI contact has an extensive file on these bastards. They've been on them for a while. I hope you won't mind if I refer to their head guy as Boyle. I just can't bring myself to call him General. Anyway, Boyle retired eleven years ago but maintained a number of militia contacts across the country. About a year ago, he set up shop in a remote area of Montana, somewhere near Thompson Rise. There's speculation the sheriff there is sympathetic to Boyle's cause as every time the bureau got close to Boyle, he was tipped off."

General Clifton glanced up from his papers, his gaze moving from one member of the president's cabinet to another. Ben imagined the general wanted to make sure he had everyone's undivided attention.

Clifton continued. "The last estimate we have says there are approximately three hundred and twenty-five men and women in the compound, all heavily armed and well-trained. Christ, they have perimeter radar and four hundred square miles of thick forest around them.

"A month ago, BATF went to federal court for a search warrant, but they were shot down. Not enough probable cause. The good news is ARA has little use for foreigners, so it's unlikely any outside terrorist would throw in or cooperate with them."

The president made notes as Clifton spoke, as did Ben. General Clifton barely took time to breathe before he went on. "Analysis of their manifesto shows a deliberate attempt to mislead us. They are not using the shortwave for communications, and there's a lot of chatter, all right, but nothing of any substance.

"We have people checking the Internet. Thoughts are they may have a secure server, encrypted, probably with a dummy home page of some kind, but that's a huge job. Even if we find it, I doubt the decryption codes on file are valid, so we'll have to hack in."

Ben wasn't surprised by the general's comment. Recalling an article he had written a few months ago on *Ghost Pages*. Criminals and terrorists were using fake sites to basically hide in plain sight. These sites used cryptic logins to access hidden content and messaging. The FBI had created a task force to study it. However, one source told Ben that the bad guys had a big head start.

"Do we have someone who can do that?" President Young cut in.

Clifton held up a staying hand. "The trouble is, you can't break in and stay invisible. They'll know we're there. Maybe we'll get lucky, and someone who doesn't like Boyle's methods will seek us out and give us front-door access." The general paused briefly, looking up at the president. "Their manifesto also states Denver was destroyed. Obviously, that didn't happen. Yet. So, the question becomes, is there a bomb? Everyone available is looking. We started in the skyscrapers because of Chicago and New York, but no luck so far." President Young did not acknowledge his reference to the Denver bomb.

Ben wondered if the staff at the paper had remained in the office or scattered to the wind. He made a note to reach out to his chief editor after this session was over.

General Clifton wasn't finished and continued. "What I'm worried about is the forty other states with strong militia groups. I have received information about scattered activity in and around some military bases, some minor sabotage, that kind of thing. If they get organized, there could be forty thousand well-armed crazies spread all over the country. We need to walk a fine line. We get too aggressive, and we risk being the spark that sets them off. But ignoring them is equally dangerous. I think our best bet would be to position our forces near enough to make a quick response but not so close as to spook them."

Sid asked, "General, what about their threat of more strategic detonations?"

Clifton turned to their NSA leader with pursed lips. "We're in the middle of a complete nuclear inventory right now. I hasten to add that one suspicious log entry has been found in North Dakota. Six warheads due for destruction in April of 2000. The log indicates they were shipped out to Texas for destruction. However, we can't find the receipt for delivery on that end."

Larry put down his coffee. "What's the tonnage on them?"

Ben edged closer to the table, staring directly at the general, attempting to gauge his reaction to Larry's loaded question.

General Clifton glanced first at Ben and then the president. "It's preliminary, probably just a clerical error. I don't think it warrants any more discussion."

President Young sighed audibly. "Come on, General. If you know the tonnage, give it to us."

The general searched his notes with obvious reluctance. "One fifty-megaton and five twenty-megaton warheads."

"So, the fifty on LA and a twenty each for DC, New York, and Chicago." Sid rubbed his forehead as he spoke.

President Young added, "That leaves two twenties out there somewhere."

If Ben read him right, General Clifton was becoming agitated. "Let's not jump to conclusions. We don't have all the facts yet."

The Secretary of Defense, who appeared to have been listening to the exchanges with rapt attention, leaned forward in his chair. Larry's gray ponytail shifted across his back. "General, do you think anyone outside the government could obtain enough bomb-grade plutonium to build five or six large devices?"

"And if they did," Sid interjected, "could it be kept quiet? It would have to come from many sources, be transported, stored, and assembled."

Ben was scribbling quickly in his notes, trying desperately to catch the nuances of this new information.

"It would be almost impossible," the general conceded quietly. "Almost. But to imagine they used our own bombs on us, that the ARA had people inside the service willing to help them… That scares the shit out of me."

Imagining it took a lot to scare Terry Clifton, Ben's shoulders slumped, and he sunk back a little deeper into his chair.

"I'm sorry, Madam President. Excuse my language." The tone of the general's voice said she'd earned his respect now.

"Don't worry about it, General." President Young chuckled. "Since early this morning, I've had an urge to run outside and shout, 'Fuck you, Harvey Boyle.'" Her admission sent a ripple of tight laughter and nods of agreement around the room.

Ben was happy the president had such a tight pulse on the room and, unlike Robbins, knew when to lighten the mood.

When the laughter subsided, Sid spoke. "We have to find those warheads. Possessing those is their only leverage. Knowing he doesn't have them or no longer has them, we could take out Boyle, and the rest would fall quickly."

"Can we look for a radiation signature using the satellites?" Larry asked General Clifton.

"Yes, but we're likely to get a bunch of false positives."

"Get started on that right away, please, General," President Young instructed just as Bobbie reentered the room.

Bobbie leaned close and whispered something in the president's ear. "Great. I'll take it." The president moved the black telephone in front of her. "Bobbie, put it on speaker for me." Bobbie quickly pushed a few buttons and nodded.

"Hello? Hello, who is this, please?" a voice with a thick Asian accent crackled over the small speaker.

"President Young and my cabinet," she said into the phone louder than necessary.

Ben was a bit bemused to hear he was a part of *her cabinet* but knew why she didn't take the time to go around the room with a stranger on the phone.

"I'm sorry. I do not know any President Young. Who is this?" the still anonymous voice said flatly.

"Is this line secure, Bobbie?" the general asked.

"Absolutely." Bobbie's usual brief but firm response left no room for doubt.

"This is General Terrance Clifton. Have you heard of me?"

"Yes, I heard of General Clifton. But how do I know you are he?"

"Go to your Crisis Cabinet and get the emergency orders," Clifton barked. "We'll wait. Do you understand?"

"Yes. Hold on, please." Sounds of the receiver clunking onto a desktop came over the speaker.

"What the hell is going on with this guy?" the president asked no one in particular. If Ben wasn't mistaken, she was not happy about his reluctance to accept her authority.

Ben studied her face closely. He was starting to get a good handle on her emotions from the position of her eyebrows. A good reporter needed to write more than just the words spoken. His readers wanted to be with him in the room and feel what was happening.

General Clifton grinned. "Damned fine man. He has procedures, and he's following them. If everyone had as much respect for procedure, I doubt Boyle would have gotten his hands on those bombs. I like this guy already."

The voice on the line returned, "Okay, I got them."

"Please open them and verify," General Clifton said, putting on his official tone. Eagle, seven, alpha, tango, bravo, three, three, five, eight, eight, two, zero. Do you need me to repeat?"

"No, sir. Verified. I am very sorry. This is Dr. Chu Dun."

"No need to apologize for following procedures, Doctor," the general replied. "Madam President, Dr. Chu Dun."

She nodded in appreciation of the general's introduction. Ben figured she could have done without his smugness. "Hello, Dr. Dun. We are in need of some information on radiation and its effects."

"Yes, Mrs. President. I can help you. I have Ph.D. from Stanford. Many years' experience radiation. Yes, I know radiation very much." Dun's voice was stronger now. His English, however, was still lacking.

Smiling slightly, the president continued. "How long can someone stay in an area contaminated by radiation?"

"Hmm... Many factors. How strong the radiation, lifetime exposure prior to event, what type of isotope. What are readings now?"

Claire frowned and leaned back in her chair. "I'm afraid we don't have that data yet. Let me be more general. How should we proceed with the rescue operations? Rotating teams or maybe by using people already contaminated?"

"No, no, no. People in area who are contaminated must get out quickly. You need someone to monitor levels and determine safe length of stay. Some areas, you stay out completely. No one goes in. Too dangerous. Many more lives lost."

"Doctor. You just got yourself a job," President Young responded, acting quickly. "I want you to coordinate all of the rescue operations. Secretary Marie Zambrano will be your contact. General Clifton will send a jet to fly you here. Is that clear?"

Ben had a few classmates that worked at Stanford's administration office. He made a note to reach out to them and get additional background about the Doctor.

"Yes, Mrs. President. When will jet be here, and where is there?" The hesitancy and tone in Dr. Dun's voice indicated he was stunned at the developments of the last five minutes.

The president now wore a full smile. "We will be in touch concerning the arrival time of the jet. As to where we are, you will know when you get here." She reached out and disconnected, chuckling softly. "Scientists... Marie, when you speak with Dr. Dun, please tell him it's madam, not missus."

Marie smiled slightly and nodded.

"General, it's vital we find those warheads quickly," the president said, returning to business. "Work with Larry and Sid on a tactical plan for the capture of Boyle's compound. If you need to move troops into position, do it quietly. We should try to identify any other areas of concern. Potential hot spots. However, let there be no misunderstanding. You do not have carte blanche. No fishing expeditions."

Claire straightened and let her gaze reach everyone at the table before she continued. "We will not become the new world order monsters they preach about. Our government still plays by the rules, and the Constitution has not been suspended. If you have any, and I do mean *any* doubts about the legality of your actions, contact the attorney general. I trust his judgment completely. If there is a person alive who knows the Constitution better, I don't know them. You can be sure of one thing, however. No idiot in Montana would qualify."

Judge Bostow nodded. "Thank you, Madam President." Larry, Sid, and General Clifton all followed suit, acknowledging her admonition.

"Why don't you three get started then, and we'll finish up the rest of the agenda?" President Young paused before continuing. "Before you go, what thoughts do you have on my television address?"

General Clifton and Sid exchanged glances. Finally, Sid spoke. "We were hoping you might consider radio only."

Ben immediately noticed both Sid and Terry visibly shift in their chairs.

"Both. I meant to say both radio and television. What's your concern about television?"

"Well," Sid began, "it's just that we've looked at the ramifications and possible outcomes, and there's some danger of someone tracing the signal back to us."

Studying Sid's posture and tone, Ben thought the NSA leader was obviously waltzing her.

"Come off it, Sid, and get to it. We don't have time for this crap," President Young snapped, her patience obviously running short.

"General," Sid said, looking down the table.

Clifton sighed. "Madam President, we have analyzed the implications of the sites chosen for destruction. It is our belief Boyle intentionally avoided hitting the south." General Clifton played with his pen as he spoke.

"Meaning what?" she asked.

"I have read some of their dogma. Talk of minorities taking over the country. The South is an important base for them, or should I say the *White South*." General Clifton's words hung in the air.

"Are you telling me you're worried the South won't support me because I'm black?" President Young exclaimed.

Ben hadn't seen this fire in the president's eyes before, and he held his breath, expecting the worst.

Looking up from the table and making eye contact with her, General Clifton straightened in his chair. "We just wanted you to be aware of the possibilities."

President Young smacked the table and leaned forward, her patience clearly at its end. "Godammit, just answer my question."

"Yes, Madam President, that is our concern," Sid responded, taking General Clifton off the hook.

"And you're a woman, a black woman," Clifton added.

Except for the president's pen tapping on her notepad, the room was completely quiet. All eyes focused on her. Time passed slowly, painful seconds enhancing the tension.

Ben pushed his chair back away from the table a few inches. He didn't want to be directly in her line of sight. It was the first time today he was a bit frightened about the consequences for Larry and Sid for challenging her.

Finally, she turned her chair away from the table and stood erect. Walking around the table, she looked at every one of them, her stare intense. Reaching the door, President Young opened it and began to leave. Halfway out, she stopped, turned, and reentered the room, closing the door behind her.

"No. I will not succumb to this madness. The time has come for people in the United States to decide if they still want a constitutional government. For me to hide from them, not let them see my black skin, deny my heritage, deny my sex, deny the Constitution… No. I won't be a party to that."

Reaching her chair, she resumed her seat at the table. "Tonight, at seven-thirty Mountain Standard Time, the new president of these United States, a *black woman* from Denver, Colorado, will address the nation on television." For the first time today, Ben thought she looked tired.

"Gentlemen, you are excused," President Young snapped.

General Clifton, Larry Franklin, and Sid Green gathered their notes and quietly left the room.

Ben wanted to say something to try and ease the tension, but even his long experience coming up with the right words failed him now. "Thank You, Madam President," was the best he could do. He gathered his notes and followed the others out.

ARTICLE VI

Virginia, January 20, 2001, 5:44 PM EST

"I can't reach anyone on this thing," Mike said as he slammed his flip phone closed.

Billy walked back toward the Explorer. "EMP probably knocked out the cell sites. We need to get moving soon. I feel a bit naked out here. What should we do with his body?"

Bo's body now lay on the shoulder of the interstate, wrapped in a gray tarp from Billy's gear. Mike wished it had been large enough to cover Bo's shoes too.

Sally had finished cleaning the glass and blood from the interior of the car and joined them. "What are you going to do with him?"

Mike didn't understand why it was his decision to make, but he made it anyway. "He'd be worse off where we're going. Let's move him off the road a bit. We can send someone back later to get him."

Sally and Billy each took an end of the tarp, moving Bo's body gently down the hill while Mike tied a red rag to the Explorer's jack handle and shoved it down into the dirt just off the pavement. "Damn shame," he muttered.

Sally visibly shivered and looked away from the body lurking in the darkness. Wasting no time, she turned and climbed back up the hill. "Come on, let's get moving."

Once situated in the Explorer, no one spoke. Mike watched in his side mirror as the red flag became smaller and smaller until, finally, it was swallowed by the darkness.

Several miles later, Sally broke the silence. "Do we have any kind of plan? I'm a little uncomfortable just driving into God knows what."

"I just want to help the survivors, if there are any." Mike was starting to lose his energy under the stress of the day's activities. "Everything has happened so fast, so out of control. I'm wide open to any suggestions you two might have."

Billy asked, "We know Quantico should have some survivors, and the troops there will be on our side. What do you say about heading toward them?"

"I know I have a personal stake in Quantico," Sally began, sounding pleased it had been someone else's suggestion, "but it does make sense to me."

"Okay by me," Mike chimed in. "Sally, can you get us there?"

"Yes. I-95 will take us right to it, about twelve miles ahead."

"Did anyone get lunch yet?" Billy asked, already digging in his bag for food.

"I could eat the tires off a dump truck," Sally quipped, her Georgia drawl hanging in the air.

Mike chuckled. He remembered the cookouts at his house outside Atlanta, friends from the FBI and CDC gathered for good food and horseshoes. They let off steam and traded war stories. Sally could out-eat and out-drink every man there but still maintained the charm and wit of a true Southern Lady. Everyone seemed to be feeling a little better now that they had a plan of action, and Bo's corpse fell farther and farther behind them.

"Sure, I could eat," Mike replied. "What do you have?"

"Dried beef tips, dried chicken fingers, dried carrots, and Twinkies." Judging by the crooked grin on his face, Billy appeared to be having fun listing the menu for them.

"Twinkies," Mike and Sally both exclaimed simultaneously.

"Sorry, not enough to go around. Someone's gotta eat a Ding Dong or

Little Debbie Pie."

Sally smiled at Mike and quipped, "That Billy really knows how to pack a lunch."

About five miles from the Quantico exit, abandoned cars on the highway began to be a problem. Several times, they were forced to drive off-road to continue. Coming back onto the highway after one such detour, Sally stopped the vehicle with a sudden intense jerk. Directly in front of them, dozens of ragged-looking people stood around a small fire made from tires burning in the center of the road. The scene was eerie and straight out of a Stephen King novel.

"Jesus. Look at that." Mike reached for his medical bag.

Before he could move, Sally grabbed his arm. "Take it easy. We need to be careful here." Locking all four doors, she edged slowly forward until reaching the first group and rolled down the driver's window a few inches. "Hi, folks. Is everybody here okay?"

A tall thin man, wearing dress slacks and a shirt that was once white, stepped forward. "I haven't seen any major injuries. A few bumps, bruises, and cuts. A few people throwing up over there. Shock, I guess" He pointed to a motor home twenty or thirty yards up the road. "What in the hell happened anyway?"

This was the first eyewitness to a blast they had come across, and Billy used the opportunity to probe for data. "Tell us exactly what you saw."

"God, I don't quite know how to describe it. I was headed to DC for a job interview with the Department of Justice in their legal research department. Just driving down the road, you know, and out of nowhere, no warning or anything, this big flash of light, blinding light, even with the sunlight. Our cars just quit running. Stopped dead. It was weird." He glanced around at the others around him before giving those in the Explorer his attention again. "Then it got really wild because on these new cars, when your engine dies, well, you've got no brakes and no steering, so we just kind of bounced around banging into one another. It was like riding the bumper cars at the carnival, only you weren't sure if you were going to live through it."

He rattled on, eyes slightly glazed over as he spoke. "When we thought it was all over, *boom*! One hell of a shock wave rolled through, a hot wind and loads of dust. It rattled the windows, even moved some cars." He paused and blinked as if clearing his eyes of tears. "So, what the hell was it? An Asteroid? One idiot said it was a nuclear blast, but that's crazy, right? We would be dead already, right?"

Mike watched as Sally tried to decide how much information to give this confused soul and looked over toward him for support. Mike just shrugged and reached for the door handle. "Dammit, Mike. Don't you dare get out? You dumb bastard, if you get yourself shot, I will kick your fu—"

The door slamming shut cut off the end of her tirade, but Mike had gotten its general tenor. "Boy, is she pissed." He chuckled.

Sally bailed out of the vehicle and gave chase. "Mike, Mike!" Sally screamed. "Wait up. You could tell a person you're getting out, you know? Heading off into the night, trying to get yourself killed? You could tell me what in the hell you're doing for once. Dammit, Mike, slowdown."

Mike recognized her tone and prayed by the time she caught up with him, most of the steam would be vented. Unfortunately for him, his prayers went unanswered. Sally swished past and spun around to face him nose to nose.

She drew in a deep breath. "You know, I should wrap my hands around your neck, drag your scrawny ass back to the truck, and tie you to your seat. Knock some common sense into that bookworm brain of yours."

Mike stood quietly for a moment. "You finished?" he asked, trying hard not to grin.

"Yes, but I meant every word. Do that again, and I'll shoot you myself." She'd nearly shouted her words in his face, and Mike knew Sally wouldn't react like this if she wasn't frightened.

"Good, then shall we go forth and do good deeds for mankind?" he replied, keeping his voice artificially cheerful.

"Smart ass," she shot back, trying to hide her own grin.

"I love you too, Sally."

"You're going to love my boot where the sun doesn't shine if you don't get somewhere a little more secure."

Mike sensed her words were for an old friend, a good friend, one she planned to keep alive. And he felt the same way about her.

"Hello...? Hello, I'm a doctor. Is anyone sick here," Mike called out into the darkness.

The voice that returned was weak but close. "Over here."

Sally moved in front of him, drawing her Berretta. "I'll go first. Hang back a little," she whispered. "Come out into the light, please," she commanded. Two shadowy figures stumbled from behind the motor home. A woman in her late sixties and a young girl.

Mike rushed past Sally toward them. "Hi. You two not feeling well?" He kept his voice calm and soothing as he knelt down in front of the little girl. She appeared to be no more than four or five, with long blonde hair and big green eyes, swollen from crying. Her face and little pink dress were covered with dirt, except beneath her eyes, where her tears had carved out a path down to her chin.

"Grandma says I'll be okay, but I've been throwing up a lot and made a mess in my underpants," she told him, crying just a little.

"I'm Doctor Mike. What's your name, sweetie?" Mike asked with his emotions barely under control.

She stopped crying and straightened her dress a bit. "Amanda. My grandma said we could go see the parade for Mr. President, but there was a big noise, and now we can't go because our moving house is broken. He has a white house, too, you know?"

"He does? I'll bet it's a big one too." Mike was using the time to check her pulse and blood pressure. "Sally, shine that flashlight over here on the gauge. Your grandma is a smart woman. And you're going to be just fine. I have some really good medicine to help make your tummy better." Her eyes were big, watching him retrieve the cysteamine tablets from his bag.

"Do you need anything else?" Sally asked softly.

He turned toward her, speaking in a whisper. "Could you find someone to stay with them and maybe some clean clothing?"

"We have clean things in the motor home, but I would appreciate someone to help with Mandy." Apparently, Amanda's grandmother had no trouble with her hearing.

In his haste to care for the child, he had ignored her. "I'm sorry. I didn't mean to be rude. Doctor Mike Jenkins. And you are?"

She managed a weak smile. "Thelma Fletcher, and don't worry. You didn't offend me. I'm so pleased you're here to help us."

"How are you feeling?" Mike asked.

Thelma glanced at Amanda. "Pretty good. Same symptoms as her."

Mike picked up on her use of words that Amanda would not understand. He winked at her. "Good, but maybe we should give you some medicine anyway."

"Yeah, Grandma's tummy hurts too," Amanda interjected.

"Where were you when the shock wave came through?" Mike asked Thelma.

She looked slowly down at the ground. "Outside the camper. I was afraid someone might hit us with their car, so we jumped out and got off the road. Is that why we're sick?"

"No. Just the first ones to get sick, but you will also be the first ones to get better." Mike smiled. "Okay, Amanda, can you swallow this like a big girl?" He gave her half of a tablet and a can of orange juice.

"Sure, Doctor Mike. I can do it." After a few attempts, the pill went down.

"Sally, why don't you watch Amanda for a minute? I'll take Thelma over to the truck for her pill."

"Sure, I'd be glad to." Sally sat down on the ground and began playing with Amanda's hair. Having children never seemed to fit into Sally's plans, but seeing her with Amanda left little doubt in his mind that she would have been a great mother.

Mike held Thelma's arm as they walked. "You both have a mild case of radiation sickness. The medication should help. The good news is I don't think you'll see any long-term effects, but you should expect a mild relapse in five or six days."

"What about her parents?"

Puzzled, he said, "I'm not sure what you mean. Are they with you?"

"No. They went to Washington two days ago for the pre-inaugural parties. We were to meet them this morning." Thelma's lips trembled as she swallowed. "They're not coming back, are they?"

Mike couldn't speak the words. He shook his head no and squeezed her arm. She laid her head on his shoulder and cried.

Billy had been checking out the rest of the group for any serious injuries and gave Mike the rundown. "Mostly bumps and bruises, but one man does have a broken leg. I think we got it set okay, and it's in a homemade splint. This young lady has some medical training," he added, indicating a young woman standing near. "She's a certified nurse's aide in a Florida nursing home. Most of the bandages over there are her handy work. Holly, this is Doctor Mike Jenkins."

The young woman could not have been more than twenty-five, with brown curly hair. She was short but definitely not petite. Her big blue eyes looked tired, and from the amount of blood on her blouse, deservedly so.

"Boy, Doctor, I sure could have used you a few hours ago," she said.

Mike smiled and shook her hand. "It looks like you did just fine without me."

"Can you stay?" she asked, hope echoing in her voice.

"No, Holly, I'm afraid not," Mike spoke softly, trying to comfort her as much as possible. "There are a lot more people up the road who need me. But I'll leave you some medication in case anyone else becomes ill."

"It's radiation sickness, isn't it? I've seen it after chemotherapy treatments."

Mike was impressed by her composure and knowledge. "Yes, but the cases are mild. It shouldn't get too bad. I really would appreciate it if you could find someone to stay with Amanda and Thelma over there by the motor home."

Holly smiled. "Of course, I will. Several nice people have offered to help."

"Thank you for all you're doing, Holly. I need to get going, but just so you know, we're hopeful the Marines up the road came through this thing okay. If they did, we'll send you back some help." Mike hoped he could come through for her.

Billy and Sally had already returned to the Explorer, but Mike took a minute to say goodbye to his girls. "Someone should be by soon to help you care for Amanda," Mike said as he hugged Thelma. He gave Amanda a big kiss. Looking at her little face, he wished Harvey Boyle were here to see the pain he had inflicted on this innocent child. He bent over, handing her one of his business cards. "Give this to your grandma and tell her if she ever needs anything to call me." He would have told her himself but was afraid of the lump in his throat.

Sally slowly pulled the Explorer around the motor home. Caught in the headlights, they saw Amanda blowing them a kiss. "She is so cute. Will she really be alright?" Sally asked.

"For now. But her chances of getting cancer are about fifteen times higher than they were this morning." Mike smiled and waved goodbye to them.

Billy leaned forward between the front bucket seats. "That rise up ahead probably saved their lives." He pointed at the incline up the road.

Billy's statement proved to be prophetic. Topping the rise, the full magnitude of the damage began to emerge. Small brush fires fanned by the increasing winds danced and leaped like some perverse spirit celebrating its victory, and for the first time, buildings began to show signs of the horrific event. Windows facing the blast had shattered, becoming thousands of lethal fragments, ripping and tearing at the occupants of the cars littering the highway. Some were still sitting upright inside the vehicles ,little if any skin on their faces, looking as if they might drive away at any time.

A few bodies lay on the roadway where they fell, or were dragged, features distorted from the pain and shock witnessed seconds before death. Mike's stomach turned and rumbled. He was a medical doctor and should be used to death and gore. But not like this. A human being couldn't see this carnage without feeling sick. Burned human flesh hanging from facial bones shattered by the blast, even babies still strapped in their car seats, the plastic seats melted around them, engulfing their helpless bodies. He wanted to bottle it up and send it to Montana, make Boyle drink it, feel it. Die from it.

"As we get closer, it will get much worse," Billy whispered.

Mike couldn't hide his shock. "God, Billy, how can it get worse?"

"At ground zero and for several miles outward, everything is virtually vaporized. Gone."

The pressure appeared to be getting to Sally, too. "Okay, enough. Can we just get to Quantico and find out if anyone is there?"

Travel on I-95 was slow and treacherous as they dodged abandoned cars and dead bodies.

"Heads up," Billy shouted. "Straight ahead at the bottom of the hill."

Flashing blue lights pierced the darkness, where several vehicles blocked the interstate. Dark-colored vehicles, dark-colored jeeps. Marines.

"How do we play it?" Mike asked, deferring to Sally and Billy in these matters.

Billy placed his M-16 on the floor. "Slow and easy. They'll be awfully nervous. No matter what happens, stay calm." Sally eased them toward the roadblock, stopping just fifteen yards short of it.

They must have come from behind them, off the road somewhere, because no one in the vehicle had seen them approaching, and without any warning, the barrel of an automatic weapon was thrust into Sally's open window. She froze, half expecting to die.

"One move, and you're all dead," the voice of a young, scared Marine shouted at them. "Now turn off the engine and get out slowly."

Doing as he said, Sally moved at a cautious speed. She slowly reached for the ignition and gently turned the key. After the motor stopped, a horrible thick silence filled the air.

Finally, Billy spoke, his voice firm and reassuring, "Easy, son. We're on your side. I'm ATF, she's FBI, and he's CDC. We're going to get out now, so please be careful with that weapon."

"Yeah, yeah, just get out. Lay face down on the road, hands to your sides," the Marine barked, obviously not moved or calmed by Billy's plea.

"Okay, but I want to let you know in advance that she and I are carrying side arms. Government Issue side arms. The federal government. Do you understand?" Billy asked softly.

"Yes," the Marine shouted. "Now get out."

Slowly, hands raised, they slipped from the vehicle, stretching out flat on the still-warm pavement, small pieces of debris and glass beneath them.

In an instant, a flurry of activity commenced, shouting voices from all directions, the distinct sound of boots running toward them and clanking rifles.

Mike was terrified. The darkness, the noise, it was too much. He struggled to reach his feet, but a Marine's boot sent him back down hard, glass digging into his cheek. "Don't try that again, or you're fucking dead." The voice belonged to an older, more firm man.

Mike opened his eyes. The world spun, and white flashes darted in front of him. His focus returned slowly, and he saw Sally spread eagle just a few inches away from him.

"It's okay. Just relax. We're going to be fine. They're just being careful. Don't worry." Sally's words were soothing, and Mike let his muscles relax, sinking into the pavement, flat, invisible. Closing his eyes again, he traveled back to Atlanta, a warm fall evening, sitting on the back porch with his beautiful wife, her golden hair blowing slightly in the breeze. With the smell of his newborn baby filling his nostrils, his thoughts were only of what great adventures lay ahead for them. It was the most perfect day.

"Mike, get up. Mike. Come on, it's okay. Get up." Returning to the present, Mike realized Sally was tugging on his arm, imploring him to rise up off the highway.

"I'm sorry if I hurt you. Let me help you." The Marine with a deeper, more mature voice, grasped Mike with one hand, effortlessly pulling him to his feet.

With one quick glance, Mike judged the hulking man to be six feet four and one-half inches tall and about two hundred forty-five pounds of pure muscle. If the Marine Corps had been looking for a perfect specimen soldier, this one was it. His ebony skin glistened, highlighting his rugged and pronounced features. Dark, searing eyes absorbed everything around him, the product of years of intensive military training, no doubt.

Mike tried to pull himself together, embarrassed by his loss of control. "No, I'm alright. Just give me a second. Are you from Quantico?"

"Yes, sir. Sergeant Thomas James Wilkinson, a/k/a TJ, United States Marine Corps. I'm in charge of this squad."

Mike would have known he was in charge even if he hadn't told him. TJ's presence, his stern voice, the way he handled himself… TJ would have come in handy at the last roadblock.

Mike sucked in a deep breath and exhaled slowly. "Well, Sergeant, I can't tell you how happy we are to see you. I'm Doctor Mike Jenkins from Atlanta. The Center for Disease Control sent us to assess the damage and help if we can." Mike reached out and shook TJ's hand. It was the firmest he had ever felt.

TJ's face changed. Large lines formed on his forehead, and his eyelids closed slightly. "Assessing the damage? That's easy. Those fucking Russians blew up the whole damn place. Nuked it. I'd say they had at least one direct hit on Washington, tore us up pretty good too. Did we get off a counterstrike?"

Mike had not considered that they'd been cut off from the outside world. Of course, they thought it was the Russians. Who wouldn't? "Maybe we should talk privately, Sergeant."

Mike took him by the arm, and even through the heavy uniform jacket, it felt like a tree trunk as he led TJ a few feet away from the rest of his squad. "I need to brief you, and I figured you could decide how and what to tell your men," Mike started, unsure how to break the news to him. "It wasn't the Russians or even the Chinese. Ever heard of the ARA?"

"Sure. Crackpot right-wingers somewhere out west," TJ replied, looking skeptical.

"Montana," Mike said, nodding.

"Yeah, that's it, Montana. What about them?"

"They did it," Mike stated, watching TJ's face closely.

"Are you sure? How? Why?" TJ was clearly confused and starting to boil.

"Yes, we're sure, and there's more. New York, Chicago and LA all hit this morning as well."

"Jesus. Oh, God. LA? How bad is it in LA? I mean, what part?" TJ's stern gaze had turned to panic and grief.

"You got someone there?" Mike inquired.

"Yes. My family. Almost all of them moved to Englewood last year. Oh, dear Jesus. No." TJ slumped as he got the last words out.

Mike didn't know how to comfort him, what to say to this huge man trying to hide his tears from his squad. "I realize this is a shock, Sergeant, but we have work to do. Even though we can't help your family right now, we can help the families here. Save whoever we can, make a difference. That's why I risked my life to come here. What do you say?"

It worked. TJ quickly straightened his massive frame, a visible lump in his throat as he swallowed. "Yes, sir. I'm sorry about that display of emotion. It won't happen again. I'll inform my men of the Washington bomb and who set it off. As for the rest of it, until I brief the captain, they don't need to know. I would appreciate your cooperation on that."

"As you wish, Sergeant, and I'm sorry about your family." Mike patted the side of TJ's arm and checked his face for understanding.

Nodding, he turned and walked briskly toward his men. Mike made the short walk back to the group gathered by the Explorer. As he stepped behind one of the soldiers, flashes of light came from the brush fifty yards up the hill. Something warm splattered his face, and the young man in front of him came crashing back, knocking Mike to the ground beneath him.

"Sniper. Get down!" TJ's voice filled the air.

Bullets ricocheted off the asphalt, one striking the young Marine on top of Mike. *Why didn't he cry out? Why doesn't he get up?*

"Get that fifty going now, Roberts," TJ ordered. "Kraft, take Whisner and Meach. Flank them from that ridge. Doc, you okay?"

"I think so, Sergeant, but this soldier won't get off of me."

TJ shouted back to him, "That Marine is dead, Doc. Stay there and use him for cover."

Mike's stomach turned with the realization that the warm splatter on his face had been blood from the Marine. "I can't do that, Sergeant. Get him off of me now."

TJ's voice lowered, dry, cold, and unbending. "Now listen very carefully to me, Doc. He's already dead. We can't help him now, but he can help you stay alive. You told me you came here to save lives, and you can't do that if you're dead. What do *you* say?" TJ had just turned the tables on Mike by using reason in an unreasonable situation, removing the emotion and concentrating on the objective. Damn him.

"Alright, I'll stay put but hurry."

Mike had just reconciled himself to lie still under the dead Marine, and then panic struck him again. What about Sally and Billy? Where did they run to? Why weren't they talking? Were they safe?

ARTICLE VII

Denver, Colorado, January 20, 2001, 2:55 PM MST

As the twenty-minute break was ending, Ben made his way back into the conference room. He had attempted to call his editor, but the damn Marine in the lobby wouldn't let him use the phone, and he was instructed to get written permission from the president or no call. It was frustrating as hell. He was in a position to do important work and couldn't even make a call. He imagined the paper was going crazy waiting for his copy. He would need to get the president aside for a meeting to work things out soon.

Ben's mood wasn't helped by hearing a closed-door meeting between Sid and Larry would prevent any update on Chris from taking place. He began to wonder if he was in too deep to change his mind and get back to his life.

For now, he needed to return to the meeting.

With everyone seated and looking calm, Claire moved to the last items on the agenda. They weren't as explosive but equally important. Ben had not considered most of the challenges facing the country. Washington, New York, Chicago and Los Angeles were important financial and transportation hubs. Planes and trains had to be re-routed or canceled, and some airline carriers lost large numbers of aircraft and vital personnel. The FAA national radar was down, and just like last year, regional ones had to be patched together. Y2K had left a few good things behind, though.

The military would also help direct traffic using AWACs flying twenty-four hours a day. Repair sites, spare parts and qualified mechanics were also at a premium. Some relief was forthcoming through training facilities from across the nation. Aerotek schools called, offering their instructors and skilled students to help fill in.

Avoiding radioactive clouds would be a top priority for everyone in the skies and on the ground. Many rail lines had been destroyed, and important switching stations lost, but most of them would be replaced by longer, more out-of-the-way routes. It was the general consensus around the table that America would not come to a stop, but its pace would be severely hampered for many years.

Economically, the wounds were deeper and more serious. The Treasury Department, Department of Printing and Engraving and the primary United States Mint were all destroyed. The New York Stock Exchange, American Stock Exchange and Chicago's Commodities Market gone. Important national and international banks in New York, Chicago, and Los Angeles gone. Media headquarters for most of the major television networks and newspapers all gone. Trillions of dollars of "paper wealth" had been vaporized. These problems would not go away quickly and could severely erode public confidence in the economy, without which the effects might rival the great depression or worse.

Ben thought about his investments, almost all in the market. It was almost certain that they were worthless today. He was getting too old to start over, and his plans of moving somewhere warm and playing golf seemed impossible to imagine now. He had been so worried about writing this story. Never thinking that maybe there wouldn't be a newspaper to print it.

How the government would pay for rebuilding the cities, the massive rescue efforts, and fund Medicare, Medicaid and Social Security, not to mention national defense, was all in doubt. Though most of the hurdles required more time to study and clear, some decisions were made. Banks would reopen, but strict limits would be placed on the amounts withdrawn. The remaining two mints would work around the clock printing Federal Emergency Notes to pay the military and other essential employees. Foreign aid would be temporarily halted, and food stores would be protected from vandals, but there would be no rationing. Not yet.

The last item they covered was creating a new Congress. A call would be placed to state governments asking them to appoint, with all speed, new congressional representatives and senators. Advice and consent were mandated by the Constitution, and President Young needed their support and ideas.

Ben certainly missed the mini tape recorder, his hand cramping badly from scribbling notes throughout the extended meetings. A long time had passed since he had relied on his shorthand, and this was not the time for errors when it came time to decipher it. As the meeting wrapped up, he cleaned up a few spots in dispute with his memory and folded up the pad.

"Ben, could I see you a moment in private?" President Young asked quietly.

Startled by her request, he came close to stuttering his response. "Of course, Madam President." Perhaps she had heard of the dustup with the Marine at the front door. It was a meeting he wanted, and now he had it.

She led him out a second door near her chair, striding into the smallish office complete with a Presidential Seal and a large bank of telephones. Ben surmised it was her private office. "Have a seat, Ben." President Young took her place behind the large oak desk as he complied.

"Thank you, Madam President."

"Could you do me a favor?" she asked, looking serious.

"Yes, of course, name it."

"Call me Claire in here."

Ben stumbled for words like a rookie on his first assignment. "Well, it's really not appropriate, you know. For me, anyway."

"I know, I know. But forget about that. I need to feel normal for a little while, please."

"Alright, Claire, you win. But then you always do, don't you?" Ben smiled. She might not admit to it, but she knew he was right. She was a natural and had become a good leader in a short amount of time.

"If you only knew." She chuckled, returning his grin. "Care for a cigarette? I quit a year ago, but what the hell. Cancer is the least of my concerns today."

"What about the hulk out there in a Marine uniform? He threatened to break my lips if I smoked down here?"

"I've got him covered. Being the top bitch around here has some privileges," she quipped, placing the lit match to the end of her smoke and inhaling deeply. "God, that tastes like crap, but I know the next one will be better."

Ben, too, was introducing the long-awaited toxic smoke to his lungs. It burned and tasted bad, and still, it was heaven. "So Claire, if we're talking favors, I need one from you. If I can."

President Young looked up at him, smiled and began to speak. "We can certainly chat about it in a few. But first, there is something we need to discuss. I know Ashley passed along my instructions that no one censor your stories, but I would like to ask for some consideration on this black-white issue. Thing is, I kind of lost control out there and said some things I probably shouldn't have. I know it's not their fault racism is still with us. However, Terry can be so pompous sometimes that I needed to take him down a notch or two. Hell, he might actually believe a black woman can't do this job. Not sure I blame him."

"You're too modest. I watched you handle that meeting and control those people. Your decisions were decisive and right on target. I was impressed." Ben could hardly believe the conversation he was having with the president.

"Thanks. That's nice of you to say, but can I count on you for some discretion?" She put out her half-smoked cigarette in a small pop can.

"And did I mention you're always to the point?" Ben smiled slightly. "I never intended to use it, Claire. We'll have plenty of time and ink to debate that issue when this madness is over."

She rocked back in the overstuffed black leather chair, her feet coming to rest on the open desk drawer. "Good," she said, nodding slightly. "I want to make sure you have all the facts on what lies ahead. You'll be a target for what you know and what you write. Just be careful. Let Ashley take care of you. She's the best street agent in the region. I went to school with her mom, not five miles from here, a long time ago. A very long time ago."

Listening to Claire talk, Ben wondered if the order to kill him if he got out of line had come from her or Sid. "Don't worry about me. You have enough on your mind."

"Now, what is it that you need?" Claire asked.

Ben sat a bit straighter in his chair. "I need to call my editor. They're waiting for something, and I need to make it happen soon."

"You have it written down? Something I can read?"

"I do."

Claire looked at Ben closely for a second. "Okay, get it to Bobbie. If it looks good to me, I will approve the call. Recorded call, you know?"

"Thanks," Ben said. "And yes, I assumed they would be."

The president's chair popped back into an upright position, and her feet hit the floor. "Well, back to the salt mines or is that cotton fields?" she added with a wink. Standing abruptly, she stretched her hand across the desk. It was Ben's cue to leave.

"Thank you, Madam President, and good luck." Ben shook her hand and headed for the door.

Just before he turned the handle, she spoke again. "Do you trust Robbins?" It was a shocking question coming from her.

Ben opened the door slightly and, from over his shoulder, replied, "About as far as I can throw this bunker." He walked out, closing the door behind him.

ARTICLE VIII

Western Montana, January 20, 2001, 4:33 PM MST

The front door squeaked open and then slowly closed. The silence was so intense. Jamie imagined General Boyle standing inside the door, waiting for her to emerge from her hiding place in the closet. He'd be wearing that smug smile on his face, and those cold, terrible eyes could see her right through the wall.

She sat there frozen with fear. After all, he was willing to kill a million innocent people just to get rid of Ken, to get him out of the way, and she was responsible for that.

If only she had seen Harvey's true character earlier, seen the madness, been faithful to her husband.

How long should she wait before moving? When would it be safe? Ten agonizing minutes passed, and still, she heard no sound of anyone in the cabin.

Slower than she had ever done anything in her life, Jamie turned the handle and began to open the door. It creaked loudly, and once again, she froze with terror. After several seconds of silence, she pushed the door the rest of the way open. Her eyes struggled to adjust as light flooded in from the brightly lit cabin. She was alone and would live a while longer.

Luckily, no one seemed to notice as Jamie slipped into the crowded room. It was the largest structure in the compound, massive and majestic. A great open room built completely of logs harvested from the surrounding forest, in the center sat a raised stage equipped with audiovisual capabilities.

Countless times they had gathered to hear the general speak for hours or view movies about government murders at Waco and Ruby Ridge.

Tonight, she felt quite different about what her role would be in the "Great Conflict." Although her emotions were confused, her mind was made up.

There was only one way out of the compound. She would go with the troops out the front gate in the morning as part of the ground assault forces. Outside the gates, Jamie could find a way to vanish and then do what she had to do. Instantly the enormous crowd snapped to attention as General Boyle climbed onto the stage. He began to pace the small platform, hands behind his back, chest out, head back, just like always. Only this time, it sent a chill through Jamie. Suddenly he stopped and turned toward his troops.

"Tonight," his booming voice resonated, "we stand on freedom's doorstep. The Great Conflict has begun. Not since 1776 has such a bold blow for liberty been struck. The corrupt government is breathing its final breath, and it shall not survive." He paused briefly to allow time for the mandatory roar of approval, stopping as quickly as it started when he raised his hand. It was so clear to her now, the blind obedience to him, every word from his mouth gospel, every word from the government lies. His world was black and white, no gray, only right and wrong, and he was always right.

The truth must be somewhere in the middle, Jamie surmised. The government had done many evil things, but it wasn't all evil either. After all, it was made up of people, some of them bad and some of them good. Neither was any one man all good and without a hint of evil. If only she could get up on the stage, remove the mask from his face, and tell them the truth. Maybe they would listen. But in her heart, she knew they would not.

"…No longer will we stand by helpless while vermin line their pockets at our expense, slowly killing us with taxation and regulation. God has handed us the power to strike out at evil politicians, lawyers and bankers. I can tell you Washington DC, New York, Chicago, Los Angeles and Denver have already fallen. Tomorrow, we move on to Portland, Seattle, Salt Lake, Sacramento and Boise. By nightfall, we should have control over the entire Western United States."

Jamie noticed he did not mention how the great cities had fallen or about his plan to split the country into regions. Secrets, it seemed, were also a part of the new government.

"Major Hollis has divided you into five platoons," General Boyle continued. "Those assignments are posted in your barracks. Your mission will be to assist the militia and overrun the local authorities."

He paused for obvious dramatic effect, Jamie mused, while scanning his loyal followers, then allowed a slight grin to emerge. "It is our belief many of them will come over to our side as the outcome becomes clear. Within a week, our numbers will swell to over fifty thousand armed patriots, but only the select few of you gathered here have the privilege of standing on this hallowed ground. This is the new birthplace of American freedom, and I have chosen this building as the site for the coming constitutional convention. Judges or Congress will not abridge our new constitution, it will not be circumvented by any president, and it will not bow to foreign governments. It will answer only to God."

Harvey stood erect, thrusting his arm in a perfect salute. "Good luck, God speed and let freedom ring from every mountain in this great country."

The crowd returned his salute. Thunderous applause and cheers greeted the general as he waded through the center of the crowd, shaking hands and exchanging hugs.

Jamie had been so close to participating in this perversion, not for liberty, but a fight to transfer power. Her moment of clarity had come just in time, and she would not wait to hug the general but slipped out the rear door and returned to her barracks.

Her heart sank, searching the list of platoon assignments posted on the board. Beside her name, it simply read *Compound Security*.

General Boyle planned to keep her close. Under his control, she would have to find another way out.

ARTICLE IX

Virginia, January 20, 2001, 7:09 PM EST

Thirty minutes had passed since the brief but terrifying firefight with the ARA, and still, there was no sign of Billy and Sally. TJ calculated they must have sought cover in the brush off the road, and disarmed by the Marines, they were unable to prevent their capture by the ARA. A few hours ago, four of them started out in the Explorer intending to help, but everything had gone wrong, so terribly wrong, and now he was the only one remaining.

Devastated, Mike asked, "Sergeant, when do we go after them?"

"Hang on, Doc, I'm waiting for two additional squads to move up for support. The tracks indicate they're heading northwest toward the FBI compound at Quantico. If they've captured that, it's going to be a hell of a lot tougher to dig them out." Mike's head slumped. "Don't worry," TJ added, "if they're alive, we'll get them back."

If they're alive. *By God, they had better be alive*, Mike brooded to himself.

A few minutes later, TJ approached him with a determined look in his eyes. "My support units are in place. I've got them coming in from behind, and my squad is taking the front and recon. Stay by the radio. We'll keep in touch."

Mike grasped at his arm. "Hey, wait. I'm going with you."

"The hell you are. You're not trained for it, not dressed for it, and not armed." TJ effortlessly released his arm from Mike's grasp.

"That's bullshit. Give me a coat and a gun, Sergeant. It's my team in there. I'm going."

TJ looked into Mike's eyes, seemingly sizing him up. "And if I say no?"

"I'll follow you after you leave."

Looking down at his watch, TJ barked, "You've got two minutes to find a tactical vest, helmet, and sidearm. No M-16. I don't want you shooting me, for chrissake. Now move."

Mike moved swiftly, obtaining the necessary equipment from the fallen Marine. It was eerie seeing the fallen man's pale features looking back at him, half of his forehead missing. Mike would have to try to ignore the bloodstains covering the heavy jacket.

TJ had two Marines stay with the body of the fallen soldier. "I'll be back to get him," he told them quietly.

Mike rejoined TJ and moved with them out into the night, still not sure why he had insisted on going. He stuck close to TJ, feeling a little safer with him nearby, quickly learning the hand signals he used to position the men.

The weight of the heavy vest, helmet, and pistol wore him down as they trudged along. The good news is it was warm. For some reason, Mike was just noticing how cold the January night had become. Topping the crest of a heavily forested hill, TJ motioned them to stop and crouched down. Mike was nervous but also thankful for the opportunity to rest.

TJ crawled forward on his stomach another ten yards or so, stopping next to a large tree. Moving smoothly back and forth, he scanned the area in front of him with his night-vision binoculars. Returning to the squad, he motioned them to come closer.

Even whispering, TJ's voice was firm as he relayed the information they would need to make the assault. "About two clicks out, four guards out in front of the main building, no movement anywhere else. Donnie, drop back about fifty yards and radio the other squads to cover the rest of the compound. We'll take the main building. Tell them not to move in unless I give the okay. Clear?"

Donnie nodded and gave TJ a thumbs-up. Turning, he headed out to radio the orders.

"Now, the rest of you, I want you to spread out. Fifteen-yard intervals, we'll crawl in. If possible, the outside guards will go down with no fire. Whisner, Meach, Thompson take one each. I'll take the other. After the guards are down, join up again, and we'll recon the building up close. Should it go sour, move in fast. I don't want to give them time to harm anyone inside. Any questions?"

One by one, the Marines gave the thumbs-up to TJ. Mike nodded and did the same. Slowly and silently, they crawled forward down the slight slope toward the front of the FBI building. Fifty yards from the first guard, TJ motioned Mike to stop and wait.

Mike watched TJ slide effortlessly on his stomach, not making a sound. Losing sight of TJ in the grass, Mike turned his gaze to the guards silhouetted against the walls of the building. His entire body tensed when four new shadows leaped from the ground with the muffled sounds of a struggle and a short but distinct grunt from someone. Moments later, all the shadows fell out of sight, and it was completely silent.

Hearing the rest of the squad moving forward, Mike began to crawl, the building growing ever larger as he moved in. TJ was crouched over the body of one of the guards, a young man dressed in army surplus green, with ARA written on the sleeve in black marker. His automatic weapon lay a few feet from his outstretched arm, and blood rushed from the gaping wound in his neck.

All Mike could think at the moment was that this guy was someone's husband, brother or son so bitter toward his life and government he chose to throw in with a lunatic, waging war on his own country. Mike would have liked to talk with him, find out how he came to this, how it could have been stopped. Nevertheless, just like the young Marine lying back on the road, this young man's life was over almost before it started.

"What a fucking waste," TJ whispered to himself.

Mike remembered as a boy sitting and listening to his father talk about Korea, the tragedy of a country ripped apart by political philosophy, families torn from each other's arms, their spirits broken. He told Mike how lucky he was that our civil war had been fought many years before. The United States has learned its lesson and will never again suffer at its own hands, his father would proclaim. For the first time, Mike was thankful his father had passed and could not help wondering what kind of world awaited his own son.

The main FBI building was mammoth in size. Mostly concrete and bricks, it had survived the blast nearly intact, although some of the windows had been shattered by the shock wave. Searching it without being detected would be difficult, if not impossible.

TJ led the soldiers behind a small outbuilding nearby. "We're going to go in together. It's too risky to split up. We'd probably end up shooting each other. Whisner, Meach, take point. Thompson and I will follow up in the rear. Clear floor by floor and go easy. Remember, not everyone in that building is a target. Make sure you see a threat before you fire."

Single file, they moved back across the open courtyard, stopping in front of the main entrance, double glass doors with stenciled letters reading *Federal Bureau of Investigation, Guard on duty at all times*. Mike could hear himself breathing and his heart pounding inside his chest, but he would not panic this time. Sally and Billy needed him, and he would not let them down.

TJ and Thompson held the doors open as the squad slipped quietly inside, taking cover behind concrete planters in the main lobby, and waited for any sign of movement. Whisner and Meach wore night-vision goggles to help illuminate the dark interior rooms, and an eerie green light leaked out around their temples.

It was all surreal, like a hundred movies he had seen.

Methodically they moved from one room to another, the tension and exertion causing sweat to pour down Mike's face and into his eyes.

Toward the interior of the building, Whisner raised his hand and then stretched it out flat. Mike stopped and crouched close to the floor.

Light streamed across the carpet from underneath a closed door. Mike jolted as shadows broke the beam, indicating someone was in the room. One at a time, they moved closer to the doorway.

Once the entire squad was in place, TJ slid a small mirror under the edge of the steel door. For several minutes, he studied the layout of the room. Mike didn't understand all the hand signals TJ used to make his report but knew enough to be afraid. At least five targets, five people who must be killed. Several non-targets, at least three who needed to be saved. Mike would wait outside in the hall. This wasn't about courage. His inexperience might endanger the Marines, something he wouldn't risk.

He made brief eye contact with TJ, a visual message passing between them. Mike knew he would do everything in his power to save his friends.

Using his fingers, TJ counted down the seconds until entry. At zero, one forceful kick from him sent the door flying open. Like water rushing through a levee break, the squad flew in the open doorway. Within a second, gunshots were being exchanged. Too many to count.

Two bullets came crashing through the wall, just missing Mike's head. "Jesus, that was close." He rolled away from the wall to lay flat on the floor.

The shots went on for more than a minute, then nothing. Smoke rolled from the office door as Mike crawled toward it. His 45 Auto pointed to the spot where a man would exit but shook so bad he would never have hit him.

"Doc, you better get in here." It was TJ's voice, and Mike was glad to hear it. Leaping to his feet, Mike ran into the hazy opening, his eyes burning from sweat and smoke. Slowly, like awakening from a dream, the grizzly scene came into focus. Dead bodies were everywhere, moist blood and brain matter dripping off the walls. It was mind-numbing. Maybe he was having a nightmare and would wake up soon. However, it was all too real, and he could not imagine how Billy and Sally could live through the crossfire.

"Over here," TJ yelled from the far corner.

Mike stumbled over the dead ARA soldiers. His feet didn't seem to have any feeling in them like lead slowing him down. Maybe he should have stayed in Atlanta with his family, protected them, and raised his son.

Reaching TJ's side, the hostages were visible. Mixed in with two others, Billy and Sally were lying face down on the floor, side by side, their hands and feet bound, not moving. Mike felt his stomach tighten with the same gut-wrenching feeling he had when the doctor told him of the death of his first baby. She had been just two hours old. Born with only half of a heart, she put up one hell of a fight to live. He would never forget the look in his wife's eyes. It was like a part of her soul had been ripped out, stepped on and thrown away. He caught her occasionally holding their son, telling him of his sister and crying softly.

Mike knelt down beside Sally, stroked her hair lightly and checked for a pulse. She was alive. "Help me turn her over," Mike yelled as the Marines gathered in a small circle around them. He removed the black cloth covering her eyes and the tape that sealed her mouth. Not yet used to the bright lights, she opened her eyes slightly, her discolored tongue wiping much-needed moisture onto her thin lips.

In a hoarse whisper, she said, "'Bout fucking time you got here."

Mike smiled, his eyes watering slightly. "Just like you, laying around when all the shit is going down. Are you okay? Did they hurt you?" he asked as he finished untying her.

"No, I'm fine. But they hit Billy pretty hard. Bastard is tough and put up one a hell of a fight."

Mike squeezed her arm and turned his attention to Billy. Two Marines had rolled him over and removed his gag and blindfold. Mike moved closer, picking up the rebel handkerchief that had been used to blindfold him.

"Morons," he murmured as he threw the rag as far as he could. A large bluish-purple lump was raised over his left eye, and numerous scratches and cuts covered the rest of his face. After removing the rest of his bindings, Mike checked his pulse and breathing, then leaned down close to his ear. "Billy. Billy, can you hear me?" Mike whispered. Billy did not respond to his coaxing, and Mike needed to know if he was comatose. He retrieved smelling salts from his small first aid kit, broke open the small package and placed it under his nose. It worked a little too well. This hulking man, who had moments ago been resting like a baby, bolted up and swung, catching Mike right on the chin with a crushing right hand.

ARTICLE X

Denver, Colorado, January 20, 2001, 4:42 PM MST

Now that Ben had the president's permission to use the phone, he called his editor at the paper. Jake wasn't thrilled to hear that the call was recorded but was glad to get the story. After Ben finished dictating the long story, he promised to call back soon and hung up.

After pausing for a brief moment, Ben picked up the phone and began dialing. He decided to call the governor's Chief of Staff, Helen. Few people had her private number at home, but Ben knew it by heart. With any luck, she could help him answer some of the nagging questions surrounding Robbins' activities. Even the president sensed something was not quite right with his behavior.

Helen was almost sixty and a longtime friend. She had always been careful but straight with him. Under different circumstances, she might have become more than a friend. But that was not to be. Politics had been her life for thirty years, and a post as Robbins' chief of staff her assignment for the last six.

If a mouse farted in the basement of the capitol, Helen not only knew the color of the mouse but what it had to eat the day before. And that's why Ben counted on her.

After a few rings, she picked up. "Helen Foster," she answered, the fatigue in her voice clear.

"Helen, it's Ben Bleser. How are you holding up?"

"Christ, Ben, I can't even find it, let alone hold it up." Her warm laugh rolled from the earpiece. "What about you? Heard you were in the dungeon with the big boys. Oops, sorry. Big boys and girls."

Ben laughed at her wit. "Yeah, it has been quite a day. Listen, hon, I was trying to finish up my story, you know, get it sorted out. I couldn't get the governor aside to ask what happened to his trip to Washington, so I thought you might be able to fill in the blanks."

"Wish I could, Benny boy, but the truth is he never said. When he came popping in last night, I asked him, you know, what happened. The most I got was 'long story' and a wave of his hand. Don't know if he had a bad dream and is ashamed to say or what."

"Hmm... That is strange," Ben mused aloud for her benefit. "You okay with that?"

There was a short pause on the other end of the line. Helen never said anything without considering the consequences. "Sure. Why wouldn't I be?"

"No reason. Just trying to make sense of it all and put the pieces together. You know me."

She was a good friend, but he wasn't about to tell her of his worries. Nevertheless, she sensed his radar had fixed on something. He knew by the hesitancy in her voice. "Okay, but if you find out anything I need to know, you will call, right?"

"You bet, old girl. Well, better go and put this to bed." Ben chuckled.

"Someday, you'll have to put this old girl to bed," Helen cackled, knowing full well she made him blush. Ben was far too preoccupied to be embarrassed by her remark. "In my dreams, babe. See ya later."

"Bye, Ben. Please be careful," Helen said in a more serious tone.

He waited for the sound of her telephone disconnecting before hanging up, a habit he acquired while dating his wife, one he hadn't been able to break.

Looking out of the corner of his eye, Ben saw Ashley in a low chair to his left, long legs crossed, her black skirt riding high up her thigh. She was glorious, and he swallowed hard as she uncrossed her legs, offering a quick glimpse of the white silk underwear she wore underneath. It was such a wonderful contrast to her black nylons he couldn't help but stare.

Slowly, she rose from her chair, pulling the skirt down as she went. A devilish smile flashed across her face, and once again, he had been caught in the act. It appeared, however, she was not at all disappointed by the attention.

"Find out anything?" Ashley asked him.

"Huh? What do you mean?" Ben fumbled, not knowing what to say.

"About the governor," Ashley said, smiling, obviously aware that Ben had lost his train of thought.

Ben felt his face redden, and he chuckled. "No. It seems no one knows why the esteemed Governor Robbins opted out of the big dance. But I can assure you of one thing, I will find out."

She moved over toward the desk where he was seated and sat sidesaddle on its edge. "Do you always get the full story, all of the data you need to make up your mind about something?"

Before now, he hadn't noticed how warm it was in the bunker. Loosening the tie around his neck did seem to help a bit, but not much. "I can usually tell when someone has something to say but, for some reason or another, holds back." He hoped she wasn't talking about journalism because he certainly wasn't. "When that happens, you just have to stay focused, don't lose sight of your objective, and push until they slip or give in."

Ashley moved a little closer to him and smiled. "You mean it's that simple, just focus and push...until they...give in?"

Ben was afraid his heart might burst out of his chest. He could barely breathe as he stood and faced her as she sat on the desk. Her tongue eased out of her mouth, and she licked her lips lightly. Slowly he placed a hand on each of her soft shoulders, gently pulling her toward him. The moment he had dreamed of since they met was inches away. She tilted her head slightly and closed her eyes. Just before he touched her luscious lips with his, a loud knock on the door echoed around the small room.

Ashley pulled back and opened her eyes. She smiled at Ben, raising her right eyebrow. "Damn. Duty calls."

Ben sighed heavily and moved back, allowing her to rise and answer the door.

It was one of the Marine guards. "They want you back in the conference room Mr. Bleser. Now."

Reluctantly, Ben turned and followed the Marine down the hall to the conference room, glancing back over his shoulder at Ashley standing seductively in the doorway. "This had better be good," he said to the back of the guard's head.

"I have no idea, sir. I'm sorry," the stoic Marine responded.

Ben chuckled. He needed to learn not to think aloud down here. Larry, Sid and General Clifton sat around the conference table, talking softly.

"Gentlemen." Ben nodded as he entered and sat down
beside Larry.

Larry leaned toward Ben. "Nothing on your boy yet, but we're still checking. Sorry."

Although his heart sank, Ben forced a smile. "Thanks. I really appreciate your help."

President Young popped out of the back office. "Gentlemen, thank you for coming." She settled in her chair. "Larry, what do you have for me?"

"The Rapid Strike Force from Camp Pendleton will be moving into place twenty miles from the Montana compound and waiting for orders. Should be there by zero-four hundred tomorrow morning. The general and I have come up with a plan for taking the camp when the time comes. News from the South is more than a little unsettling. The Alabama National Guard has moved in around one of our bases, heavy armor and all." Larry looked up from his notes at the president. "It appears our fears about the South may have been true."

"Have you talked with the commander there, General," she asked, ignoring the remark about the South.

General Clifton didn't look up from his notes. "Yes, Madam President. He's a little nervous about the loyalties of southern soldiers on the inside but assured me the situation is under control for now. The Guard has shown no signs of aggression, but if we attempt to leave the base, I can't guarantee anything."

President Young rubbed her forehead. "Okay. I'll limit my address tonight to radio. Let things settle a bit so we can get better organized. Do not view this as a weakness on my part. I'll do what's right for the country, nothing less. We'll deal with the issue of my race and gender at another time. Move on."

Ben jotted down her comments. He might not be able to use them now, but someday the country would be proud of this great woman. She would not let her pride stand in the way of what was right, a sure sign of greatness in any leader.

"Larry, any communication from the Governor of Alabama? What are his intentions?" Sid asked, leaning forward in his chair.

"No. We've tried several times to reach him, but I can't find anyone there who'll tell me squat. He definitely hasn't made any public statement, but I heard through the grapevine that the Guard's orders are to prevent the mobilization of any federal troops stationed there."

Larry sipped from the blue ceramic coffee cup in front of him. "I don't think they're stupid enough to come barging in. Wouldn't make sense, and they could sit out there for a long time. I think most of the Patriots outside of Montana are waiting to see if Boyle can make this thing happen. You know, before they do something that they can't undo? Funny thing is I can't seem to locate Robbins to ask for his help on this."

President Young reached over and pressed the intercom button. "Bobbie, find Robbins for me, please," Claire requested, not expecting or waiting for a response.

Sid took his glasses off and set them on the table. "So, what should we do, Terry?"

The general stood and paced slowly around the room. "This is no time for anything rash. We stay alert and stay put. However, I would like permission to make plans to send in reinforcements if needed."

President Young looked up at him. "Of course, General. We won't hang anybody out to dry. Make whatever plans you need. I know you'll be discreet in their deployment."

General Clifton retook his chair. "Thank you, Madam President."

Ben was pleased to see the respect between the two of them had been restored. They were both powerful and proud, strong as allies, weaker as enemies.

Larry shuffled through more of his notes. "We have more problems in Texas. There's a small civil war going on there between the Secessionists and the Americans loyal to the country."

"Who has the upper hand now?" Sid interjected.

"Right now, it's the Rangers, but they're better organized than the Free Texas Collation. Can't say what will happen if they do get their act together."

President Young tapped a pencil on her pad. "Anything we can do to help?"

"We have Fort Hood on alert," General Clifton chimed in, "but we're trying to keep our presence down to a minimum. They don't need any fuel on the fire right now. It would be a lot better if this could be settled by Texans, but if they ask for our help, we'll be ready."

The president nodded in agreement. "How is the search for the other devices going?"

Terry paused briefly and sighed before he answered. "First off, we're almost certain the seven warheads that left the Dakota's never reached Texas. Someone in the pipeline destroyed the manifest shipping orders and then forged the destruction certification. Had to be an inside job. The colonel in charge of the division was under Boyle for ten years. I'm sorry to say we have not been able to locate him yet, he was supposed to be in DC, but that may be just a cover story."

"My sources say he never got on that plane," Sid said flatly.

Ben was certain now of Sid's background and knew who his sources were. What puzzled him was how would Military Intelligence know the colonel didn't get on the plane unless they had been watching him?

"Was he under surveillance?" Ben blurted out.

The room drew silent. Sid ignored Ben's question, and no one else spoke. General Clifton continued his report. "It takes some time to reposition the satellites to make the sweep, but—"

"Madam President," Ben interrupted, cutting Sid off, "I would like an answer to my question."

Sid bristled in his chair. "Listen up. This isn't a fucking press conference, so shut up and write."

"With all due respect, Sid, I was not talking to you. Well, Madam President?" Ben could hold his own in a battle of words.

Sid was visually livid and stood from his chair with his palms flat on the table. "Madam President, my ass. I was talking to you—"

"Gentlemen, we do not have time for this," the president hissed through clenched teeth. "Sid, I'd like to hear the answer to Mr. Bleser's question."

Sid pumped his right hand in and out, making a fist. "Yes. Okay?"

"Thank you, Sid," Ben said in the most sarcastic tone he could muster.

"Fuck you, Ben," was Sid's only response.

President Young shook her head. "If you two are finished, maybe we can put away the testosterone for a while. General, please continue."

General Clifton glared at Ben. He had not made any friends in the last few moments, but he was still a reporter and was going to act like one. If they wanted a puppet, they had chosen the wrong man, and they had better know it now.

"As I was saying, it takes some time to get things online. By zero one hundred or zero two hundred, we can start."

The red light on the telephone blinked. President Young pushed the intercom button. "Yes, Bobbie?"

"I'm sorry, Madam President. The staff informed me Governor Robbins received a phone call about twenty minutes ago, and he left. So far, his office hasn't heard a word from him. We're still checking on where he went."

"Okay, Bobbie, thanks. Let me know the minute you find him." President Young clicked off the phone.

Ben was already on shaky ground, but he decided to speak up anyway. "I don't think you'll find him."

President Young stared at Ben, clearly floored by his statement. "Why not? What do you know about this that I don't?"

Ben leaned back slightly, uncomfortable with the position he'd placed himself in. "Just my prior experience with Governor Robbins. The holes in his story about DC, the bomb in Denver not going off, and his attitude toward you. Way too many coincidences for me. I don't like the implications if he's left the city."

Sid looked down at his pad and spoke quietly. "I hadn't had a chance to brief you in private yet, Madam President, but I think Ben may be right."

"Alright, let's get one thing real fucking clear right now." President Young rose slightly out of her chair and leaned directly into Sid's face. "You will *not* withhold anything, and I do mean *anything* from me. Do you understand, Sid?"

"Yes, ma'am, very clear." Sid's face had turned beet-red.

"Larry, Terry, that goes for you too," she added, glaring at them. "Now, let's start over. I want to know everything all of you know about the governor."

ARTICLE XI

Western Montana, January 20, 2001, 6:06 PM MST

Tension mounted inside Jamie. Her stomach ached, and the sound of grinding teeth filled her ears. How could she get out of the compound in time to prevent the destruction of Denver and Ken's death? It seemed impossible. She cursed herself for being so selfish and thinking only of Ken. What about the three million men, women, and children living in the Denver metro area?

For far too long, she had thought only of herself, not considering what might happen to others because of her actions. She wanted to believe the stories she heard on the shortwave and low-power AM radio station in Deer Path. After all, they had expert guests on all the time, people who had witnessed the terrible crimes against the constitution, like the ex-CIA operative who had been present while others conducted experiments on unsuspecting citizens.

They administered mind-altering drugs in combination with torture and brainwashing, transforming them into assassins and spies to be sent back into society to create havoc and civil disobedience. This infiltration technique was designed to flush out other operatives and ensure the government a willing public, ready to accept new laws denying rights to law-abiding American citizens. A conspiracy at the highest level, but no one seemed to care.

It was shocking learning of the dozens of executive orders signed in secret by president after president, nullifying important constitutional rights. Neither the courts nor Congress could overturn the treason committed by them. Either the liberal media refused to believe the stories, or the large New World Order corporations were controlling them.

Important medical knowledge was being withheld, including cures for cancer and heart disease. The cures would have crippled the powerful healthcare industry and eliminated the need for socialized medicine, something the government wanted badly. Researchers had been killed, or their minds turned to mush with potent drugs, and large pharmaceutical companies were paid millions to steal the patents on new drugs but never produce them. Videotapes passed between the Patriots clearly showed proof of the murders of two young boys in Arkansas to hide drug running by the CIA. The ties to this cover-up led straight to both the Brush and Clayton White House.

Murder, the destruction of records, and perjury were rampant in the highest levels of government. New World Order conspirators were controlling the international banking cartel and planned to bring down the economies of the world. By creating large paper wealth in the stock markets and incurring a large debt no one could repay, they could decide when the crash would come. Acting as saviors, they would step in and save humanity with their one-world government. Foreign troops were already in the United States, training in secret, waiting for the order to march into American cities. What little money Jamie had, she'd converted to gold and weapons.

The evidence was clear, the American public was prepared to sleep through the takeover, and action had to be taken. The founding fathers had not sat idly by while England ruled this land with tyranny. They were inspired by God to create this great nation and fight the great fight for freedom.

Jamie's sister tried to convince her that the founding fathers were just men fighting to create a better life for themselves. After months of haggling, white male landowners created a compromise document protecting the rights of, oddly enough, white male landowners leaving women with virtually no rights whatsoever and Afro-American slaves as three-fifths of a person. If God inspired these men, he was certainly a white male landowner in heaven.

The liberals had gotten to Jamie, poisoned her mind, and she had refused to see or speak to her sister since. If only she could call her right now, tell her how much she loved and missed her.

So much had changed today. This wasn't the way it was supposed to be.

The dream of freedom had become a nightmare, a sick, tragic opera with her on the side of the villain.

A loud knock on the barracks' door startled her. Before she could respond, the door flung open wide, and General Boyle strode in from the night.

He turned and closed the door firmly behind him. Turning back toward Jamie, his eyes transfixed on hers. "Were you at the rally?" he asked, his voice stern and fatherly.

Jamie tried to sound upbeat, hoping her eyes wouldn't tell him everything she had been thinking. "Yes, sir. I was near the back. Great speech."

He pretended to check out the room, walking slowly from one bunk to another, occasionally bending down to check the tension on the green army blankets stretched across the small mattresses. Slowly but deliberately, he made his way to her location by the window.

"Not as comfortable as the cabin?" he whispered in a haunting growl. His large rough hand was now tracing its way up her arm.

Jamie fought the urge to recoil. She wanted to run, get far away from this monster, but she couldn't afford to raise his suspicions. He must think everything was okay until the time was right. "Yes, I suppose, but I did it for you. People were starting to talk, you know, it didn't look good."

The general reached behind her head, releasing the rubber band holding her hair back. "Shake it," he demanded. She shook her head gently, allowing a full head of auburn hair to tumble down over her shoulders and forced her sexiest smile. "Take off your shirt."

"Here? General, someone will come in." Jamie grasped for any reason not to comply with his demand.

"The door is secure. Now get that shirt off," Boyle commanded. The tone was dripping with disdain for her, and his eyes flashed hot and angry.

Jamie was beginning to fear him. He had never been so gruff and forceful. Her hands trembling, she began to undo the buttons on her uniform.

"You're taking way too fucking long," Harvey barked out as he tore away at the material, causing her buttons to fly in all directions, bouncing and rolling across the wooden floor. He ripped the light undershirt down the middle exposing her breasts. Jamie instinctually covered herself with her arms, startled and ashamed of the situation she'd put herself in.

He grabbed both her wrists and squeezed hard. "What's the matter, Jamie? You think I haven't seen those before?" His words hung in the air, but he expected no response from her. Resigned to what was about to happen, she let her arms fall to her side. The torn shirt slid off her shoulders and onto the floor.

"Now the rest, and don't take all night." It was an order, one she knew now had to be obeyed. Within seconds, her boxer shorts hit the floor with the rest of her clothing, her body stark white under the intense barracks lighting, the cold night air causing her nipples to become erect against her will. She felt dirty and wanted very much to cry or scream.

Jamie looked up at him. His erection was visible through his pants, and the leer on his face evil and threatening. Fear overwhelmed her shame. What was he going to do to her? How much did he know?

Slowly he looked her up and down, his chest rising ever faster. Jamie imagined the adrenaline from the rally still coursed through his veins. His rough hands moved across her breasts, gently at first and then squeezing hard, pinching her sensitive nipples. Jamie felt a sharp pain shoot through her body.

"Ouch, Harvey. Easy, dammit," she cried out.

It was a grave mistake. He removed his hands from her aching breasts and swung them down to his sides. His lips pursed, and his eyes narrowed. Suddenly and without warning, the general backhanded her hard across the mouth, sending her sprawling onto her bunk. His eyes flared with anger and excitement. "Don't use that tone with me, bitch."

Who was this man? Power had made him dangerous to everyone within his reach, and she was clearly within his reach.

Jamie could taste the blood flowing into her mouth from a small cut inside her lip. It wasn't the first time she had tasted blood. Many times, the hand-to-hand combat training exercises would turn more violent than necessary. It almost seemed normal, something she could think about, tune out his presence in the room. She had insulted him by moving out of the main cabin, and now it was time to pay for it. Pay with shame and humiliation, but hopefully not her life.

As General Boyle freed his manhood from his field greens, he shouted, "Spread your legs, whore," and crawled up on the bunk between her thighs.

He thrust inside as he came down on her. With no preparation or excitement to aid in the entry, it was rough and painful. Jamie bit the cut on her lip to avoid crying out in pain.

His breath smelled of Southern Comfort, and his body of sweat and dirt. A full day's stubble on his chin dug into her shoulder as he humped and grunted on top of her, the pain inside increasing with each thrust. Thankfully, his excitement was great and his power to hold back short. The liquid he expended inside her at least helped reduce the friction and pain as he twitched and shook like some prehistoric animal before collapsing limp and heavy.

"I…love…you…Jamie," he gasped between breaths.

Jamie closed her eyes, tears streaming down her cheeks. Maybe he would do her a favor and kill her now.

The general rolled off her and stumbled to his feet, his weapon now limp and glistening with semen, dangled from his fly. He moved close to the bed, hovering over her. "Clean that up." he snapped.

Jamie's body felt like it was weighed down as she struggled up on one arm. She almost vomited, taking him into her mouth. Finished, she collapsed back on the bunk, weak and sick to her stomach.

"Get dressed. I have something wonderful to show you. I'll be outside. Hustle up." A moment later, the bunk door closed behind him.

Great sobs welled up in her body, the sadness and pain mixing together, tearing at her soul. She wasn't sure if she could get dressed. Barely able to see through the tears, Jamie struggled to find her clothing, but she would do anything to prevent him from coming back into the barracks.

Her hands shook so badly that she made no effort to close her shirt using the one remaining button. Hurrying toward the door, Jamie made sure not to look in the direction of the mirror mounted on the wall, afraid of what she might see in its reflection.

General Boyle stood leaning against the barracks exterior wall with his arms folded over his chest and a large cigar, its end glowing red, clenched between his teeth. Jamie wanted to kill him, wipe that smug look off his face, shove that cigar down his throat and have him choke on it.

Taking a large puff from the sweet-smelling weed, he removed it from his mouth. "You look like shit," he spit out, his voice again full of distaste for her. Removing his coat, he said, "Here. Take my jacket and cover yourself up."

Jamie shivered in the thin January Montana air, although she was sure the traumatic encounter with the general had a lot more to do with it. Although the jacket smelled like him, it warmed her, and she was glad to have it.

"Where are we going?" she asked weakly.

"You'll see," was his only response.

They walked toward the communications building. The only structure Jamie had not been allowed in. It was tucked away about a hundred yards from the other buildings in a small dense patch of pine trees.

The trail leading into the trees was narrow and covered with small rocks that crunched under their feet. She was certain Boyle would kill her out in the darkness, then tell everyone she had run away during the night.

Maybe instead she could somehow escape, they would have more trouble tracking her this year with the warm, dry winter. Last year she would have been trudging through two feet of snow that anyone could follow.

Two slivers of light pierced into the black night from small openings in the concrete bunker. Dozens of wires poked through the thick walls, then dipped below ground, making the trip to the antennas mounted atop a nearby ridge. A small generator hummed away, providing a separate power source for communications. General Boyle entered a five-digit code number on the keyless entry system, and the heavy steel door swung open.

An incredibly small room filled with row after row of two-way and shortwave radios greeted them. In the corner, a man sat working at a PC, apparently connected to the Internet. Jamie thought it strange he was retrieving messages from The Happy Gardener home page. However, she didn't have long to ponder why.

General Boyle stood by a door leading into what she assumed was the war room, as she'd heard others refer to it. "In here."

The war room was filled with handmade redwood furniture, eight chairs and a beautiful round table. A large multi-colored map of the UNITED FREE STATES OF AMERICA covered the entire front wall.

There was something different about this map. The states hadn't changed, but new lines had been drawn and shading added. General Boyle flipped a switch near the back of the room, and two large lights flooded the map.

"Now you can see the grand plan. Our new country," he said proudly, strutting up to the map.

Without pausing, he launched into his dissertation. "The main problem with the federal government is its size and inability to recognize the cultural differences between regions of this great land. I've solved both problems. We'll remain a united nation for purposes of national defense, but other than the original constitution and its ten amendments, each region will make its own laws. Four Senates will pass legislation for their own region, no House of Representatives. Each state will have an equal say. Besides, the House has always been too large and unmanageable, prone to corruption and deceit.”

Jamie listened intently, but not for the reasons she hoped he thought.

“Each region will have its own president and army, with all four presidents sitting on the national defense council.” He was like a kid showing off his science project, proud and excited.

“Let me show you the new map. The Western Region ends here on the eastern borders of Montana, Wyoming, Colorado and New Mexico and includes Alaska and Hawaii. The Midwest Region stops at the Mississippi River. The Northern and Southern Regions are split along the Mason-Dixon Line. The great thing about this concept is each region has a similar history and like-minded people with common goals and needs. If the coloreds aren’t welcome in the southern region, they can move to the west or north.”

Jamie was aghast. He had never used that word before, not within her hearing. There had been some discussion of minority rights and laws, but Jamie thought it was about everyone’s rights being disturbed and compromised.

How many more surprises did he have in store for her? “So that’s why you didn’t bomb any cities in the south?” Jamie wished she hadn’t asked the question as soon as the words left her mouth. But Harvey was too far into his world to notice the tone.

“I will not destroy the South. That’s been done before. If Lincoln had allowed nature to run its course, all of this would not be necessary. After almost one hundred years, the states had made decisions about where they stood on most issues. Just because they didn’t agree with those in the north and wanted to create a new nation was no reason to destroy them. Now one hundred and thirty-seven years later, they have a chance to complete the process, take back control of their lives.” He paused, staring at the Southern Region on the map.

Jamie was sure it was no accident the shading was Rebel Gray.

ARTICLE XII

Virginia, January 20, 2001, 8:12 PM EST

"Shit, Billy, you nearly broke my jaw," Mike mumbled. He remained flat on his butt where he'd landed when Billy struck him.

TJ smiled at him, his M-16 cradled in his hulking arms. "Could have been worse. I almost smacked you back there at the roadblock."

Mike grimaced at the thought of it. "Are you feeling any better, Billy?"

Billy stumbled to his feet. The purple lump on his head appeared ugly and painful. "Guess so. Maybe I should have gone along peacefully. Bastards really got their jollies by cracking my head. If any of them are still alive, I'd like to have a word or two with them alone."

Mike tried to smile, but the pain in his jaw wouldn't allow it. "I need to check you for a concussion Billy. You were out hard, and that isn't a good sign." Even though he was pissed at Billy, his medical training still kicked in.

Billy felt the lump on his forehead. "Nope, I'm fine. Let's go."

Sally clasped Billy's arm and stood beside him. "Don't be an ass, Billy. Let Mike check you out."

Billy pulled away from Sally's arm, wobbling a bit as he steadied himself. "I said no, and I meant no. Leave me alone."

"Mike, don't you think you had better check on them?" Sally said, pointing at the two remaining bound figures on the floor.

"Who are they?" Mike asked, moving toward the first still stranger and kneeling beside him.

"I don't have a clue. They brought us in blindfolded. I didn't even know they were here with us." Sally's legs were still a bit unsteady from being tied up so tight, and she collapsed into a nearby chair.

"TJ," Mike began in a direct firm voice, "take Sally out in the hall. Now."

"I don't take orders from you—"

"Dammit, TJ, please get her out of here," Mike ordered, whirling around to glare at him.

Sally leapt from her chair. "Mike, what is it? Mike? Oh, God, no," she sobbed as TJ half dragged her out of the room, his arm the only thing keeping her upright.

Billy knelt beside Mike. "Is it her ex?" he asked in a quiet tone.

"Christ, yes, it's Jeff. They shot him in the head. Looks like after he was gagged, he was executed. I don't want Sally to see him this way. No one should have to see that." Mike was crushed for her. The bullet had entered low on the back of his head and exited through his mouth. It was a gruesome scene, and Mike didn't want her to remember him this way.

"Here, let me cover him with this." Billy had retrieved a blanket from the corner of the room, and he quickly placed it over the body. It was the second time tonight they had covered the body of a friend. Maybe it was time to head back. Get out alive while they still could.

"This is crazy. Should we go back to Atlanta?" Mike asked Billy.

"I'm not going to tell you what to do, Doc, but I am not going to let these traitors run me out before I've had a chance to do what I came here to do. We need a lot more information on the size of the bomb and the damage."

Mike dropped his head. He was so tired, the day having zapped all his energy. He knew Billy was right about going on, but he wasn't sure if he could go with him. He wasn't even sure he wanted to.

Billy checked the other hostage. "This one is dead too, Mike. I wonder why they didn't kill us?"

Mike stood staring at the two bodies. "The real question is why the hell they had to kill them?"

"My guess. They were here at the FBI building. They knew they were agents and represented who they were fighting. They weren't sure yet about Sally and me. Maybe thought we might be useful. Shit, who knows?" Billy shook his head slowly as he finished speaking.

"Let's move, Doc," TJ said, tugging on the sleeve of Mike's bloodstained jacket. "We still have to make Quantico Station before we can get some sleep."

The last thing Mike wanted to do was to face Sally out in the hall, but someone had to tell her, and it might as well be her best friend. He walked back to the doorway, more aware now than before of the carnage beneath his feet. Bloody footprints were spread between the bodies of the fallen ARA terrorists.

He couldn't bring himself to call them soldiers after what they had done to Jeff and the other FBI agent. War or no war, cold-blooded execution was an act of terrorism and murder. His feelings had changed drastically since he ached for the dead guard outside in the courtyard. No longer did he feel their pain or anger, only disgust at their actions. It should not have surprised him, though. For thousands of years during these sorts of struggles between men, it had happened just this way. Rage built up by the people who felt powerless, lashing out at the symbols of their oppression.

Whenever power changed hands by revolution, more times than not, it was bloodier and crueler than the events leading to it. Perception was reality, and to these people, the entire government was evil and ungodly, bent on destroying their lives. Not individuals or humans, things, evil things to be eliminated. No matter what was done, if it served to accomplish its overthrow, it was just.

At least now, Mike knew where he stood and what he was willing to sacrifice to stop them.

Sally sat against the wall, curled up like a ball, her arms covering her face.

It was so contrary to the Sally Mike knew. Confident, proud, defiant. This lunacy was changing all of them. Mike knelt and wrapped his arms around her, a quiet embrace of love and pain that lasted for several minutes. When she was able to gather herself, he was confident the three of them would be even more united and determined to move forward, their bond sealed in the blood of Bo and Jeff.

Mike rubbed her shoulders and spoke softly to her. "I'm so sorry, babe. I know you still really loved him. So did I. But we must go now. I don't know how safe it is for us here."

She peered up at Mike, her eyes puffy and red. "Can I see him, please?" she asked, her voice weak and pleading.

"You don't want to do that, Sally. The Jeff you knew is gone. Putting yourself through that won't bring him back. Trust me this once." Mike kissed her lightly on the forehead and helped her to stand.

Billy had just emerged from the room and walked over to them. Mike hoped he would join them in an embrace, but he remained distant, not even looking at them. Mike sensed something had changed in Billy. More than the injury to his face, his eyes were different somehow. It sent a chill down his spine.

After a few moments, TJ cleared his throat, making eye contact with Mike. A tilt of his head toward the hallway was all the communication needed for Mike to understand it was well past time to go.

Mike squeezed Sally's shoulders. "From this point forward, we stick close and watch each other's backs. I've lost enough friends today, so we all have to make it out of here safely, okay?" She nodded and managed to smile at him. For now, the pain and grief were their bond.

Sally looked over her shoulder at Billy. "You with us?"

"Don't worry about me. From here on out, it's shoot first. Fuck these idiots," he replied as he turned and walked away.

Mike had no idea how to respond to him. After making sure Sally was ready to go, he walked over to TJ and thrust out his hand. "I can't thank you enough for saving them."

His hand now fully engulfed Mike's as TJ smiled in return. "Anytime. That's what they pay me for. I'm just glad you didn't want to hug me."

"I was going to, but figured I would never get my arms around you." Mike chuckled, shaking TJ's hand vigorously.

"Good call. Now let's see if we can get your scrawny ass back out of here without getting it shot off."

With that, TJ made small circles in the air with his right index finger, and his squad began moving back down the hallway. TJ and two other Marines waited for Mike, Billy, and Sally to proceed them before bringing up the rear.

ARTICLE XIII

Western Montana, January 20, 2001, 7:21 PM MST

"Do you want to stay and hear my address over the shortwave at seven-thirty?" General Boyle asked Jamie, his eyes indicating to her that it was not a request.

She wondered if it might be a good time to try to escape from the compound but knew she wouldn't get far in the cold dark night, dressed like this. "Sure. That would be nice."

Nothing could be further from the truth. On the other hand, maybe she could find out more information about his plans, information she would need to help them. *Them.* It sounded so strange for her to want the government to stop him. The truth was she wanted anyone to stop him, maybe even by her own hand if it became necessary. Thankfully, he did not notice when she recoiled from his touch as he walked past her back into the small transmission room.

One of the most defining and eerie moments in American history was about to take place. At seven-thirty PM MST, General Harvey Boyle would talk with his supporters over the shortwave, and President Claire Louise Young would address the rest of the nation using AM and FM stations. Jamie was sure that not since World War II had so many Americans huddled together with their families around their radios.

General Boyle told Jamie that when he learned of the president's address, he intentionally scheduled his at the same moment. To steal her thunder, he'd said.

However, Jamie knew him better than that. He simply didn't want his supporters listening to any version of the facts that might conflict with his own.

A radio near Jamie was configured to record the new president's speech for General Boyle to hear later. It was just loud enough for Jamie to hear from her position, and she would be able to listen to both at once.

The shortwave operator sounded a long tone before speaking into the microphone. "Patriots and loyal Americans, General Harvey Boyle."

From the small speaker on the radio, Jamie heard, *"Ladies and Gentlemen, the President of the United States of America..."*

"Good evening, fellow freedom fighters, patriots and other Americans. Tonight, I speak to you with hope in my heart that a new America is within our reach...."

"My fellow Americans, tonight I speak to you with pain in my heart for our great nation and hope we can begin to repel the forces working to tear it apart..."

"Not since the great civil war has an opportunity for restoring the constitutional rights of our citizens and its states, something the founding fathers would have been extremely proud of, been so close at hand..."

"Not since the tragic civil war that so devastated our people has our country been so divided, something the founding fathers worked hard to prevent..."

"No one regrets the loss of life this morning more than I. However, peaceful attempts to regain control of an unbending federal tyranny has been unsuccessful. It was time to act and take it by force..."

"Millions of innocent Americans perished today, the result of a carefully planned attempt to transfer the power of your government to a military tyrant. Unable to accomplish his sick plan through the ballot box, he has resorted to the destruction of American cities and the helpless men, women and children living there..."

"We can never return to the way things were before this morning. We must move forward toward our goals. Those who choose to join us and become part of the second revolution can start by taking control of your own neighborhoods and towns..."

"You, as Americans, must trust your instincts. The decision to support

our constitutional system and government or follow a madman bent on all-out civil war is yours and yours alone. This government will only attack armed troops attempting sabotage or terrorism. No federal troops will roam the streets..."

"Soon federal troops, mixed with United Nations foreign troops, will descend on your home, taking your food, guns and freedom. If our struggle inspired by God himself is not successful, you will live under the control of a one-world government police state forever..."

"You must stand strong with your neighbors and family against this menace to our long history of free elections and peaceful transition of government power. Do not let this lunatic lure you into sharing his conspiracy fantasies about a one-world authority..."

"If you love God and your country, lift up your voice and guns and join me in this great battle for freedom. Give shelter to your Patriot friends and give no aid to the wicked government about to receive a fatal last blow..."

"I can assure each and every one of you we will prevail if it is your wish for us to do so. No enemy, from without or within, has ever toppled our democracy, and today is not the day that it will. Pray for those who have already died on both sides and for the loved ones left behind to grieve..."

"Because of our actions today, a message has been sent around the globe. A message of freedom and change. It is a message they do not want to hear, for they know the power of the United Free States will soon be used again to promote freedom for all citizens of the world..."

"Our actions in the coming days will send a message to the world that freedom is worth suffering for, worth fighting for. It is a message they need to hear loud and clear from you, the American people..."

"I wish Godspeed to all freedom-loving soldiers of this great nation. God Bless our cause, and goodnight."

"Let us pray together for our nation, for the strength to overcome this greatest of all tests of our faith and our nation. God bless you all, and

goodnight."

Tears streamed from Jamie's eyes as she absorbed the emotions now flooding her mind. She could not survive another day like this one and wondered if the nation would crumble with her.

General Boyle finished the glass of Southern Comfort in front of him and stood up from the small table holding the microphone. He was beaming and proud, his chest puffed out even farther than normal.

"Come on, Jamie. You're spending tonight in the cabin," he barked as he strutted through the small doorway into the darkness.

ARTICLE XIV

Denver, Colorado, January 20, 2001, 7:42 PM MST

"You should try and get some sleep," Ashley said softly from behind as they walked down the brightly lit hallway.

The sound of her voice made Ben's legs a little less sure of their course, and he struggled to plod on. As he stopped at the door to his small quarters, she came up close behind him, repeating her suggestion. Ashley's' warm breath fell softly on the back of his neck, and he closed his eyes, trying to hide the shivers running through him. How could she have known the effect that had always had on him? Was it written somewhere in his file? It didn't matter because now it was written all over his face and body.

"Are you going to stand out here all night dreaming of me? Or are you going to invite me inside?" Her tone was like a blowtorch heating his entire body as she lightly caressed the small of his back with her fingers.

Guilt assailed Ben over feeling like this when there was so much grief and pain all around him. Including his own. Maybe that's why it was so intense, so unreal. He was done fighting it off. Done feeling numb. He fumbled with the door handle and burst into the small room, his heart racing and his face flushed and hot.

Ashley smiled broadly at his unease and slowly stepped in, closing and locking the door behind her.

"You know, of course, that we shouldn't do this," she said while sliding her jacket off her shoulders and letting it drop to the floor.

Ben opened his mouth to respond to her statement, but no sound was forthcoming. Instead, he moved close, kissing her hard on the mouth. Her lips were soft and moist under his, small pillows of sensation moving in perfect rhythm with his. Why had they waited so long for this moment?

Ashley's tongue desperately sought out his raising their passion to a new level, a passion Ben hadn't known for many years, stirring his mind and body. She had no trouble noticing his arousal and pressed her hips hard against his.

His legs almost buckled as she began a gentle sensual rhythm moving side to side. Ben reached around her placing his hands on the small of her back, pulling her even closer. It was the foundation of a deep groan from within her, throaty and animal-like.

Their embrace intact, they fell back, almost missing the small bed. Ashley's legs wrapped themselves tightly around Ben, her skirt forced above her waist. He was nearly overwhelmed by the feeling, even through his pants, of her silky nylons rubbing against his legs.

Conscious of how rapid her breathing had become, Ben eased his mouth down onto the softness of her neck, the scent of her perfume engulfing his nostrils. His head began to swim and spin. What little thought process he still possessed evaporated. It was instinct now, passion unchecked.

With a deliberately light touch, Ben constructed tiny slow circles on her neck with his tongue. Ashley, too, was losing control, new powerful moans erupted from within her, and she stepped up the tempo of her hips against him.

Ben traced across her shoulder lightly with his fingertips, allowing them to slowly move down the front of her blouse toward her breasts. When the palm of his hand reached her erect nipple, she gasped and grabbed his hand, squeezing it hard enough to cause Ben pain.

"You can't do that," Ashley panted in a husky whisper.

Ben looked at her for some explanation of her sudden reluctance. Ashley's eyes slowly opened, revealing they were filled with passion and longing. "I don't understand," he said.

Sighing deeply, she uttered, "If I let you touch me there, I won't be able to stop."

"Did you want to stop?" Ben asked, not wanting to hear the answer.

"I'm not sure, but if you touch me there, I won't be able to."

Ben looked directly into her eyes. They were mesmerizing. Slowly without losing eye contact with her, he lowered his mouth, kissing her smallish breast through the silk blouse. Ashley's response was swift, feverishly opening her blouse and unsnapping the front catch on her black lace bra. Her breasts rose and fell rapidly as she interlaced her fingers into Ben's hair pulling his mouth down instantly to them.

"Now I might have to kill you," she said, sounding as though she could barely speak. "But not until after you make love to me."

Ben raised his head and smiled devilishly. "After I make love to you, I might just let you."

He was only half kidding and made love to Ashley like it might be his last act on earth.

Her body responded like no other woman he had ever touched. Time after time, she climaxed, shuddering and groaning until Ben could hold back no longer and joined her in the ecstasy of the moment. For a few precious seconds, the world didn't seem so screwed up. Ben almost lost consciousness during the intense orgasm and struggled to regain his senses.

Although, according to Ashley, she didn't want him to ever move from his position atop her, Ashley sighed contentedly when he rolled off and turned to rest by her side. No doubt, the release of his weight allowed her to breathe again.

Spent and tingling, they lay tenderly stroking and kissing each other. Finally able to speak again, Ben said softly into her ear, "Thank God we weren't disturbed this time."

Ashley's face broke into a large evil grin. "It wasn't just luck, you know. I threatened to kill anyone who did."

"Can I ask you something?" Ben's finger now drew imaginary shapes on her bare stomach.

"Don't worry, I'm on the pill," Ashley replied flatly.

Ben chuckled softly. He hadn't even considered that aspect of their lovemaking. "No. No, not that. I've been laying here trying to figure something out. Why me? Why now?"

"God, you do ask tough questions." Ashley looked away from him to stare at the plain white wall of the small room. "I guess I've been so busy with my career plans. You know, always going the extra mile, taking extra duty, there just hasn't been any time for fun or love. When all this happened this morning, I suddenly wondered if I would ever get the chance again."

Ben smiled slightly. "Uh-huh. Sounds familiar."

Pausing briefly, she looked back at Ben. "I hope you know," she whispered, "that the minute I started studying your folder, I wanted to meet you. All the tragedy in your life, the way you have risen in your field, without stepping on others or selling your soul. A man of integrity and honor, hardworking, dedicated. All the traits I look for in a man, it was like I had known you for a long time."

Ben gazed deeply into her magnetic blue eyes, the bright overhead light enhancing every detail inside them.

Ashley pulled his head closer to hers, lowering her voice so far it was barely audible. "When I saw you for the first time in the elevator, you were so handsome, so funny, so in control, so afraid, so exciting. I told myself right then, don't let this one get away. We all could have... Hell, what am I saying? *Should have* been dead this morning."

"A lot of people died this morning, good people, friends..." Ben's voice trailed off.

"I know, Ben. I hope you get some word about your son soon. I've been saying prayers for him all day." She lightly stroked Ben's stubble-laden face.

Ben took her hand and looked into her eyes. "Do you think I should be there looking and not here?"

"Well," Ashley started. "I think that, like you have all of your life, you should be where you can help the most people. Make some sense of what is happening in their world. I've read some of your work. It's good. Makes a difference. Don't beat yourself up."

"Thanks. I didn't mean to bring the mood down. As I remember, you were about to say more glowing things about me," Ben quipped.

She flashed a smile he hadn't yet seen, the kind that melts away troubles, erodes defenses, and plunges men into love. "Yes. Yes, so I was. Let's see, did I mention handsome?" She giggled and tilted her head to the side.

"Uh-huh," Ben said, grinning and laying his head back down on the pillow.

"What about exciting?"

"Uh-huh."

"Hmm...funny?"

"Yep."

"Strong?"

"Nope. You missed that one. But don't let that stop you." Ben was enjoying her attention almost as much as he had a few moments ago when they made love.

"Smart? Oh, wait, maybe not smart," she cooed, smiling even wider.

Ben bolted upright, threw his hands around her small waist, and began tickling her with all the energy he retained. "You're going to pay for that one, Agent Prescott," he howled as they rolled back and forth on the small cot, laughing uncontrollably.

Still tired from lovemaking and the day's stress, they soon settled back down on the bed. Ben's mind suddenly turned more serious. Should he ask her? Did he really want to know?

"Would you...? Well, you know, if they told you to, even now?" The question was so uncharacteristically vague and cryptic Ben hardly could believe he, of all people, had asked it. However, Ashley knew just what he wanted to know. He could see it on her face and in her eyes. He imagined she had been asking herself the same question over and over again.

Her head turned away from him, and she rose to her feet, slowly gathering her clothing from the floor. A muffled "I don't know" tumbled from her mouth. "I really don't know," she said, repeating the answer as much to herself as Ben.

The room was silent for several minutes while Ashley dressed. As she reached the door, she paused and said, without turning around, "Let's hope we never have to find out." And with that, she quietly opened the door and disappeared into the hallway.

Ben lay motionless on the bed staring at the ceiling. What he would give to be in the Bannon Club right now, the hot water pulsating against the back of his neck.

ARTICLE XV

Virginia, January 20, 2001, 9:44 PM EST

"Dammit, TJ, slow down," Mike yelled. Sally had been struggling to keep up with the blistering pace the Marines were setting through the underbrush. For the last fifteen minutes, Mike had been forced to half-carry her, a job made more difficult by his own fatigue. The trauma of being held hostage, combined with Jeff's murder, had taken its toll on her, and Mike was uncertain how much farther they could travel without rest.

TJ raised his hand, signaling the group to stop and made his way back to the rock where Sally and Mike now sat. "What's the problem, Doc?"

"Sally isn't doing well. Her damn legs are like rubber, and I can't carry her anymore," Mike informed him, half yelling, half-pleading his case to this hulking man, who, by all appearances, never tired.

TJ slowly scanned the surrounding brush, his index finger tapping on the stock of his M-16. "I don't know, Doc. This isn't the best place in the world to be if shit hits the fan again. I would sure like to make it back to the base tonight." He paused and waited for some reaction, but Mike simply stared back at him, hoping TJ could see his resolve. "Okay, okay. We'll rest here for thirty minutes but not one minute more. Find some place for her to lie down and keep quiet. Understand?"

"Thanks, TJ," Sally said weakly.

"It's not going to get any warmer either," TJ snapped, apparently still trying to win the argument.

Mike nodded and managed a brief smile. "Thirty minutes."

Four separate times TJ pointed to one of his men, then pointed two fingers to his eyes and the direction he wanted them to go. The four men crept silently into the darkness to stand watch over the group. Mike wondered how many young men on both sides of this madness would spend the night crouched in the darkness, waiting to kill or be killed. There was little doubt in his mind that the ARA wasn't a match for the United States Military machine if it held together. However, no one could know what might happen when the rank-and-file soldier discovered who the enemy really was. Would American soldiers really kill Americans? It was a chilling thought.

There was a great deal of unrest in the military. Fallout from the 1999 budget cuts, and constant excursions into harm's way around the world, usually without a clear-cut mission. The loss of over seven hundred men in the middle east in March of last year, before being ordered to unceremoniously pull out in the middle of the night, caused nearly one-third of the command staff to retire or resign. Enlistment was at an all-time low, and there was even talk of re-instituting the draft. If the enemies inside the country were successful in bringing the government down, the enemies from outside would be waiting for them too.

"Have you got any water?" Sally asked in a weak voice.

"Here, take mine," came Billy's quiet voice from the shadows.

"Where the hell have you been?" Although he was relieved that Billy wanted to help, Mike was annoyed about not seeing him since they left the FBI headquarters. "I could have used a hand with Sally."

Billy stepped out of the shadows, an automatic weapon taken from one of the dead ARA thugs slung over his shoulder. "Keep your voice down. I've been out on the right flank, hoping to pop a couple of caps into one of those assholes." His face was still swollen and bruised from his encounter, but his good eye was intense and angry.

Mike studied him for a moment. "That isn't what we came here for, Billy. Why don't you stick with us from now on?"

Billy looked past Mike into the darkness. "Seems to me the plan has changed a little. I sure didn't come all this way to get killed or watch you get killed. I'm not going to let them do anything else to us. Next time they'll have to kill me, but not before I kill a bunch of them first." Billy threw his canteen at Mike's feet, turned and disappeared into the night.

Slowly, Mike reached down, picked up the canteen, removed the lid, and handed it over to Sally. "He's losing it. We need to get back on track, back to what we came here for. Maybe they should have sent someone else, someone better suited for this. I'm not sure I can finish it."

Sally took a long drink from the canteen and fixed her eyes on Mike. "I don't want to hear any more of that kind of talk. Billy will be fine in the morning. They scrambled his brain up a little, and he's pissed. Let him blow off some steam and play soldier. When the time comes that we need him, he won't let us down. Okay?"

Mike paused and stared at the spot where Billy had disappeared. "I hope you're right. We'll need him tomorrow when we get closer to the blast zone. I don't know enough about these bombs to do it without him, and we can't just guess, you know?"

"He's never let me down before."

It took a moment for her words to sink in, but Mike was not so tired that her meaning went over his head. Though they had been close friends for many years, Sally had always kept a certain amount of information from Mike. He understood about her job and why that was necessary, but this was different. He was a part of it, involved.

"What do you mean by before?" he asked, staring directly into her puffy eyes. Even before she answered, he knew she hadn't intended to use those words. Fatigue had caused her to be careless and let the truth slip out. He could see she was angry with herself.

"Let it go, Mike," she said quietly, turning to look intently into the dark Virginia night.

Mike had no intention of letting it go, and he pushed harder for an answer. "Sally, this is not subject to negotiation. You will tell me everything, and I mean *everything*."

"You don't want to know. Not yet."

Mike moved to stand right in front of her and bent close to her face. "I'm not going to budge from this spot until I know it all. Please don't push me on this one, Sally. I won't tolerate any more secrets."

"All right, all right. Now get out of my face. Even tired, I can still kick your ass." Her tired eyes had come to life, and Mike backed away.

"Billy and I worked together several times before," she began. "We go back to the Oklahoma City bombing days. Truth is, I couldn't have put that whole case in the box without his help. He had a few moles inside the movement, deep cover stuff. The BATF was looking at explosive violations and weapons charges on a few of the chief wackos. After they took out the Federal Building, Billy tried hard to dig out which members might be involved. But when he lost one of his agents, shot in the head, he backed off to let things cool down for a while. Late in ninety-eight, after McVey and Nichols had been sent off to prison, Billy cranked up the heat again. I had been working on the case, too, of course, coming in from a completely different angle but making good progress."

"Did Billy know you were working the case?"

"Just let me finish, please. One night, I had a meeting scheduled with a West Texas rancher. I heard that he could help me identify one sect I had been looking for. When I arrived at the restaurant that night, Billy was waiting for me. He didn't trust me at first, but after a few hours, we began to share our information. Between what he knew and what I knew, we pieced together the facts and started down the road to solving the case."

Mike struggled to keep his anger under control until she spilled it all. "So why haven't I heard of him before? Why did you and the Bureau take all the credit?" Mike asked in the most acrid tone he could muster.

Sally peered back at him, her eyes narrow and black. "Fuck you, Mike. That was politics all the way. I lobbied for a joint arrest, but the BATF was laying low at that time, and there were a few questionable tactics used by Billy before I came on the scene. He was a SEAL in the gulf war and was used to results over procedure, so it was decided to bury their role in the investigation. Still, Billy got a good promotion and a bump in pay. Besides, I think he's more comfortable in the background anyway."

"So, what else? Why the hell didn't you tell me you had worked with him before?" Mike knew Sally wouldn't hide this information without good reason, and he was determined to find out her reasoning.

"We're covert. I had orders not to tell you."

Mike was losing the battle to control his temper. "Covert? Covert? I don't even know what that means. I'm not *covert*." His voice got louder with each word.

Sally stood and took him by the arm hard enough for it to hurt. "Keep your voice down. We aren't alone here, you know?"

From behind him, Mike heard the distinct sound of an automatic weapon being cocked. "Listen to her, Mike. She's right." Billy stepped from the shadows again, this time with his M-16 pointed near Mike's midsection.

Mike turned to face him directly. "What are you going to do, Billy? Shoot me?"

"Sit down and be quiet," Billy's response was unusually terse and impersonal.

Sally moved between the two men facing Billy. "It's okay, Billy. I've got this under control. Just relax and put the gun down, okay?"

There was a firm yet calming tone to her voice, and Billy eased the weapon down to his side. "Okay, but I don't want everybody in the state knowing who and where we are. How much does he know?"

Sally relaxed a little, moving back to sit on the rock. "Just that we know each other and that we haven't been straight about why we're here."

"And she was about to tell me all about that," Mike quickly added. He didn't want Billy's presence to stop the flow of information.

Billy walked over and sat next to Sally on the rocks. "You sure you want to hear it?"

"Yes. All of it. You at least owe me that," Mike said as he stood facing them, his hands hanging limply at his side. He felt a little sick to his stomach. He had risked his life for them, trusted them. What secret had they been keeping? Why hadn't they trusted him enough to share it before now?

"Two safes. We're going in to locate two safes," Billy stated flatly.

"What safes? Jesus, you mean I risked my ass and got Bo killed for a couple of safes?" Mike felt even more sickened by the revelation. Suddenly he didn't know who these people were. Mike hadn't ever felt closer to a friend than he had with Sally just a short time ago, and now he wondered if he would ever be able to trust her again.

"It's important, Mike. These aren't just any safes. One at the DOD and the other at the US Mint," Sally explained.

"What's so damned important about those?"

Billy stood and stepped closer to Mike. "Come on, Mike. Think about it. The plates for all the US currency and our strategic defense plans. Can you imagine how many people would like to get their hands on that? The plates alone could bring down the economy if the wrong person got to them before we did."

Mike knelt on the wet ground and rubbed his temples. "Didn't everything get obliterated by the blast?"

"We don't think so," Sally answered. "Both safes were fortified, designed to survive a blast like that. Besides, neither is close to what we think was ground zero. What we're concerned about is the possibility that they might have been exposed or compromised by the blast." Sally was regaining her strength and sounded much stronger.

"It's important," Billy interjected. "I'm sorry we couldn't tell you before, but it wasn't our call. So can we count on you to help us out?" Billy's tone was calm and warm.

Instead of making him better, Billy's sudden turn in mood made Mike even more unsure about trusting him. "And if I say no?"

"Then you go back alone," Sally responded without hesitation.

"Or not at all," Billy added.

Mike knew without asking the meaning of his comment. "How would you get out if I take the chopper?"

"You don't have a chopper. It went back to Atlanta as soon as it dropped us off." Billy once again began pacing back and forth in front of Mike.

"Would it be too much to ask how you planned to get out?"

Sally knelt beside him. "A military helicopter. Tomorrow night just outside Washington. We need to get the contents of both safes and be there at sixteen-thirty hours."

Before Mike could say anything, TJ strode briskly up to them. "Okay, times up. Let's move out. Now."

For a few brief seconds, the three looked at each other. Mike sized up the situation, deciding what to do next. He spoke first. "Thanks, TJ. We're ready to go."

TJ looked at Mike as if he sensed something was off. "Everything okay, Doc? You look worried or something."

Rising up off the ground, Mike smacked TJ on the shoulder. "Yep, all good. Let's get going."

Sally reached out, squeezed his arm, and whispered, "You did the right thing, Mike. I owe you one." Billy said nothing and slipped quietly back into the night.

Mike wasn't yet sure if he would help them complete the mission, but for now, his options were limited, and he trudged along, not knowing what daylight would bring.

ARTICLE XVI

Western Montana, January 20, 2001, 9:40 PM MST

For the second time today, Jamie crouched behind a closed door attempting to listen to one of the general's conversations. This time, however, it was a little less nerve-racking since he knew she was in the cabin.

She was somewhat relieved that he felt comfortable enough to speak with Major Hollis while she was there. It was now clear he did not suspect that she was in any way disloyal to him. He must be as unaware of her intentions as she was of his before yesterday, and she hoped to keep it that way for as long as possible. Cautiously, she placed her ear against the heavy oak door and strained to make out the words filtering in from the other room.

"The only thing I want to hear from you is that it's done," General Boyle stated flatly.

"Well, not exactly, sir. The team has located the bomb, but so far, they've been unable to get to it."

Boyle had never taken bad news well, and this was no exception. "Why the hell not? Who did you send down there, a bunch of halfwits?"

Major Hollis's tone was steadfast as he laid out his case. "No, sir. I sent the best team we have. But they can't take on a company of Army regulars. I'm not talking about the National Guard. These guys are from the elite Rapid Strike Force Division."

There was a brief silence, and Jamie could hear the general pacing around the small room. "What the hell is the RSF division doing there? Do you think they found the bomb? Isn't Young from Denver? Yes, of course, she is," the general said, answering his own question. "'You know what? I bet she's there."

"Why would she stay there when there could be a bomb?" Major Hollis asked. "That would be crazy. Suicide. Wouldn't they head for Omaha or Cheyenne Mountain? Hell, even keep her airborne?"

"Maybe, but I think she might just be stubborn enough to stay in spite of the threat. And besides, she's a darkie. You know they don't like it underground."

General Boyle's statements carried the weight of indisputable fact, and Jamie was pretty sure Hollis wouldn't challenge him again.

"Okay, so what do you want done now?" Hollis asked.

"Well, this does change things quite a bit. I hadn't planned on taking her out of the picture this easily. Send down thirty of your best men. I want them on the road tonight." Boyle sounded excited, and he spoke quickly. "Have them get to that bomb, and detonate it as soon as possible. I want Denver out of the way for good. There are now so many great reasons for turning that cow town into a pile of dust. If this works, they'll be totally disorganized for at least a week, more than enough time for us to move in and clean up."

Jamie heard a small handclap as the general finished speaking, something she'd heard many times when he was pleased with himself.

Jamie knew Hollis was a soldier and loyal to Boyle and his cause. Nevertheless, when it came to these kinds of decisions, he always pushed for clear orders. So she wasn't surprised by his next question.

"So that we're clear on this, General, you want the bomb set off as soon as they can get in and get out?"

"No. I want the bomb set off as soon as they get in." The flat, firm response from the general chilled Jamie to her core.

Major Hollis cleared his throat. "General, with all due respect, I'm not sure I can order those men to commit suicide. I can *ask* them. Let them know your wishes. But I can't order them to do that. I'm sorry, sir."

Jamie cringed, expecting the worst. She even had thoughts of the general shooting Hollis right there in the cabin with his sidearm. What happened next surprised her as much as anything had all day.

"You may be right, Hollis," the general said slowly. "Alright. Ask them to take the site as quickly and quietly as possible. Then detonate the bomb as soon as it's safe to do so."

"Thank you, sir. Even though many of our patriot brothers will lose their lives tomorrow, at least they'll have a fighting chance."

Suddenly Jamie's heart stopped. Out of the corner of her eye, she saw motion from outside the small window beside the bed. Absolute terror gripped her. She flung herself away from the door and toward the small closet.

One of the guards had his face just inches from the window, staring intently at her. She was dead. The general had set her up, placed her in a position to drop her guard and had her watched. Soon he would be informing the general of her actions and pay her a deadly and painful visit.

Frantic now, Jamie looked around the room for a weapon to protect herself. Maybe she could use a chair and hit him when he came through the door. Both the windows were in the view of the guard, and the only door led straight to Boyle and certain death.

She looked back at the window to see if the man, now discovered, had left his post. To her great surprise, not only was he still there, but he had also moved closer to the window and was making some kind of motion to her. Was he trying to tell her she was going to die? Taunting her? Was he getting sick pleasure out of this?

Carefully, still watching the bedroom door, she moved to the window. When she got close enough to see the man clearly, Jamie recognized it was Stuart Williams. Stuart made the trip with her from Deer Path nearly two years ago, and they had remained close friends while at the camp. Why had Boyle chosen him to seal her fate? And why had Stuart agreed to spy on her after all they had been through?

However, nothing was quite what it appeared to be today, and when Jamie reached the window, she realized the motion Stuart was making was for her to be quiet. He looked just as nervous and afraid as she was, constantly glancing from side to side, his eyes darting and frightened.

Jamie quietly opened the small window a crack. "Stuart, what the hell are you doing out there? You scared the living shit out of me," she whispered.

"Alright, calm down. We don't have time for a nice long talk." He glanced around again, then said, "Listen. We talked a lot about the world we wanted to help create. I know you can't be going along with this madness. Killing millions, not caring who they are. Meet me in the morning near the back gate at zero-six hundred. We've got to get out of here as soon as possible. I have some information the other side needs, and I want you to cover my back. Did you hear anything through the door?" Stuart asked, talking quickly and quietly.

Jamie wanted so much to trust him, to have an ally to help her. However, this sounded too pat. How did he know she wasn't going along with Boyle? It could just as easily be some kind of trap, an attempt to bring her out in the open and find out how much she knew. She decided to play it safe for now. "Maybe I'll be there. If I can get away. Oh, and I didn't really hear much. I was just curious about what to expect tomorrow."

Stuart frowned and shook his head. "Okay, if you need to play it that way, I understand. I wasn't sure about coming here either. I'll be at the back gate in the morning at zero six hundred sharp. If you're there, then I'll know I was right about how smart you really are. If, on the other hand, one of Boyle's goons is there to put a bullet in my head, well then, I guess that will be it for Denver and who knows how many other cities. You'll have to decide if you can live with that. I can't stay here any longer. Goodbye." With that, Stuart turned and crept silently off into the darkness.

Jamie's stomach rumbled and gurgled. The stress of the day, combined with not eating since breakfast, was beginning to take its toll on her body. How would she ever sleep? Her bones were so tired, and she wanted to escape the madness for a time. Be able to make up her mind about what to do with Stuart and his plan after she rested. She collapsed on the bed, pulling the comforter up around her weak and shivering body.

It seemed like only a minute or so later, the door to the bedroom creaked open.

"You asleep?" Boyle asked her from the side of the bed.

Jamie wasn't sure if she had slept or not. "No. Not anymore," she responded, her voice groggy and tired.

"Great. You know, this has been the best day of my life. I'm not sure I'll be able to sleep. I've known victory before, but not like this. Yesterday, the world was going along smoothly about to become a socialist one-world government. But tonight, they've been served noticed that not all of us are going to follow without a fight." He had moved to the window and stared out into the night.

Jamie rolled over slightly so she could see him better. "So, what's next?"

A slight smile passed across his face as he turned to face her. "We'll build a new country and a new world. Freedom will be the order of the day. No man will have to scrimp and save just to pay his taxes. Crime will disappear as a true justice system is re-instituted, swift but fair. The government will become what it was intended to be, protection from outside threats and a fair-trade referee. Everyone will know that God is the only power that supersedes my great nation."

Apparently, Jamie's fatigue caused her to take unnecessary chances because she bluntly asked, "*Your* great nation?"

He didn't even flinch. "Just as the founding fathers were responsible for making this great country what it used to be, I will be the author of the new words our great-grandchildren will live by and whisper in their nightly prayers. Since God chooses who shall be his sword here on earth, who am I to question his will? Not since He gave Moses His laws has He entrusted so much human destiny to one mortal man."

How could Jamie have been so blind to this man's dangerous ego?

The general sat down on the edge of the bed beside her. "The world can be yours, Jamie. I'll give it to you."

She looked into the eyes of this man who claimed to love her and intensely hated so many others. "What about Ken? I'm still married, you know?" Jamie knew she was walking a fine line with Harvey, but for the first time today, she had no fear. If she was supposed to die at his hand, so be it.

"I didn't let an entire government shut me down. I sure as hell won't let one drug dealer come between you and me."

Jamie was sure he believed it was something she wanted to hear him say. Having come this far, she would see it through to the end.

"How will you stop him from coming for me when the prisons are emptied?"

He rose, moving back toward the window, where he clasped his hands together behind his back, a sure sign to Jamie that he was contemplating how much to tell her. "What would you say if I told you, after tomorrow, it won't matter what he wants?"

"What do you mean? What's going to happen tomorrow?"

"Justice."

 "Justice for who? Ken?"

"Yes, and for that woman who has insulted every American by illegally seizing power, challenged my motives and killed my Patriot brothers. Did you know she sent me a message?"

"No, I didn't, Harvey. What did it say?" Jamie had him relaxed and talking and wanted to get it all.

"She said, 'The United States Government is alive and well and will never surrender to a terrorist.' Me, a goddamned terrorist. Shit, the nerve of that black bitch. Oh, and you will love this. She's extended an opportunity, for a limited time, of course, for me to give up. If we stop now, she'll guarantee fair trials for all. What a joke. Ask Tim McVeigh if he got a fair trial or a dozen other Patriots who are sitting in a prison cell somewhere. She doesn't have a clue what it means to be free, really free."

Jamie was always amazed at how he could talk to himself, half preaching, half pouring out his thoughts and feelings. She continued to prime the pump. "What did you expect her to say?"

The question seemed to take him by surprise, and he looked back at Jamie with a slightly puzzled expression. "Well, I'm not sure. I never really gave it much thought. I guess, considering we hit them so hard this morning, that they might want to try for some kind of settlement. Maybe trade Montana and a few other states for peace. Maybe I gave them too much credit for being smart enough to know they're already beaten. Oh well, doesn't matter. Soon enough, they'll become painfully aware of their miscalculation. Then it will be too late for mercy, too late to stop the tide of freedom rolling across the landscape."

Finished with his oratory, he undressed and slipped into bed beside Jamie. "I want you. I need you. Please make love to me," he whispered.

In the last few minutes, Jamie had learned how much easier it was to be with him if she played her role. One way or another, this would be her last night with him, and she would do what was needed to survive and meet Stuart in the morning.

Her soul was already gone, and it could not be repaired. Ken's life was the only thing she had left to live for. She rolled over and faced this man who had murdered millions of people.

"Of course, Harvey. I would love to."

ARTICLE XVII

Denver, Colorado, January 20, 2001, 9:57 PM MST

Ben stumbled down the corridor toward the conference room. He hadn't been asleep for more than a few moments when the guard woke him. At least his time with Ashley hadn't been disturbed. At Sid's request, the Marine had summoned Ben, Larry, Terry and President Young for an impromptu meeting.

"We found Robbins," Sid told the small group gathered in the conference room.

President Young had obviously been asleep also, as her eyes were puffy and her hair slightly mussed. "Where?"

Sid removed his wire-rimmed glasses. "Aspen. He's hiding out there in the cabin of one of his rich buddies from New York. I got a call from an old friend who lives in the area. He spotted Robbins having dinner with some friends. Said he seemed really nervous and was wearing a hat pulled down to cover his eyes."

Larry leaned back in his chair. "Are we one hundred percent sure it was him?"

"No doubt," Sid said without hesitation. "I used another source to confirm it."

"Well, let's pick him up and bring him back," General Clifton interjected.

Sid nodded. "We can do that easy enough."

Ben was beginning to feel like flirting with fire in these meetings was part of his calling because he couldn't hold back. "Are you sure that's wise? I mean, what authority will you use? This is the Governor of Colorado you're talking about. Can you prove anything yet?"

Larry seemed to ponder Ben's point for a moment before speaking.

"Yeah. We don't want to step outside our authority, and this could get ugly if he decides to use the guard against us."

President Young sipped from the coffee cup in front of her. "Sid, can we send someone up there to talk to him? Ask him to come back down here so we can work this out?

Sid rubbed his tired eyes. "Well, Claire—oh God, I'm sorry—Madam President, it's pretty late." Sid had traveled in the circles of power for most of his life and saw his breach of etiquette as nearly unforgivable.

"Forget it, Sid." Claire waved his concern away. "Go on, please."

"I really am sorry, Madam President. I certainly meant no disrespect."

She smiled warmly at him from across the table. "Sid, it's okay. Hell, it sounds a lot more natural to me than that fancy title, anyway. Come to think of it, it was the first time today that I was sure someone was really talking to me. Do me a favor and forget it, okay?"

Sid relaxed into his chair a bit and nodded. "Thank you. Now, where in the hell was I?" Everyone at the table chuckled at Sid's quip. It was a side of him they hadn't seen yet. Humble, human, and maybe even a little amusing. "Oh yeah, Robbins." Straightening in his chair again, he continued. "I don't think we should tip him off. If you aren't comfortable bringing him back down, then we should put a tight watch on him. Maybe tap a phone or two. Not for the sake of prosecution, just to see if we can gather some information on his plans."

"I'm not comfortable with the taps," President Young said quietly, almost to herself. "I know we can probably make a good case for them, but if we're wrong, there would be hell to pay for a long time."

Pleased she had reacted to the possibility of taps in that way before he had raised his own objections to them, Ben stepped into the conversation again. "History never rewards those kinds of tactics. If anyone cares, I agree with you, Madam President." Ben paused. "However, we do have other ways to tie him to the ARA if that's what's going on here. More legal ways. His phone bills are public records, and we can get our hands on those without a big scene. I have a source at the Capitol. Last year, the Tenth Circuit ruled that email sent over state computers was also fair game. Not to mention his travel records. I'm willing to bet he's met face-to-face with these idiots, and it wouldn't have been in Colorado either."

President Young nodded, appearing to consider Ben's suggestions. "Sid, do you agree with Ben? Do you think we can build a solid paper trail from Robbins to the ARA?"

"Everything and everyone leaves tracks," Sid replied, scratching notes on his pad.

"Good. Then we go with that. Keep a close eye on him for now while we close the paper noose on him. Ben, will you help Sid gather the information?"

"As long as it's clear that I work independently of his group. I won't share or compromise my sources. After all of you are long gone, I'll be stuck here with my ass exposed and my name ruined."

Sid shot back, "If he'll share his entire work product and promise not to print it, then it doesn't matter to me where he gets it or who gives it to him."

"Okay, okay, let's not start that crap again, gentlemen." President Young shook her head. "Ben, you may gather your information however you want. No one will interfere with that. Nevertheless, you can't use it yet. After this is over and done with, you can write that best seller boiling inside you. I'll send Ashley to look after you."

"No. I won't take her." Even Ben was surprised at his tone with the president, who looked up from the notebook where she'd been scribbling some notes and slowly laid down her pen.

"It wasn't a request, Ben."

He shifted slightly in his seat. "Having her along is no different than Sid going along to take notes."

"I understand how you feel. You've made that very clear. My job is to make sure you don't get killed. You must know that by now, it's no secret what you're doing down here with us. Anyone wanting information about what's going on or just wanting to shut you up might be a threat to your safety and possibly even ours. So, despite your protests, she's going with you, and that's final."

Ben had always been a thoughtful speaker, but the strain was beginning to wear on him too. "And if I say no?"

They had all seen the president's anger earlier in the day. Now it was Ben's turn to be the recipient of it. Her eyes narrowed, and she visibly ground her lower jaw. "If she doesn't go, you don't go."

It was too late to turn back now, and Ben was determined to find out where he stood. "With all due respect, Madam President, I am a private citizen. You cannot make me take Agent Prescott any more than you can make me stay if I choose to leave." He stared directly into the president's now intense brown eyes.

President Young rose from her chair and moved around the table toward Ben, stopping beside him. She leaned over until her face was inches from his. "With all due respect, Mr. Bleser, we are fighting for the life of this country. You will do as I say, or I will have you thrown in prison for a long time. Is that clear now?"

Ben did not look up at her, but he could feel her stare burning through him. "Yes, Madam President. Very clear." Now wasn't the time to anger her further. He could decide how to handle having Ashley along later.

"Thank you for understanding." The words she spoke didn't match the tenor of her voice. Claire was clearly not at all pleased about having to flex her authority over him.

She moved back to the head of the table and sat down hard. "General, will the troops be in place in Montana by morning?" she asked, her voice quiet and under control again.

"Yes, Madam President. They'll be ready. I don't think we have a good handle on the whole layout yet, but it looks like a tough assault. The forest is rugged there, and the threat of one of the bombs being in the camp is very real. We've been getting a strong positive from the satellite. If we do go in, I can't guarantee they won't detonate it."

Looking exhausted, President Young rubbed her eyes. "Well, that would solve the compound issue, wouldn't it?"

"And kill a few thousand of my men," General Clifton shot back.

"Oh no, General. I apologize. I didn't mean I *wanted* them to detonate it. I was just talking aloud. The decision to go in will be yours and Larry's. After we decide if it's feasible to take it, you two will be in control of the operation."

The General nodded. "Thank you, Madam President. We won't let you down."

Ben thought the general's response might have been the humblest thing Terry had ever said to a civilian. It was in stark contrast to Ben's showing of bravado a few minutes earlier, and he was more than slightly embarrassed. "Madam President, I'd like to apologize for my behavior before. I've been a crusty old reporter too long, and I meant no disrespect."

She smiled slightly and gave him a nod of acceptance. "It's alright, Ben. We're all tired and a bit on edge. I'll tell Ashley to cover her ears at all times."

Ben was glad to see the president's wit and humor were still intact. "Deal," he said, chuckling softly.

"Okay, let's wrap this up. We have a Cabinet meeting in four hours." President Young rose from the table. "Ben, can you stay for a moment? Oh, and Larry, ask Agent Prescott to step in here, please."

Moments later, Ashley strode into the small room and stood awaiting her instructions. She still looked fresh and evidently had not been sleeping. "You wanted to see me, Madam President."

"Yes, Ashley. Please have a seat."

Ashley slid a glance in Ben's direction before taking a seat across from him.

"Ashley, Ben is going outside to gather some information we need. I want you to look out for him, watch his back. This is not an assignment to report back to me or anyone else about what you see or hear. Your only job is strictly security. Do you understand?"

Ashley sat erect and maintained eye contact with the president. "Of course, Madam President. Do I have shooting authority?"

Uncomfortable with the calm tone of Ashley's question, Ben squirmed a bit in his chair.

President Young looked at Ben. "Yes, you can do whatever is necessary to get him back safely. Also, if, in your opinion, Mr. Bleser is doing something counter to the good of the United States, bring him back, or shoot him, if you must. Ben, I wanted you to hear my orders to her as I gave them. I didn't want there to be any misunderstandings about the goals of the mission. So, you both understand, then?"

Ben and Ashley nodded as Claire looked at them.

"Good. Then, I trust there will not be a repeat of what happened in Mr. Bleser's room tonight. Until this is over, that is. After that, you two can run away and get married for all I care."

Ashley's eyes lowered to the table, and Ben felt all the blood drain from his face. It seemed President Young had a good handle on everything that happened in the bunker.

Ashley spoke softly. "I am sorry, Madam President. If you need to re-assign me, I'll understand. It was inexcusable."

"Ashley, you know how much I care about you and your mom. I don't care who you sleep with, but I do care if you must think before you act in a crisis. Just keep it in check until this madness is over. And don't think I wouldn't like to grab that big Marine in the lobby and escape for a while if I could. Now get out of here. I need some sleep." President

Young reached out and gave both Ben and Ashley a pat on the hand.

After President Young had closed the door to her private office, Ben turned to Ashley. "Guess there aren't any secrets down here, huh?"

She looked back at him and grinned. "No, I guess not. But for the record, I would do it again."

ARTICLE XVIII

Virginia, January 21, 2001, 5:32 AM EST

Unable to fully open his eyes against the glaring overhead lights of the small room, Mike squinted to see his wristwatch. Pain shot through every muscle he attempted to move. Surely, someone had beaten him while he slept.

The glowing green digital letters read *5:32*. Less than four hours since he had crawled into the cramped bed for some much-needed rest. Mike had never been a "morning person," and after several unpleasant encounters early in their marriage, his wife had learned to give him a wide berth until the coffee kicked in. Above his desk at work, someone had even tacked up a sign reading, INSTANT HUMAN: Just add coffee.

It was always his own damn fault, too. Staying up until three or four in the morning working on a research paper or preparing a CDC report due for release was common practice. The wee morning hours were his favorite of the day. No phone calls, faxes, appointments, or meetings, just the still of the night air and some soft jazz playing in the background. All his most inspiring speeches and reports were written during those quiet times.

"Come on, Mike. It's time to get going," Billy barked, standing directly overhead and looking down at Mike. His eye had taken on some interesting shades of purple and green, but the swelling had eased somewhat, and it appeared that at least he could see out of it.

"You go ahead," Mike groaned. "I'm going to sleep for a couple of days."

"Right. Come on, Mike. We don't have time for this crap." Billy poked Mike with his boot.

"Go away," Mike growled as he rolled over, turning his back to Billy. He didn't like the tone of the agent's voice and wasn't going to snap to attention for him or anyone else today. Yesterday had taught Mike more than a few lessons about being the nice guy all the time.

Billy apparently didn't appreciate being ignored. "You've got one minute to get up out of that bunk and get dressed."

Mike was beginning to boil. Billy's tone was that of a father to a child. However, the hard poke in the middle of Mike's back was more than he could take.

Mike sprung from the bed, wildly swinging his fist, catching Billy square on the jaw.

It was a tossup as to which man was more surprised. Going by the expression on Billy's face, he was completely shocked that Mike would hit him, and Mike couldn't believe he hadn't been sent flying backward from the force of the blow. Billy stood right where he had been, staring directly at Mike with his one good eye now narrowed.

Mike stood cocked and ready, looking into Billy's flaring eye, carefully watching for any movement of the agent's hands, bracing himself for the crushing force that was sure to come.

Billy only grinned. "I think you'd better stick to verbal battles, Doc." He turned to leave the room and shot over his shoulder, "We leave in thirty minutes."

Mike almost wished Billy had hit him. Walking away was an insult to Mike's manhood, and something deep inside made him yell out at Billy as he closed the door, "I'm not afraid of you. Don't push me too far." It was a hollow remark because, deep down, Mike was very afraid of Agent Forest and what he was capable of. And they both knew it. Thankfully, Billy did not return.

Mike sat back down on the edge of the hard mattress. No wonder his body hurt so much. His waterbed at home was cool and forgiving. This cot was not. Thinking of home and his family still tucked safely in bed and sound asleep made him long for them more than he thought possible.

His wife would have been up several times during the night to check on their son, pull up his blankets, change him if he was wet, and feed him if he was hungry. How much Mike desired that he could be there to help her. To crawl back in bed, cuddling close, his leg partially wrapped around hers, the smell of her hair in his nose as he kissed her bare shoulder.

Molly's skin was so soft, its texture caressed his lips like soft silk. Often, she would stir slightly when he kissed her there, moaning quietly and snuggling into him. It was one of those moments where the world seemed somehow perfect, and warm contentment would flow over him like a wave. Deep blissful sleep was always close behind. God, he missed them both.

The time had come for him to decide if he would turn back or move ahead with Billy and Sally. The easy answer was for him to go home. He didn't owe them a damn thing. Not after what he had done yesterday. Saving their lives, risking his. If he did leave, he wouldn't carry any guilt about them. But how many more little Amandas were out there? Could he turn his back on them?

Mike got up and moved to the shower. Maybe the hot water would help him think more clearly. He turned the knob, but nothing happened. Only a single drop formed on the shower head and dripped harmlessly to the floor. "Perfect. Just perfect. No shower, nothing but bloody, dirty clothes and body aches everywhere. How in the hell did I get here?" Thankfully, he hadn't slipped so far that he answered his own question aloud.

"Glad to see you're alive," Sally said as he emerged from his bunkroom into the larger area of the bunker.

"The jury is still out on that one," Mike shot back. "Where the hell is the coffee?"

She chuckled as she rose from the table to meet him halfway. "Right here, your highness. I was up early slaving over a hot stove so it would be ready for you." She handed him a tiny paper cup.

"So, I take it this is instant?"

"Yes, I'm afraid it is, but I did boil the water." Her smile was as warm as ever.

Mike, however, hadn't forgotten how she had deceived him. "You're a regular comedian this morning." His attempt at a smile to accompany the remark was halfhearted and disingenuous.

The grin slipped from her face. "Yeah, and you're the asshole I know and love," she shot back, returning to her seat at the table.

"Morning, Doc," TJ said.

Mike hadn't noticed him sitting in the corner until now. "Morning, TJ."

TJ leaned back in his chair, his hands interlocked behind his head. "Did you sleep well?"

"Considering the bed is like granite, and I couldn't shower, no. But thanks for asking."

TJ laughed out loud, a booming laugh that filled the room. "Damn, Doc. I thought all the talk of how pissed off you are in the mornings was just chatter. I guess, if anything, they may have soft-peddled it a bit. Drink your coffee quick before I decide to shoot you and put you out of your misery."

Mike couldn't help but grin. "Okay, okay. I get the message." As Mike made his way to the table, Sally pulled out a chair for him beside her and Billy. He ignored the gesture and instead went straight to where TJ sat and joined him. "Did you get any sleep?" he asked the sergeant. Though Mike didn't look back at Sally, he could feel the daggers shooting from her eyes.

TJ sighed. "Not much. We needed to go and get Corporal Moore's body back here. Couldn't leave him out there beside the road. Then I had to write a letter to his sister. Hell, I'm not sure she's even okay or still in Omaha. But, that's what you do for your men."

For the first time, Mike thought TJ looked tired. Desperately wanting to change the subject from the dead Marine, whose coat he still wore, Mike leaned forward in his chair. "Did those two tell you what they're up to?"

he whispered.

TJ glanced over Mike's shoulder at Sally and Billy and leaned even closer to Mike. "No, sir, they did not. Why don't you tell me?" Before Mike could answer, TJ's eyes moved up and behind Mike's shoulder.

"Is this something we should hear too?" Billy asked.

"The Doc was about to brief me on our little mission this morning," TJ replied, leaning away from the table.

"Oh, he was, huh? Well, Mike, go ahead, don't let me stop you."

Mike didn't look at Billy but sipped from the small cup. "No, Billy. I think since it's your mission, you should explain it."

"You'd better be careful how you play this," Billy said, his voice lowered.

TJ rose slowly from his seat and stood face-to-face with Billy. "I think you've got that wrong, sir. You had better watch how you talk to the Doc and with the amount of respect you show me. See, I come from the streets of Detroit. Out there, people don't just get respect because of who they are. They have to earn it. Yesterday, this man earned mine. That means he only has to ask me, and if it's in my power, I'll help him. You, on the other hand, never even said thank you. That means you probably don't respect me, and people who don't respect me have to be careful they don't make me mad. We clear?"

"You going to let him fight your battles?" Billy asked Mike, ignoring TJ's question.

In a flash, TJ grabbed Billy and placed him against the wall sliding him up so that his feet didn't touch the floor. "See what I mean? You just pissed me off. You think you're a tough guy. You threatened my friend. Now, can we talk about this mission we're going on?" It was a voice TJ probably hadn't used since he left the street.

Billy's face was bright red, and his hand moved down the side of his leg toward his boot. "Put me down, Sergeant, or you'll be very sorry," Billy said through clenched teeth.

"Listen real close, cowboy. Yesterday the Doc told me about what happened to LA, and there's a pretty good chance my entire family is dead. So I don't give a shit what happens to me. Now if you should happen to reach that knife in your boot, I will rip out your windpipe and then shove it up your ass. You decide." TJ tightened his grip on Billy's throat, whose face turned even brighter red.

"Okay, let go," Billy managed to whisper.

TJ gave him one more squeeze and released his grip. Billy slid down the wall and sat on his butt, rubbing his neck and trying to regain his breath. TJ reached down and slipped the seven-inch knife from Billy's boot. "Why don't I hang on to this for a little while?"

He grinned, then returned to his chair. "Okay, let's have it. Where are we going and why? I think Doc will gladly tell me if you aren't being totally honest with me."

Mike nodded and looked down at Billy. Billy swallowed hard and began to speak in a low voice. "We're on an important mission, and I'm going to trust that it won't go any further until we get to our destination." TJ didn't acknowledge whether it would or wouldn't. Billy scowled and continued anyway. "We have orders from the highest known authority still alive yesterday morning to get the contents of two safes out of DC. Ten plates from the US Mint and plans for our strategic defense. We have an extraction planned for twenty-one thirty today. An Army chopper will pick us up just west of the city."

"Is that the truth, Doc?" TJ asked, not taking his eyes off Billy.

"As far as I know, TJ, it is. I only found out last night on the way here. However, his timing of the extraction doesn't match what he told me yesterday. Even though I put my ass on the line for them, they didn't trust me enough to share that much until then." Mike glanced back at Sally, who had remained silent during their entire exchange thus far. Instead of returning his stare, she looked down at the tabletop and played with her cup.

"This authority you speak of, who is it?" TJ asked.

"I'm not in a position to say right now," Billy responded quietly.

TJ grinned. "On the contrary. You aren't in a position not to."

It appeared Billy had learned that crossing TJ was not in his best interest because he began speaking almost instantly. "The acting Director of the NSA."

TJ sat quietly without speaking for a long moment. "Okay. I'll brief the colonel, and if he gives the go-ahead, I'm in. We'll take a small squad in an armored vehicle."

"Will you need a doctor, TJ?" Mike asked.

TJ grinned at Mike. "Wouldn't think of going without one."

Mike downed the last bit of coffee from the small cup. "Then count me in too."

"Good," TJ announced. "Head down to the end of this hallway. On the left will be the supply officer. Tell him to issue you anything you need. I'll go speak with the colonel." TJ rose to leave the room. "Oh, and by the way. If anyone so much as lays a hand on the Doc here, I will cut their throat myself." With his warning still hanging in the air, TJ disappeared into the dimly lit hallway.

An hour later, TJ, Mike, Billy, and Sally joined ten Marines in a small, armored vehicle. The four of them sat in the front with the driver while the rest of the squad climbed into the more protected rear portion. Mike felt a little strange, dressed in full Marine battle dress, but it was better than wearing the same blood-stained clothing from yesterday.

"TJ, has anyone been into the city yet?" Mike asked.

"No. We're going to be the first. That is as far as our side is concerned. Can't say how many of the idiots are there waiting to greet us." TJ's tone said he was only partially kidding.

"I'm more concerned with what this little box has to say," TJ said, pointing to the Geiger counter between his legs. The needle on the gauge was already dancing slightly, showing triple the normal amount of background radiation.

ARTICLE XIX

Denver, Colorado, January 20, 2001, 11:26 PM MST

Emerging from the underground bunker didn't make Ben feel as good as he thought it might. Maybe the engulfing darkness or the thought of making a case of treason against the governor of his home state was the root of his uneasiness. But something wasn't quite right. He had learned to listen to that little voice inside and instinctively reached out for Ashley's arm.

"What is it?"

"I'm not sure, but the hair on the back of my neck is standing up. Let's be damn careful what we drive into. Okay?" Ben gave her arm a soft squeeze.

Ashley pulled the long black Buick out of the parking garage and waited for the barricade blocking their way to be removed. "Relax. I won't let anything happen to you. I'm not finished using your body yet, and if I don't get my way, someone's day is always ruined."

The grin on her face helped Ben to relax a bit. "Helen isn't going to be pleased that I'm calling this early," Ben said as he pressed the send button on the cell phone.

"I can't believe you'd call your old girlfriend with me in the car," Ashley quipped, the green glow from the dashboard lights revealing an evil grin on her face.

Ben chuckled. "Hey, they all want me. But I'm— Oh, hi, Helen. It's Ben."

A groggy Helen had likely been sleeping soundly before Ben's call. "What in the hell do you want? I'll tell you this, it had better be damned important," she shot into the earpiece.

"Yeah, I know, babe. Sorry about it being so early. Can I shoot straight with you?"

"Sure. What's up?"

Ben wasn't comfortable using an open cell phone. "It's Robbins. I think we have a problem, and I need your help to find out for sure. I don't want to say too much more on this thing. Can we meet?"

There was a brief pause before Helen responded. "Who's *we*?"

"Me and an agent providing security for me." Ben glanced over at Ashley. She tried to look mean and patted the bulge her gun made in her jacket. Ben smiled and shook his head. "So, can we meet somewhere? I would hate to see you involved in all of this when it comes down."

It was a veiled threat, a heads-up to her that she had better go with the flow or risk being at the wrong end of a bad situation. Ben knew that even half asleep, Helen wouldn't miss its meaning. "How bad is it?" she probed.

"Your worst nightmare. Come on, I know you suspect him too. I know you better than to think you agree with what he's doing. If you protect him now, your head will be on the block with his. Is that what you want?" Ben was on dangerous ground with her right now, and he knew it. If he spooked her, she might tip Robbins off and clam up. It was a risk he had to take, though. She would never help him unless she knew the worst.

Once again, the phone was quiet while Helen processed the information. "Alright, but the agent stays outside."

"Inside the building, but outside the office," Ben negotiated.

"Deal. Where are you now?"

"About two minutes away from the Capitol."

"Christ. We can't meet there. Can you give me a few minutes to wash my face and slip on some clothes?"

Ben looked toward Ashley, not sure if she could hear the other end of the conversation. "Well, you can wash your face anyway. So where then?"

"Cheeky bastard," Helen said, chuckling. "Robbins still maintains his old lawyer's office over on North Ogden. Do you know where that is?

"Yes, the place where I interviewed him during the election?

"Yep," Helen replied. "Park in the back and ring the side doorbell when you get here."

Ben put the phone down on the seat. "We have an appointment with the governor's chief of staff at the governor's old office. It's over on North Ogden. The seventeen hundred block."

Ashley made a few extra turns to head toward the new destination. She was doing her best to not let Ben see how nervous she was about the meeting. He was being more quiet than normal, so she probed. "Everything okay? You seem worried about something."

Ben hesitated before responding. "She'll let you in the building, but you'll have to wait outside the office. She won't talk to me with you in the room."

"I'm not sure I can go along with that."

"You don't have any other options. The president told you to stay out of my way so I can do my job."

Ashley had hoped that this wasn't going to become a battle between them. The president told her privately how stubborn Ben could be. She would have to play this by ear. "And to keep you safe," she added.

Ben flashed a smile. "I'll be safe with Helen. She's a political animal down to her bones. She and I go way back. Been through a lot of crap together. I would trust her with my life."

"I know, I know," Ashley relented. "But can *I* trust her? Let's see how it goes when we get in there."

Ben seemed to ignore her last comment. After giving her further directions, they arrived at the old office building. Ben pointed to a well-lit parking area. "Pull in over there, behind the back entrance."

"Okay, but let me get out first and check the area." Ashley parked the car and slipped her sidearm from its shoulder holster. Holding it low beside her leg, she slipped quickly from the protection of the car and walked quietly around the compact parking lot. Satisfied it was safe, she motioned for Ben to get out and join her.

Ben strode up a few steps to the side door and rang the buzzer. "I hope she isn't still in her PJs."

Ashley aimed a small visual dagger in his direction. "That makes two of us." She kept reminding herself of the mission. It was so obvious to her now how much her feelings for Ben clouded her judgment. She didn't want to disappoint the president or get Ben hurt.

"Breathe, hon. She won't shoot us," Ben whispered, apparently noticing the concern on Ashley's face.

"Come on up," a female voice squeaked from a speaker beside the door. Ben waited for the door latch to buzz and pushed open the heavy old wooden door. The back stairs were steep and made creaking noises loud enough to wake the dead as they plodded up.

"Guess you won't be sneaking out without me knowing," Ashley stated.

"Don't count on it. We might just take the secret elevator to the Bat Cave."

"Oh, you are funny," Ashley shot back, poking him hard in the back.

Ben jolted as a small figure appeared at the top of the stairs. The woman didn't look happy to be up so early and was dressed in a pair of Denver Bronco sweats.

"Nice outfit," Ben quipped.

"Go to hell, Ben. Since Elway retired, I only wear them after dark." Ashley had to assume this was his Helen, the governor's chief of staff. Helen didn't smile, but Ashley got the impression she wanted to.

"So where is this big tough agent?" Helen asked, her tone sour.

Reaching the top of the stairs, Ashley stepped out from behind Ben. "I'm afraid I'll have to do," she replied, gripping Helen's hand more firmly than normal. "Ashley Prescott, Secret Service. Nice to meet you."

Helen smiled, but it looked forced. "Sorry, Agent Prescott. Ben and I always kid each other. No harm meant."

"None taken."

Ben moved past Helen in the tight hallway. "Well, if this love fest is over, can we talk?"

"He is charming, isn't he?" Helen asked Ashley.

Ashley smiled at Ben. "Yeah, like a bad rash." They all chuckled while making their way down to the end office.

"Agent Prescott, you can sit in that chair over there if you wish," Helen said, pointing to a hard-back chair near the door. "Sorry, I don't have any coffee made."

"Sorry, but I'll need to have a look in there before I can let him in."

"Ashley, is that necessary?" Ben queried.

"First name basis, huh? Well, okay then," Helen said with a smirk. "By all means, snoop away."

Ashley looked inside the small office to make sure it was secure. "Where's this door go?" she asked, jiggling the locked handle.

Helen seemed annoyed with the question. "Hell, I don't know. It's always been locked."

"So we good?" Ben asked.

"Yes," Ashley replied. "Let me know if you need anything." Ashley settled in the chair close to the door.

"Water?" Helen asked her.

"No thanks. I'm good."

Ben and Helen entered the office and closed the door behind them. Ashley sat reading a copy of Colorado Business Weekly and listening to the muffled voices through the wall.

Engrossed in an article about Denver International Airport becoming the busiest airport in the world this year, the minutes passed quickly.

Suddenly, she realized the voices had stopped. She moved close to the door and strained to hear any noise. There was none, only an eerie silence.

Pulling her sidearm from its holster, she tried the door. It was locked.

Standing to the side of the opaque glass in the door, she called out, "Ben, you alright?" Only quiet answered her.

Ashley stepped back two steps and gave a door a heavy kick. As the door flew open, she burst into the room, her revolver before her. The room was empty.

Ben's tape recorder sat on the desk, still running, recording the deafening silence. Fear gripped Ashley, fear for Ben and fear for her. Where could they have gone? And did he go willingly? The door that was locked before now sat ajar.

Opening it slowly revealed another office with a wide-open door out the other side.

"Dammit! Strike two for you today, Prescott," she mumbled. He was her responsibility, and she had failed.

Ashley lifted her hand and spoke into her wrist mic. "Alert one. I repeat alert one. This is Spider. Notebook has withdrawn, location unknown. Notify OPS and send two response units to my location STAT."

Ashley reached slowly forward and turned the tape recorder off.

ARTICLE XX

Western Montana, January 21, 2001, 4:54 AM MST

Jamie awoke with a start, sitting up straight in the bed. What time was it? Had she missed the meeting with Stuart? Her eyes focused on the clock radio sitting on the nightstand. The red numbers showed the time to be 04:54. She struggled to bring her heartbeat back down to normal and regain control over the wave of panic that gripped her chest.

She glanced beside her, checking to see if Boyle had risen yet. The crisp sheet of light streaming from under the bathroom door told her he had been up for a while. Laying her head back down on the soft pillow, she tried to clear her mind of the events of yesterday and especially last night.

Today would be the most important day of her life, maybe the last day of it too. The shock of those horrid events had settled into her heart, making it heavy and weary. Today the struggle for control of the country would begin. How would the government in Denver respond? Were their troops waiting to invade the camp? Jamie wondered why Boyle wasn't more concerned about being overrun or bombed. What was keeping them from attacking?

A sudden thought had her sitting back up in bed. A bomb. Of course, he had a bomb here in the camp. The truck that arrived last month in the middle of the night and was directed to the shelter on the hill. No wonder he wouldn't let her go with him to inspect it. Is that what Stuart knows?

The door from the bathroom swung open, and light flooded over the small room. "Oh good, you're awake." Boyle's face broke into a full smile.

Jamie swung her legs over the edge of the bed, not wanting him to return to lay with her. "Well, I'm not sleeping anymore, but I wouldn't say I'm awake." She tried to sound groggy and out of it.

Boyle grabbed a freshly pressed uniform from the closet by the bathroom. "Grab a shower. I'm going to the communications bunker to see how the night treated us."

"Okay. Then what?"

Struggling with the top button on his uniform, Boyle said, "You better find something to do. I have several meetings, then breakfast with the field commanders before they leave."

"I thought they were leaving in the middle of the night."

"They were. We moved it back a few hours due to some supply issues. He finished buttoning his crisp uniform and started for the door.

Jamie breathed a sigh of relief. "Okay. I'll see you later." Still naked, she passed by him on her way to the bathroom.

"That won't work," he said as she passed. "I have work to do."

Fighting the urge to hit him, she managed a slight smile. "Well, a girl can try, can't she?" Jamie closed the bathroom door behind her and fell against it. Boyle's laughter from her parting comment still hung in the air.

Yes, today was the day. It had to be.

She felt much better once she had washed Boyle's scent from her body. She still didn't know quite what to do about Stuart but dressed warmly in case she decided to make a run for it with him.

The cold January air struck her face and sent a shiver down her spine as she stepped out the back door of the cabin. Slipping unnoticed through the trees had always been easy for Jamie, but the darkness of the Montana winter morning made it almost routine.

Twice she passed within forty yards of one of the security patrols without making a sound. Topping the last ridge before reaching the back gate, she slowed and began looking for Stuart. Crouching near a large pine tree, Jamie made a soft whistling sound. She and Stuart had used this code many times on maneuvers at the camp. After a few seconds, the soft tone was repeated back to her from no more than ten yards away.

How strange it was to be using the training they had received at the camp to try to escape it. Countless days and nights had been spent honing the skills they would need to fight urban warfare. Not two months ago, Jamie and Stuart led a small group down into Thompson Rise. They crept into town, rendezvoused at several key checkpoints mapped out by the lieutenant, and even entered the town hall, taking an insignificant item that wouldn't be missed. Though there were a few close calls with a large dog and a small but pesky skunk, the mission was a complete success. Now the mission was very real, and the students would be trying to fool the teachers.

Stuart crept silently up to Jamie. "Glad you could make it," he whispered.

"Don't get too excited. I'm not sure why I'm here."

Stuart shifted slightly, moving closer to her. "Listen, we don't have time for a long, drawn-out discussion about this. I need to get started before it gets light. There's a hole in the perimeter radar, and with darkness on my side, I think I can make it out."

Jamie studied his eyes, searching for his motives. "So what's this big news you need to get to the other side?"

"And if I tell you? What will you do then? Go? Stay?" Stuart asked, studying her face for clues.

Jamie rambled out her thoughts to him, no longer fearful of his loyalties. "I don't know, really. I want to do something. Yesterday I thought getting out was the most important thing, but now I think staying might be more helpful. Stuart, I think I figured out something. I think the crazy bastard has a nuclear bomb here. That's why they haven't come for us yet."

Stuart didn't flinch. "Yeah, I know. I saw it last week. It's triggered and ready to be fired. The sergeant in charge of it told me he could detonate it within ten minutes if he was ordered to. I asked him how he would get far enough away before it went off. You know what he said?"

"I can guess."

Stuart shook his head. "Told me he would sit on top of the damn thing and smoke a big cigar. Said if the general wasn't going to survive this thing, he didn't want to either. It's crazy. They have lost their fucking minds. I sure as hell don't want to die for that wacko."

"He wants to take out Denver just to kill my husband."

"That's why I need to get out of here. I know exactly where the Denver bomb is and when they plan to explode it. That's for certain."

"God, Stuart. How the hell did we get into this mess?" Jamie asked as she sunk back against the tree.

"Don't be too tough on yourself. We had our reasons. There are a lot of things wrong with this world, and we wanted to help change them. How could we have known this man was capable of such wanton and senseless death? He wants the same thing we're fighting against, uncontrolled power."

Jamie didn't speak. She couldn't through the lump in her throat.

Stuart continued. "Oh, he talks a good game, all right. Liberty, freedom, milk and honey, blah...blah. Nevertheless, when it comes right down to it, he kills millions of innocent people, more in the blink of an eye than they have in over two hundred years." Stuart paused, staring out into the night sky. "I would put a bullet in his brain right now if I thought there weren't a couple of dozen idiots under him ready to follow it to the end. They have to be stopped. All of them."

"I'm staying," Jamie said flatly.

"But why?" Stuart asked, almost pleading. "What do you have to gain by staying here?"

Jamie reached out and touched his cheek softly. "Leave that to me. Go now. Tell them what they need to know to stop the other device from being set off. I'll take care of the compound. Tell them to pull back and get far from here. By tonight, Boyle and this camp won't be a problem for them."

"I won't leave you."

She forced herself to smile. "You have one minute to get the hell out of here, or I'll start screaming my head off for help. Understand?"

Stuart looked at the gate and then back at Jamie, tears filling his eyes. "Okay. But I hope you don't think people aren't going to know what you've done here. I love you. Goodbye, Jamie." Stuart gave her a quick kiss on the cheek, turned, and slipped silently across the small opening in the trees and over the back gate.

Jamie sat watching the gate and the surrounding area. "Bye, Stuart. I love you too," she whispered into the darkness.

ARTICLE XXI

Virginia, January 21, 2001, 6:50 AM EST

Mike's head bounced hard off the top of the half-track roof. "Shit. TJ, do you think the driver might try not to hit every hole he sees, please?"

"If you would put that seat belt on like I asked you to, maybe you could stay in your seat."

Mike had always rejected wearing seat belts. The cops in his hometown were regularly giving him warnings and tickets for not wearing one. Nevertheless, it seemed nothing could prompt him to change his ways. To him, it was an issue of personal freedom the government had no business being involved in.

Suddenly, a large explosion next to what had been passing for a roadway threw the half-track six or seven feet to the right. Dust and smoke covered the front windshield, and small rocks pelted the heavy metal roof. Once Mike had regained his place in the seat, he reached down and quickly snapped himself in.

"Jesus, Billy. What was that?" Mike shouted.

"Mortar or RPG," TJ responded. "Either way, it's not good. What do you say we get the hell off this road, Corporal?"

Snatching up the radio, TJ called in the helicopter gunship standing by to cover their entry into the city. "Make for that pile over there," he snapped at the driver. The half-track stopped with a jerk behind what remained of a stone structure. "Stay put, everybody. I'm going to check for damage."

Mike's stomach churned, thinking about what might still lie ahead of them. Was it going to be like this all the way? Idiots shooting at them and never knowing if the road would keep going.

He surveyed the scene around them. It was more than clear the nuclear bomb blast still had maintained a great deal of force when it passed through this area. Three bodies, or at least parts of bodies, were strewn around the base of the stone wall. The one closest to him was missing it's head and one arm. The flashfire that followed close behind the blast wave had blackened everything in its path.

Billy's voice sounded strange as he spoke from the back seat. "If you ever tried to imagine what hell is like, you can stop. It looks just like this."

After a short silence, Mike said, "How much radiation do you think is out there?

"A lot more than we should be getting, that's for sure," Sally replied, speaking for the first time since they'd left the bunker. "And it's in here too, you know?"

"It will only get worse," Billy added softly. "My badge is already red." Mike looked down at his own Personal Radiation Monitor. It glowed bright red.

The sound of the helicopter was deafening as it roared over them. A large explosion a sparse few hundred yards away spelled the end of whoever had fired on them. It seemed Marine justice was swift and deadly, and Mike was damn glad they had stumbled across TJ last night.

The door to the vehicle flew open, and TJ jumped in. "We're okay. Let's move. Now, Corporal." TJ glared at the Marine when the metal tracks spun directly over the torso of a dead woman. "Jesus Christ, man, watch where the hell you're going."

"Sorry, sir, I didn't even see it. Uh, I mean her."

TJ didn't respond, and Mike ventured he was trying damn hard not to think of Los Angles and the fate of his family. Somewhere near Englewood, a Marine might be looking at body parts that once were his loved ones.

Studying him, Mike saw TJ's fingers tense and relax on the trigger guard of his weapon as the muscles in his jaw flexed tight. Just before he spoke again, his nostrils flared wide. "From this point forward, we're shooting first and asking questions later. Everybody understand?"

The Marines answered with a crisp, "Yes, sir." Mike, Sally, and Billy simply nodded and said nothing.

The landscape they faced was far different than it had looked yesterday morning. No part of any building or structure had escaped damage. Pieces of carved stone and concrete alike had been tossed around like tumbleweeds in the desert. Important historical monuments and fast-food restaurants shared the same fate. Anything that survived the blast had to weather the firestorm and flash wind. Little did.

The closer they got to Washington, the more severe the desolation became. Traveling through and around the rubble was bad enough, but determining where they were on TJ's map, was even harder. Anything resembling a landmark had been destroyed. After almost three hours, they came to the place where the Pentagon should be. Little remained of the above-ground structure, miles of hallways and glass had been simply blown away.

TJ ordered Mike, Sally and Billy to wait in the vehicle while he and the squad of Marines checked out the area for ARA members or booby traps.

Something made Mike look again at his radiation badge. It wasn't red any longer. "What do you make of that?" he asked Billy, holding it up for him to see.

"Yeah, mine too," he replied. "Captain back at the base said there was a nasty little storm that blew through Washington last night. Crazy that it would lower the radiation that much."

"Wish Bo was here," Sally added.

Mike was pleased to hear the news. "It means we can be here a bit longer than we thought. Should really help any survivors."

"I hope you know where you're going," TJ said to Billy when he opened the door to let them out.

Billy surveyed what was left of the huge building. "Get me down below ground level, and I think I can get us there."

"TJ, did you notice your badge?" Mike asked.

"Yeah, Doc. Meach showed me. Doesn't mean I suddenly love being here. Let's get moving."

"Is everybody's flashlight working?" Mike asked. Everyone checked the flashlights they had been issued from the storeroom in Quantico. Even in daylight, the dust and smoke particles were illuminated by the beams of light as they went on and off.

"This way," Billy said as he started off through the rubble, climbing swiftly over a concrete slab.

Mike kept TJ in sight as they made their way over and around the various obstacles strewn randomly in their path. Billy led them toward the north side of the building, where the main entry once welcomed hundreds of people a day. This great monument to war which symbolized America's power and pride, was now a rubble pit. Two Marines stood guard as Billy searched for a place to enter.

"Over here," Billy shouted. "I found it. Come on."

TJ bristled. "Hang on to your ass a minute. I decide when and where we go."

Billy stopped and glared back over his shoulder. "Yes, sir." Judging by the expression on TJ's face, Billy's sarcasm was not lost on the sergeant.

"If you want to go in alone with no backup, go right ahead," TJ snapped. "But if you want me and my men with you, then you'll let me have a look at that hole." TJ walked past Billy and used his flashlight to light up the crack in what was left of a wall.

"It's the front lobby area. The elevator shaft and stairs should be forty or fifty feet down toward the river," Billy told him in an excited voice.

"Any chance the place has been compromised by the water?"

Billy's brow furrowed. "Damn, I hadn't thought of that. Shouldn't be, but I guess it's possible."

"Thompson. Meach. Recon that hole. Check for signs of water and good air." TJ motioned them into the opening.

The two young Marines disappeared into the opening without hesitation. After a few minutes, the crack of M-16 gunfire echoed from the darkness. Everyone hit the ground, and TJ waved up two more Marines. TJ trained his M-16 on the opening as a light flashed back and forth across it.

"It's okay, Sarg. It's me," shouted one of the young men.

"What the hell were you firing at?" TJ snapped.

The first Marine out of the dark smiled slightly. "Rats. Meach hates rats."

Sighing heavily, TJ glared at the two young men. "Well, what else did you find besides rats?"

"Rough going, but no sign of water and the air is dense but okay," the second Marine rattled back.

"Can we get going now?" Billy asked dryly, again pushing his luck with TJ.

An evil smile crossed TJ's face. "Sure, you go right ahead. We won't be far behind."

Billy didn't respond to TJ's crack but disappeared into the blackness of the hole.

"Okay, move out," TJ ordered his men. "Thompson, Meach, take up the rear. Oh, and Meach. If you see a rat, don't shoot it. Besides, if we shot all the rats in Washington, who would run the military?" TJ winked at Mike.

It was just what Mike needed to ease some of the dread he felt entering the dark recess. He fell in behind TJ, sliding down a piece of concrete slab into the belly of the building.

Though a small amount of light came in through various openings, it was as dark as night inside. The beams from the powerful lamps cut through it like a laser beam. It was the eeriest thing Mike had ever seen.

Signs and parts of the office building had remained intact, but the dust and fire made it seem like it might have been a thousand years old. They could have been explorers checking out the ruins of lost people. However, the occasional body reminded him that this was a fresh event. People had been going about their normal routines yesterday morning. Eating a bagel with their morning coffee or walking to an office somewhere in this massive, seemingly indestructible fortress. Who could know if they had time to know what happened. Thankfully most had not. Mike wondered if anyone on the levels below had survived.

After about fifteen minutes of searching through the hallway, they found the entrance to the twelve elevators. Two bodies lay right beside one of the doors, their arms covering their heads in a feeble attempt to survive the blast.

"Duck and cover," Sally said quietly.

Two of the Marines worked on prying a set of elevator doors open for a long time and made no noticeable progress. Suddenly, with a loud bang, the doors popped open. A hot, dense black smoke poured from the shaft engulfing the two men and filling their lungs with toxic fumes.

TJ leapt quicker than a cat from his position some six or seven yards away. With linebacker-like tackling precision, he grabbed them one in each arm, pushing them to the floor and away from the opening.

"You alright?" TJ asked after he had righted himself.

"Yeah... Sarg... Thanks," the young man nearest to him managed to say between coughing and gagging. The other marine, however, said nothing.

"Klein. Klein, are you okay?" TJ shouted.

Mike moved swiftly to the side of the motionless young man. He reached for his lower arm and checked for a pulse. "No pulse. Get me a kit. Hurry." Mike began CPR, coughing and choking as Klein's lungs gave back the toxic smoke remaining in them.

TJ ran to Mike's side, handing him a first aid kit. "Alright, Doc, get him back," he demanded.

Mike laid the kit down on the floor beside Klein. "It's too late. The heat seared his lungs. They're burned deep inside. No way they'll pass any air. I'm so sorry."

"Dammit. I should have gotten to him faster," TJ said, slamming his fist into his own leg.

"Wouldn't have mattered. It hit him the second that door popped open. There wasn't anything you or anyone else could have done." Mike laid his hand on TJ's shoulder.

The hulking Marine's eyes narrowed and focused deep within Mike's eyes, then opened wide and bright. "Okay, then that's that. Meach, help me move Klein over in the corner. We will take him back up on our way out."

Although TJ had been a rock so far, Mike couldn't help but wonder if he might lose it sometime soon. He seemed to accept the death of Klein almost too easily. They would have to be careful how much trouble they laid on the sergeant's doorstep today.

The smoke had mostly dissipated, so they moved carefully forward to check out the damage inside the shaft.

TJ stood on the edge and shined his light into the dark square. "How far down do we need to go?"

"SUB three, two floors down from here," Billy answered.

"Whisner, tie off a line around that column over there," TJ barked. After securing a line, the group headed down the shaft one by one. Luckily the elevator car had stopped on SUB four, allowing them to use the top of it to work from. After TJ, Billy and Mike made their way to the elevator roof, TJ began forcing open the inside doors on level SUB three. Finally, he was able to force one of the heavy doors open.

Billy quickly directed his light into the hallway. A recruit who looked to be no older than nineteen stood in the hall, his handgun pointed directly at Mike's head. The sound was deafening, and the flash of the gun's muzzle blast brightly illuminated even the darkest corners of the shaft.

ARTICLE XXII

Denver, Colorado, January 21, 2001, 3:27 AM MST

"I'm disappointed, Ashley." Ashley sat at the large conference table with her head hanging, not wanting to make any eye contact with the president. She knew what President Young was feeling.

Who could forget her mother telling everyone how proud she was that Ashley had passed the test and made it into the Secret Service? President Young, who, of course, was just Claire then, had called to congratulate her, telling Ashley how proud the entire government was of her.

Now Ashley wished it was *just Claire* sitting across the table from her instead of the President of the United States. Ashley could cry on her shoulder, tell her how terribly afraid she was, tell her how much she missed her mother. However, wishing wouldn't bring her mother here.

"Yes, Madam President, I know. It was inexcusable. I should have never let him out of my sight. I was so sure there wasn't any way they could get out of there without me knowing about it. I checked the office, and that woman lied to me. She said the door was locked, and she couldn't open it. When I saw firsthand how comfortable Ben was with her, I believed her without any further reservation. It's totally my fault."

President Young moved back to the table and sunk down in her chair. "Any clues? Do you have an idea where he might be?"

"My hunch is he went to see the governor. But I have no clue where. I'm sure he had no choice. He's trying to help."

President Young fiddled with a pen lying on the table. "Sid's sources say Robbins left Aspen. They're speculating he's returned to the city. My recon reports are that the Colorado National Guard is moving toward our compound."

President Young paused, let out a sigh and went on. "You know, Ashley, things could get ugly if they move on us. Should we find ourselves pinned down here, we might not be in a position to get Ben back, even if we know where he is.”

Ashley looked up at her. “I know him. If he has any way to help us with Robbins, he will. Ben’s gut told him that in the end, Robbins would cave, and I trust Ben’s gut. If he can get to Robbins, try to talk some sense into him, then maybe it can still work out. I just think Ben never would have left unless it wasn’t damned important.” When the president raised an eyebrow, Ashley added, “You know what I mean. Not just for a story but to help all of us make it through this thing. He’s a good man with the right kind of heart.”

“I know. He would not have been down here with us had it not been clear he could be trusted. We should know within the hour if the Guard intends to take us on. Let’s pray they don’t. I can’t imagine giving the order to fire on them.”

***

In a dark office only a few miles from the compound, Ben waited for Robbins to appear. He was ashamed of himself for treating Ashley like a chump, but what else could he have done? Helen had made it clear to him that if he didn’t come alone, Robbins would never see him. The question now was, what did he want? Why meet with him if there wasn’t an important reason?

Noise from down the hall had Ben straightening in the hard back chair. Helen opened the door swiftly and strode into the office.

“He’s on his way. I’m afraid I need to leave you now. Hope everything goes well.” Helen leaned down to place a small kiss on Ben’s cheek.

“Okay, babe. Thanks. I do appreciate you sticking out your neck for me.”

Helen looked at him a bit strangely. “It’s your neck that’s stuck out, my friend. Be careful you don’t get it caught in anything sharp.”

Ben smiled, although he didn't feel happy or amused. "Yeah, not the first time. I'll be fine. Now get out of here before I give you a big wet kiss." Helen smiled and walked back down the hallway into the night.

As soon as she disappeared, several new sets of footsteps thumped down the old wooden hallway, and seconds later, two burley goons busted into the room and headed straight for Ben.

One of the men struck Ben hard in the chest just as he instinctively sprang up from his seat. A rush of air forced from his lungs erupted into the room. Ben tried desperately to suck in air to inflate the breathing sacs inside him.

He soon realized the real reason he could no longer breathe was the massive hand wrapped around his throat. Positive he would soon suffocate, and since fighting would no doubt be unsuccessful, Ben decided to relax and go passive. It seemed to work almost immediately, and the pressure on his windpipe eased. Slowly he began to get just enough air to forestall unconsciousness. The other man kept Ben's arms pinned to the floor over his head. This position, while limiting his movements, did help invite air back into his burning chest.

"Are you through being stupid?" the man sitting on Ben asked. Ben nodded and remained still. "Okay, let's just check and make sure you're clean." With that, he began an intense search of Ben's clothing.

Speaking for the first time, the other man said, "I hope we didn't hurt you, Mr. Bleser."

Having gained enough air to speak, Ben responded sourly, "That's okay. I am getting used to it. It seems for an old reporter, people think I'm dangerous."

"You are dangerous, Mr. Bleser. With your pen." The man conducting the search had been the one to toss out the retort with no humor in his voice.

The search complete, Ben now sat upright on the hard floor. "Is that what all this pushing me around is about? What I might write about the governor? Hell, I haven't written anything yet. I just have a few unanswered questions about his movements over the last couple of days. Why's he so threatened by that?"

"Alright, that's enough chatter, Phil. Let's get him up off the floor."

"Yeah, get me up off the floor, Phil," Ben added sarcastically.

"Don't start thinking you're too smart, Mr. Bleser. I have limited patience for your type," The second goon said as he snatched Ben from the floor.

Ben, too was losing his patience. "My type? You mean someone who wants the truth? Someone who doesn't believe anything is justified just because you're taking orders. That type?" Ben straightened his ruffled clothing.

The man's face tightened as he moved close. "You know something?"

"I know a lot."

"You don't know shit. When you see the governor and your face is all swollen from me pounding on it, you better tell him that you fell. Or maybe you prefer to have me break all of your fingers? Make sure you can't write those lies you call the news?"

Ben backed slowly away from the threat. "I think you'll do whatever you want with me. But it won't stop the truth from getting out."

Just as the man raised his fist to swing at Ben, a voice from the doorway boomed, "John, back off." Governor Robbins, dressed in khaki pants and a plaid shirt, stood in the doorway, looking a lot less slick than he had at the cabinet meeting the day before. He strode briskly into the office and stepped between Ben and the bodyguard. "Wait outside," Robbins told the red-faced man.

"Just give me five minutes with—"

"I said wait outside. Don't make me repeat myself again," the governor shouted, taking a step toward the man.

Ben hadn't ever seen this side of the governor and was shocked by the intensity he'd displayed toward this man who was much larger than himself. Suddenly, Ben wasn't so sure about his decision to trust Robbins with his safety. Maybe Ashley's caution had been wise? Was this to be his swan song?

Fear was a great equalizer. It placed Ben in a position to be less open about what he knew. Now that he'd seen a whole new side of Robbins he didn't know existed, what would he ask Robbins, and how far would he push? It was certainly too late to turn back now. Maybe, just maybe, he would try to be a little smarter about staying alive. He really wanted to live long enough to help President Young and get Ashley off the hook.

Glaring at Ben over the governor's shoulder, the man said, "We'll finish this little chat later, Mr. Bleser. There are a couple of points I didn't get the chance to impress on you." With that, he turned and walked out into the hall, slamming the door firmly behind him.

"What an asshole," Ben shot at the closed door.

"Walk a mile in his shoes, Ben," the governor replied.

"Meaning?"

"Oklahoma City. His wife and son were blown into tiny little pieces. He still believes the press covered for the ATF and FBI, sure they knew it was going to happen, and did nothing. Even thinks the ATF helped plan it."

"And I'm the press."

"Yes, you are. I can control him most of the time, but I would tread lightly if you see him again."

"But that's crazy. Why would the ATF be involved?"

"That's not important. The point is he believes it."

Ben moved toward a chair across from the one Robbins was now seated in. "Okay, even though it may not look like it, I really don't have a death wish."

"That remains to be seen." Robbins' words hung in the air for a moment as Ben searched his face for a sign that it was intended as some kind of joke. There was none.

"Yes, sir, I guess it does. Maybe the same could be said about you." As his words shot back at Robbins, it became evident that Ben didn't know how to play it safe.

"I sure don't want to die," Robbins said quietly, looking down at the floor.

Considering what Robbins had said only moments before, the statement stunned Ben. "None of us do, Governor."

"Millions did yesterday."

"I know. One of them likely my son Chris in Chicago." Ben wasn't about to let Robbins off the hook.

Robbins looked to be close to tears. "I'm sorry to hear that. Very sorry. My sister and uncle too. They just wouldn't be convinced to leave LA, and I couldn't tell them why they had to."

Ben's breathing became shallow and labored. He could barely force his chest to rise. "You could have stopped it."

"No. I was in too far. I told you I didn't want to die." Robbins paused and added, "They would have killed me for sure."

Ben was now torn between the anger rising within him and the need to find out everything he could from Robbins. Why was he telling him this? Did he just want to unburden his soul?

Suddenly the anger faded to bone-chilling fear. There was only one reason why Robbins would spill his guts. Ben wasn't going to live to tell anyone what he'd heard. How stupid could he be? Not only was he not going to be able to help the president, likely he would be in for a great deal of pain before he died as the goon outside attempted to find out what Ben knew.

Maybe the end would be swift. He could make the man so angry that he would kill him before he told them anything.

"What?" Robbins asked after the silence from Ben grew longer and longer.

"Nothing," Ben said as calmly as possible. "I'm just trying to soak it all in."

"Don't lie to me. You already knew what was going on, or you wouldn't be here. You're thinking about what I might do to you? You know I already have blood on my hands. Why would I hesitate to kill you? Something like that?"

"Maybe. Guess I should have thought of that before now, huh?"

Robbins studied Ben's face for a minute. "Well, we all make mistakes. The truth is I'm not sure yet what to do with you."

With an apparent opening to work something out with Robbins, Ben breathed just a little easier. "I know it must seem like there's no way out of this for you, but I've spent some time with the president, and I know we can come up with a plan to help us all out of this thing. It's never too late to do the right thing, Governor. With what you know, we can save a lot of lives. Really make a difference."

"Wow. How original, Bleser. 'We can do the right thing, Governor,'" he mocked. "'Don't worry your little head, Governor.' What now? Am I supposed to fall on the floor sobbing and tell you everything? Beg your forgiveness, and then wait to be shot for treason? You're not dealing with a two-bit snitch here, Ben. I've been around the block a few times. I know how it works." Robbins stood and began to pace the room.

Instead of fear, Ben felt anger growing inside him. "Give me a little more credit. I never thought you were stupid. We both know you can't just walk away from this scot-free. But this insurrection of Boyle's will eventually crumble. There won't be any peace until the lives lost this morning are avenged."

Ben began to boil. "Dammit, don't you remember your history? The

American people will fight you, block by block, house by house. It just can't be sustained without them behind it, and they won't be, not now, not ever. You can't change the country this way. You spilled the first blood, and the real citizens out there will spill the last."

Robbins stopped pacing but didn't say a word, which was good because Ben wasn't finished. "Do you really think they'll look at you and Boyle any different than Hitler or Stalin? You made decisions for them as if you knew what was best for them. Why? Because you're smarter than they are? The power to change the country for better or worse has always been with the public. You can't supersede that, ever."

Robbins' shoulders slumped as he returned to the chair and sat facing away from Ben. "I know that. I've always known that."

Ben rose and moved to stand in front of him. "Can I ask you something?"

"Doesn't hurt to ask."

"How did they suck you in? What made you go along with them?" Ben asked, bending to be eye to eye with him.

Robbins laughed without any hint of humor and began tapping his leg. "Well, Mr. Bleser, that would be a vacation in a federal prison. DOJ has been up my ass about campaign funding, and word was I would be indicted by this summer at the latest. It was all going to come crumbling down around my ears. All the hard work, the years of working my way up. All gone because of one weekend in Taos, one stupid weekend. You see, it's illegal to spend campaign money on hotel rooms for seventeen-year-old girls and booze."

"So they found out, and Boyle played you?"

Robbins glared at Ben. "Fuck you, Bleser. You ever get tired of standing on that soapbox of yours? You don't know shit about me. I should have let them blow you and this whole city to the moon. Hell, I still might. Go sit at my desk and take the ride with you."

Without any warning, gunshots and loud shouting erupted just outside the office door. Several bullets came crashing through the thin walls sending splinters of wood flying around them. Ben glanced back at Robbins just as he produced a silver handgun from his pocket. Robbins looked toward the main office door, then headed for another door located on the opposite side of the room. Just before exiting the room, he pointed the gun at Ben.

"You bastards are all alike. See you in hell," Robbins snarled as he squeezed the trigger.

The bullet whizzed past Ben's head just as he leapt behind the large oak desk in the corner of the room. Crashing hard to the floor, Ben scrambled to get under the heavy desk, hoping it would provide him some protection.

Ben heard Ashley's distinctive voice shouting orders to other agents just outside the door. "Ashley! Ashley, I'm in here. Be careful he has a gun," he shouted at the top of his lungs.

Ben heard the door close behind Robbins just before the main office door came thundering off its hinges.

"Ben? You okay, Ben?" Ashley cried from somewhere near the door.

Ben breathed a large sigh of relief. Never had he been so glad in his life. "Yeah, Ashley, I'm fine. I'm under the desk in the corner. Can you see Robbins?"

"No, I can't. Keep your head down until I tell you to come up." Though Ashley's voice boomed through the space, she sounded relieved to hear Ben was okay.

He gave a half-hearted laugh. "No heroes down here, Agent Prescot." Even under the circumstances, Ben knew the remark would let her know he really was okay.

After five or ten tense minutes, Ashley's long beautiful legs appeared by the desk. "Okay, come on out, Ben. It's clear. You hit or hurt? Do you need a doctor?"

Stiff and sore, Ben made his way out of the small space he had so easily crammed himself into. "No. I'm fine, really. Thanks to you anyway. And before you say anything," he continued as he got to his feet, "I would like to say that I am truly sorry. You were right about the danger, and I hope the president wasn't too hard on you." He smiled at Ashley and wanted very much to hug her. But Ben knew this wasn't the time or place for that kind of affection.

She returned his smile. "It's okay, Ben. You're safe, and I'm safe. We'll work out the rest later."

His hand still trembled as he reached out to lightly touch her arm. "How did you find me?"

"Helen called. It seems she really is the good egg you thought she was. She was worried about what they would do. Said she just couldn't live with herself if anything bad happened to you." Ashley gave Ben a sideways grin. "You realize, of course, I'll have to keep a close eye on you two from now on? I think she just might be sweet on you."

Ben returned the knowing smile. "Yeah, she's a great lady, but you don't have any worries there. Did you find Robbins?"

"Yes, we found him."

"Good. He knows everything. He was involved from the start. We just need to get him back to the compound and get it out of him. It was incredible. He just started spilling his guts. I think I know what Sid was talking about, why he suspected him."

Ashley looked down at the hardwood floor. "Sorry, Ben. Everything in Robbins' head is now splattered on the bathroom wall in there. He shot himself."

Ben sat down hard on the nearest chair, unable to speak.

Ashley said, "I don't know what the hell we're going to do now. President Young is going to have both of our hides."

ARTICLE XXIII

Western Montana, January 21, 2001, 6:52 AM MST

"Have a nice walk?" Boyle's voice boomed from the shadows near the cabin, startling Jamie and sending her jumping back a few feet.

"Jesus, Harvey. Are you trying to give me a heart attack?"

His sinister laugh told her that was exactly what he had intended to do. But why was he here waiting for her? Hadn't he said he would be busy this morning with meetings? Had he followed her to the meeting with Stuart? Or did he have her followed?

She couldn't help being thankful it wasn't completely light yet. Maybe the shadows would hide the panic on her face. She continued slowly toward the cabin and, as calmly as possible, spoke. "Yes, a nice brisk morning walk is better for the body than coffee."

"You should try a good workout. Pushups, sit-ups. You know, like me? Keeps you young."

"Yuck. Never. You know I hate to workout. Was your meeting canceled?" Jamie asked, trying to change the focus of the conversation and find out why he was here.

"No," Boyle said. "Just postponed for forty-five minutes while some new intelligence information is being analyzed. I only came back to say good morning and let you know how happy I am that we worked out our differences last night."

Jamie wondered why Boyle sounded so calm and relaxed. It seemed strange, considering the events and decisions he would face today. However, his demeanor told her he probably wasn't aware of the meeting with Stuart and her real feelings about him.

Slightly more relaxed, she carefully probed him for information. "When do the troops leave? Oh, and by the way, I'm still pissed you didn't let me go with them."

"Objection noted," he said, smiling. "The deployment hasn't been finalized yet. Depends somewhat on the new information we just received. It was planned for zero seven hundred, zero seven thirty at the latest." Boyle reached the front porch of the cabin and plopped onto a wooden bench near the front door.

"Could this new info mean they don't go at all, then?" Not wanting the discomfort of sitting next to him, Jamie sat cross-legged on the porch.

"Hmm, I guess. But I hate the thought of not hitting them before they get a chance to get their act together. Nonetheless, the reports coming in are strange. Yesterday, the scouts told us Army regulars were moving into position all around the compound."

Boyle sipped from the coffee mug he held while Jamie played with a small stick, scratching out shapes on the wooden porch. "Didn't you expect them to do that?"

Boyle lit a cigar retrieved from his shirt pocket and puffed deeply. "Yes, of course, that wasn't the strange part. This morning I just got the word they have stopped advancing. So now, why in the hell would they do that? Move in and then just stop? Most of the staff think they're trying to entice us to leave the camp. You know, draw us out into the open. I think they figured out how tough it was going to be to take this place. It's like a fortress with a twenty-mile moat of forest surrounding it."

"Yeah, it could be a ploy," Jamie said softly. She knew now that Stuart must have gotten through and told them to get the hell out of range. "What do you think they're doing?"

"I'm not sure, but if I were their commander, I damn sure wouldn't try to root us out of here. Then, of course, there is the bomb. And I think they know I have one. After all, it would make sense for me to have an ace in the hole."

Feigning great surprise, Jamie stared at him with wide eyes. "You have a bomb? Here? Oh God, you mean a nuclear bomb? Shit, where is it?"

Boyle chuckled. "A twenty-megaton nuclear bomb, and trust me, it would leave a great big hole in Montana. Unless they're stupid, by now, they've figured out where I got the devices and how many I had. So, if the satellites are still working, they've seen the radiation signature of our little friend. Maybe they only just found that out. That would explain why they're headed in the other direction so fast."

Jamie stood and leaned on the porch railing. "God, Harvey, I had no idea. Where is it, really? Up on the hill? Is that why I couldn't go up there?"

"Yes, yes, calm down. I don't want the whole damned camp to know." Boyle grinned like a proud father. "Do you want to see it? I think we may have enough time for a quick look. "

Jamie attempted to sound downright bubbly. "You bet your ass. Wow, I never thought I would ever see one. Come on. Come on. Let's go. Please, Harvey? Please?"

Boyle rose from the bench, a mischievous smile now widening across his face. Grasping her by the hand, he led them quickly up the hill toward the bunker. But before they could reach the thick forest trail, a young soldier came running toward them.

Following the usual salute and return, he managed to spit out, "General Boyle, they're ready for you now, sir."

Boyle frowned at the young man for the interruption. "Alright, tell them I'll be right there, son."

"But, General..." Jamie begged.

"Go on, soldier. You're dismissed. Get going." Harvey waved the young messenger away. "I'll be along in a second."

"Yes, sir," the soldier snapped but refused to move until Boyle returned his now rigid salute.

Jamie lowered her voice. "Harvey, let me go up and see it anyway, please?"

Boyle stood quietly, glancing at the soldier running toward the camp before turning back to her now pouting face. Completing a long draw on his cigar, he said, "Okay, you win. The password for the sentry is John 3:16. When you get to the door, punch six-six-six on the keypad. Got it?"

Jamie straightened and gave him a brief hug. "Sure. John 3:16 and six-six-six. Isn't that kind of a strange combination?"

Grinning, Boyle responded quietly, "No, not at all. The tools of the devil used for the glory of God. It's the perfect combination."

Jamie fought hard not to react to his perverse logic. "Oh yeah, now it makes sense. Thanks, Harvey. I really do owe you one."

"Yes, you do, my dear. Indeed you do. And I'll collect too."

Jamie knew his meaning and hoped he would never get the chance to collect on the debt. Half smiling, she turned to make the small climb up the hill.

"Jamie," Boyle's shouted at her back.

A chill climbed down her spine. She was so close to some kind of plan, and this was the perfect opportunity to get it started. Had he changed his mind? Slowly she turned to face him. "Yes, General?"

"Do me a favor."

"Sure. What is it?"

"Don't touch anything."

Jamie smiled at him warmly. "General, really. Do I look that stupid? Wait, don't answer," she said, holding an open palm to him. "Notwithstanding that, I certainly don't want to blow us up. Of course, I won't touch it. Now get going before they send out an armed squad to get you."

Jamie spun around before he could respond and half sprinted up the narrow gravel path leading to the hilltop bunker.

The heavy branches blocked the sun, and it was much darker in the thick stand of trees. Just before the top of the hill, Jamie lost her footing in the gravel and fell headlong into the knee-high undergrowth. Small sticks and rocks skinned her knees and elbows as she tumbled to a stop. Slightly dazed but not seriously hurt, she cursed herself for being so careless. When she paid attention and focused, no one could outmaneuver her. But when she was in a hurry, mistakes or falls were commonplace.

She had never seen her husband so angry as the time she fell off the stage while dancing. Wearing only a G-string, she tumbled into the laps of six men celebrating a bachelor party. Even though she cleared almost five hundred dollars from them before the night was over, he forced her to quit the next day.

Jamie wondered if a small mistaken step on a path in rural Montana might have meant the difference between millions of people, including her husband, living or dying. She would need to be more careful, stay focused, and not let anything or anyone stand between her and what she needed to do.

Again on the trail, she dusted herself off and checked out the small tear in the knee of her uniform. A small trickle of blood ran slowly down her leg. "Dammit, you are an idiot, Jamie. Now shake it off and get up there." Though painful, the fall had helped Jamie re-focus on what she was doing. This wasn't just about revenge on Boyle. It meant life or death for so many.

Quickly but much more carefully, she completed the last hundred yards up the winding trail. Fifteen or so yards from the small building, a sentry stepped from behind a tree, pointing his M-16 directly at her head.

"Freeze. What are you doing up here, miss? I'm afraid this area is restricted. You need to turn around and head back down to the camp right now."

Jamie stopped dead in her tracks. "Relax, soldier. I'm here with General Boyle's blessing. I believe the proper words are, John 3:16."

Slowly, the middle-aged man lowered his weapon. "Okay, soldier, but this is a little unusual. The general's careful about who comes up here."

"I know. My name is Jamie," she said, not proud of having to use her position as Boyle's girlfriend.

"Oh, so you're Jamie. I see. Yes, of course. You can pass but don't touch anything in there." He didn't even try to hide his unnecessary eye roll.

Jamie knew the whole camp had become aware of what she and Boyle had been doing for months. By giving her name, she hoped to make this guy more comfortable and maybe buy her a little more time with the bomb. "Yeah, I got that lecture already," she said, walking over to the door.

"Do you have the code?" he asked as she reached it.

"Yup," Jamie said, brushing past him.

"That's good because they didn't give it to me. In fact, I haven't even seen it yet. Do you think I could have a quick peek?"

Keeping her body between him and the keypad, Jamie quickly punched in the six-six-six code and pushed firmly on the heavy door when the electric lock beeped. Entering through the doorway, she turned to face the now advancing man. "Nope. Go back to your post," she said firmly, closing the door with a distinct thud before he could argue.

She hated to treat him so coldly, but if he had drawn sentry duty for the bomb, undoubtedly, he was an ardent believer in Boyle's cause. It would be stupid to take any chances with him snooping around.

It took only a second for her to realize that in her haste to shut the door, she hadn't located the light switch. Complete darkness surrounded her, and she jumped when a small red LED light flashed in the corner, accompanied by a prominent beep. "Holy Shit. What the hell is that?"

Beginning near the door, she began a frantic search for the switch. However, feeling up and down the walls, she came up empty. Though she should have anticipated it, the second flash and beep once again made her spring backward. It was so eerie in this small pitch-black room with a device that could wipe out twenty square miles of Montana. Moving ever so slowly toward the center of the room, she screamed out loud when something touched her face. Startled, she took a step back and screamed even louder when the sentry pounded sharply on the door behind her.

"Jamie, do you need help?" he shouted through the door.

"Not unless you know where the light is," she shouted back at him.

A flat "Nope" was his only response.

Jamie thought it likely he was getting some measure of enjoyment at her plight after how rude she'd been, and she wasn't at all pleased that he had frightened her enough to make her cry out.

"Then go away. I'm fine."

Remembering the touch of something on her face, Jamie felt around in the empty darkness. Finally, her hand brushed past a piece of string hanging from the ceiling. She pulled gently, and intense light filled the room. She had to close her eyes for a moment and slowly blink them open again to become accustomed to it.

The room was fairly small, maybe ten by twenty feet. Tucked in one corner, on a sturdy metal platform, sat the bomb. It wasn't anything like she expected. It didn't even look like a bomb at all. Constructed of black metal plates about two feet square, it appeared harmless enough. The small red LED she had seen in the darkness was in the upper portion, on the side panel facing her directly above the stenciled word *INACTIVE*. What she couldn't have seen was the green LED above the word *ARMED*.

Though the thought of this light flashing scared her to death, she hoped she would be able to somehow make it glow. Jamie assumed this heavy box was designed to help protect the device from being breached or compromised in a plane crash or the destruction of a rocket. On the right side of the box, in large bright yellow letters, the word *RADIOACTIVE* had been placed right below the international symbol for the same. On the left side were the words *Property of the United States Air Force* in smaller white letters, along with the serial number.

Now she had to find a way to get it open and arm it. There weren't any handles or knobs on the top, just a small silver inset lock. Quickly, she began to search the room for the key, seeing the only real possibility a desk in the opposite corner of the room.

Jamie began to rifle through the drawers for anything that might help her. Though she didn't come up with the key, she did find a small manual on the bomb. Stamped clearly as *TOP SECRET*, it had instructions and descriptions she would need to finish what she had started. There wasn't enough time to try and read it here, but it would be too dangerous to take it with her. She had so few options left that the choice was obvious.

Glancing at the door, she stood, unbuttoned her pants, and carefully slid the book down inside her boxer shorts. Redressed, she resumed the search for the key. "Christ, Jamie, you can be so stupid. Boyle wouldn't keep it here." She placed her head in her hands. "Think now, think. Where would it be?"

Like a truck, it hit her. The day the bomb was delivered. He had it. The driver gave it to Boyle.

The relief she felt in knowing where to find the key was offset by already having to devise a plan to get it from him. "Same old story, two steps forward and one back."

Now accustomed to the periodic beeps, Jamie didn't budge when she heard it. However, the buzz of the keypad on the outer door caused her to freeze with fear.

The door swung open wide, and Major Hollis' silhouette filled the entryway with the sun now higher in the sky behind him.

"Well, well. What do we have here?" Hollis said.

ARTICLE XXIV

Washington DC, January 21, 2001, 10:05 EST

"Everybody okay? Is anybody hit?" TJ asked as the smoke began to clear in the shaft.

"You were the only one shooting, TJ. How could we be hit?" Mike spit out as he examined the dead guard. "Why the hell did you have to kill him like that? I'm pretty sure he's on our side."

"Doc, you don't know these Pentagon types. They have orders to shoot to kill down here. Especially under these circumstances. But if it'll make you feel better, I'll let one of them shoot you first next time, and then I'll kill him."

Mike got back on his feet. "Come on. I didn't deserve that. I just think we need to try and stop this madness at some point. When do we become Americans again? Stop killing each other? This kid was a soldier, just like you."

TJ looked at the floor, cradling his M-16 in his arms. "I know, Doc. I hate seeing anyone die. But you have to remember my only job here is to keep you and my men alive. The mission is secondary. This man is secondary. One job and one mission. One mistake today, and we all might be dead. It can't be any other way. If that isn't good enough for you, let's head back right now."

"Nobody's leaving," Billy growled from a few feet away. "Not when we're this close."

TJ turned toward Billy. The sound of his rifle cocking echoed down the empty hallway. "I thought you and I had an understanding. You don't tell me what to do, and I don't shoot you."

By now, Billy had learned his lesson about pushing TJ too far. "Sorry. I just meant it seemed like a waste to leave before we get what we came for. Strictly my opinion. You can do whatever you think is best." Billy turned his back toward TJ and kept his hands at his sides.

TJ's eyes narrowed as he stared intensely at Billy's back. "I'm not the smartest son of a bitch in the world, but don't play me as a chump. We'll find your little safe, alright. On my terms and schedule. You have anything else to add?"

Billy slowly faced TJ again. "Nope."

"Good. Now which way to this safe?" TJ asked, aiming his headlamp back down the long hallway.

Billy motioned behind him with a flick of his head. "Down this way, about one hundred yards. You want me to lead?"

"Yeah, great idea, hero. You take the point. Oh, and Billy, check with the doc here before you shoot someone." TJ snorted a laugh. "Hey, I got a better idea. Let them shoot you, then open fire."

"You're a riot," Mike said flatly. "Be careful, Billy."

"Yeah, I will. Let's go."

TJ turned to face the rest of his squad. "Move out on the big hero's ass. Meach, you take the rear and clear those offices as we go."

Already several yards down the dark hallway, Billy didn't acknowledge TJ's last barb. Light smoke lingered in the air, but there was little if any, direct damage from the blast at this level of the building. Some water ran down the walls, and a few ceiling tiles had been dislodged, but it wasn't anything that would slow their search for the safe.

About five minutes later, the group gathered around a closed, keypad-activated steel door. There were no markings on the door except for a large sign reading, *No Unauthorized Entry.*

"You sure this is it?" Mike asked Billy.

"Yeah, it's the only one it could be. Any ideas on how we might get it open?" Billy laid his rifle down and felt around the edge of the doorway.

"God, no. I only open things with skin on them. Sally, you got any brainstorm ideas?"

Sally had been unusually quiet and was hanging back from the group. Without saying a word, she moved up and examined the door. Finally, she said, "Blow it."

"'Blow it'?" Mike exclaimed, not liking the sound of that. "Can't we just shoot the lock or something?"

TJ moved up close to the door. "Not unless you like bullets ricocheting back and forth across the hallway."

"He's right, Mike. This stuff is too heavy for that. Bullets won't go through it. Sure wish I had that C4 in the Explorer."

"'C4'? Shit." Billy seemed never to run out of unpleasant surprises for Mike. "I wish you had told me. Christ, you people are unbelievable. Do you recall when the bullets were flying through the truck yesterday? Might have been a good time to mention you had C4 in there."

"Calm down, Doc," TJ said, placing a hand on Mike's shoulder. "You can kick his ass later if you want. We have work to do right now." TJ knelt next to Billy. "What about a couple of grenades? Can you rig them to blow together?"

"Yes, that might work. Are thcy all on a three-second delay?"

"Five. Pull it, count one...two...three and throw it."

Billy nodded and stood. "Okay. I'll need some twine, tape and a heavy desk."

Getting back on his feet, TJ turned to two of his men. "You two, find a heavy desk in one of these offices and bring it here. Collins, go find some tape—the heavier, the better—and some string or lightweight rope."

The three Marines hurried off to complete the tasks he had assigned them, leaving only Mike's team and TJ standing close to the door.

"What about inside?" TJ asked Billy. "What will we have to deal with in there?"

"Just the safe. I have the combination. Won't take long."

TJ looked up and down the hall. "I hope you're right. The less time we have to spend down here, the better."

Sally turned to face Billy. "And if you blow yourself up opening the door?" she asked him quietly.

"Then the safe stays closed," Billy answered with finality.

"That's bullshit," Mike hissed. "Too many people have died already for this thing. You're not that important. Give the combination to Sally, just in case something happens."

"I have orders. No way anybody gets in that safe but me. Nobody."

TJ started to step toward Billy, but Mike cut in front of him. "I don't care about your goddamn orders. Do you remember, Bo? Shot in the back? TJ's men and the guard down the hall? All dead because of what you're after. Well, I can tell you something, Billy. They died for *something*, and I'll make sure of that. So, if you don't give the combination to Sally, I'll move out of the way and let TJ deal with you or maybe shoot you myself." With that, Mike raised his 45 auto and pointed it at Billy's stomach.

Billy looked into Mike's eyes and then over his shoulder at TJ. "You won't shoot me, Mike. But that crazy bastard would." Billy appeared to give it some thought. "Alright, alright, you win, now back off."

Using his hand, Billy moved the barrel of Mike's gun away from him, turned and walked away from the group. "Sally, let's you and I take a little walk down the hall."

Mike grasped Sally's arm. "Don't let him talk you into going along with him. If he won't give you the combination, walk away. Okay? You owe me that," he whispered into her ear. Sally smiled and nodded. Free of

Mike's grip, she followed Billy down the darkened hall.

"Didn't know you had it in you, Doc," TJ said after Sally and Billy were out of earshot.

"Well, I'm not proud of it. Another couple of days with this bunch, and I can kiss my nice guy outlook on life goodbye."

TJ let out a rumbling belly laugh. "God, you make me laugh. You are so far from a hard ass. Don't worry about getting that rep. Worry about staying alive long enough to get back to your soft little world. How the hell did you get here anyway?"

Mike slumped down the wall and sat on the floor. "I've been trying to figure that out. I think because I hadn't eaten yet when the phone rang yesterday. My blood sugar must have been low, and I was clearly out of my fucking mind." It was a joke, but Mike wasn't laughing.

TJ grinned and shook his head. "Come on. It was just you being you, doing the right thing, the good thing. Helping out your fellow man and all that crap."

"She's so soft, so pretty." Mike kept his gaze on the floor.

"Who is? Sally?"

"No, my wife. I met her at a party. She turned and looked at me, smiled, and it was all over. She was sitting in front of this table lamp, and the light glowed around her head and shined through her hair. As she rose and walked toward me, I wasn't sure if I was dreaming or awake. My knees even went weak and started shaking. We married just two months later. That was six years ago. But even now, late at night, when I finally make my way to bed, I crawl in beside her, and the smell of her hair, the smile on her face... Groaning slightly, she rolls toward me and places her head on my chest, her hand on my stomach. She's the most glorious person in the universe and the reason I want to live. Yet, here I am, risking my life for that pompous asshole that has done nothing but lie to me and almost get me killed. Can you explain that to me, please?"

TJ sat down on the floor beside him. "Yeah, maybe I can. Ever ask yourself why she loves you, Mike? I think if you did, you might conclude that the reason is that you're a man. A real man, one who believes all people are worth saving. Worth something to someone, somewhere. It isn't something you plan or think about all the time, just who you are in your gut. I noticed it right off, and Billy and Sally counted on it. They knew that when the chips were down, you would stay and help, do the right thing. You wouldn't be able to do anything else. That's why I'm here right now. I want to make sure you get back to that family of yours. Hell, someday, you might even invite me to dinner."

Mike smiled. "Consider yourself invited. In fact, my door is open to you whenever you can come down. I owe you my life, TJ."

"Just like you, I know what my job is, and I try to do it damned well." TJ returned Mike's smile and got up off the floor.

The two Marines had located a large steel desk and finished dragging it a few feet from the door. "Where do you want it, Sarge," one of them asked, huffing and puffing a bit from the strain.

"Leave it there for now. Hey, Billy, you about ready to do this thing?" TJ yelled.

"Be right there," Billy shouted back.

A minute or so later, Billy and Sally came back to the door. "You get it?" Mike asked Sally.

"Yes, Mike, I did. Let's hope I don't have to use it." She sounded more upbeat than before. The third Marine returned carrying black electrical tape and a small ball of twine.

Billy took the items and set the twine on the floor. "You have the grenades?"

TJ reached inside his coat and pulled out two grenades. "You sure you know what you're doing with these?"

"I've handled a lot worse," Billy replied. "Why don't you all move back down the hallway? I'll do this alone." He began to wrap the tape around the two grenades, making them into one.

A young Marine pointed toward the elevator shafts. "There's an office fifty yards or so down the way, Sarge. Steel doors, no glass."

"Okay, everyone, move out," TJ snapped. "Meach, get them down and ready. I'll be there in a few."

"I said alone, TJ. That includes you."

"Just keep working. I'll go when I'm ready." TJ stood like a statue watching him.

Billy continued working, taping the grenades to the steel door near the latch. "Whatever. It's your ass." Billy carefully tied the string around the pull pins. "I hope the tape holds." Billy rose and looked at TJ. "Since you're here, help me get this desk where it will do some good."

"You want it to deflect the blast back toward the door?" TJ asked, sitting his weapon on the floor.

Billy looked a bit surprised. "Very good, Sergeant. Let's sit it up on its end and slide it close to the door." The two men managed to arrange the desk in the doorway, making sure not to cover or pull on the twine. Billy began to slowly unwind the ball of twine as he walked back toward the office where the rest of the group waited. Only ten or so yards from the door, the twine came to its end. Billy glanced at the homemade bomb, then back down the hall to safety. "Huh. I was hoping for a bit more string."

"Want me to pull it?" TJ asked.

Billy hesitated, but only for a second. "No. I'll do it. If you could hold the office door open for me, that would help a lot."

"You got it. I'll be ready." TJ turned and made his way to the small room. "He's almost ready. Get your heads down." TJ stood, bracing the heavy door open with his foot.

Forty or so yards down the hall, Billy sucked in a deep breath as if gathering his nerve and gave an even but swift pull on the twine. The two pull pins clanked to the floor, and Billy began his sprint toward the office. When he reached the open door, he dove inside the room.

TJ slammed the door closed just as the grenades exploded, sending a savage rumble down the hall and a deafening bang against the outside of the room. The heavy door flew open, followed closely by a choking cloud of dust and smoke.

Mike instinctively reached out for Sally, and just before he grasped her hand, the ceiling in the office came crashing down on them.

ARTICLE XXV

Denver, Colorado, January 21, 2001, 8:06 MST

"Well, Ben. Your cowboy crap really botched things up. I hope you're happy," Sid said in a tone aimed directly at Ben's pride.

The president stepped in before Ben could respond to the taunt. "That's enough of that, Sid. I'm sure we all would like to change a few things in the last couple of days. Let's move on. Where is General Clifton?"

"He should be here in a minute or two," Larry answered. "He was delayed by an urgent message from Montana. He wanted to make sure he had all the facts before the meeting."

"What kind of message?"

Larry looked over his notes briefly before speaking. "I hesitate to get into it too much before the general gets here, but I do know he was insistent that the troops be moved back from the camp as quickly as possible. Of course, I agreed to that. Terry wouldn't ask if he didn't have a good reason. The withdrawal began an hour or so ago."

"I see." The president frowned. "Larry, would you go find General Clifton and see if we can get this information as quickly as possible?"

"Of course, Madam President," Larry replied, already halfway out of the conference room.

Claire looked at Ben. "You okay? Ashley said it was pretty hairy over there."

Ben tried to force a smile. "Yes, Madam President, thank you. I put myself there. It was my fault. Thank God my old friend Helen came through for me."

"Yes, you were lucky." President Young nodded. "Anything you want to share with me about your little meeting with Robbins?"

"Same old story. Politician makes a mistake and then compounds it with more mistakes."

"This wasn't a mistake, Mr. Bleser. It was mass murder and treason."

Ben was displeased with himself for his apparent minimization of Robbins' complicity. "Sorry. I know that. I told him that. There isn't any excuse for what he did. He lost sight of why he had wanted to hold office. Sank down to the level of any tyrant that uses force to maintain power. We both know your power doesn't come from the Army or Navy or any other post. It comes from the Constitution and the people."

"Right words, wrong order," President Young announced as she pointed straight up into the air. "The people and the Constitution grant the power to me in order to uphold the document. If the people decide at some point that the Constitution doesn't mean anything, no amount of power or force will change that."

Ben stared directly at her. "You are indeed an amazing woman."

"Thank you. I hope you're right. I tried to pay attention in my history and civics classes. I learned that one person can make a difference, but the average citizen makes it happen. Most people give Mr. Lincoln credit for single-handedly freeing my ancestors and reuniting the country. However, he never fired a shot in the war, didn't suffer in the winter mud, or lose a son at Bull Run or Gettysburg. He supplied the vision and the words, but ordinary men and women fought the battles. Not because they loved him or thought he knew more than they did. They died because it was the right thing to do for their country and their Constitution."

Ben and Ashley exchanged glances. Claire went on. "You can see the same lessons all around the world. For instance, when the wall fell, it didn't fall from our preaching against it but from the weight of their people no longer willing to support it. One person can lift up their voice, but only many voices can unite a country. Boyle may have been the catalyst for this insurrection, but without the help of hundreds of others, it wouldn't have come to pass."

Ben was astounded by not only her grasp of history but also how it affected the present. "That's very true, Madam President. So what happens when it's over?" he asked, trying hard to commit her words to memory so that later others might share in her wisdom.

"The hard part begins," she said, speaking softly. "Not unlike the end of the civil war, anyone committing crimes will be punished, the troops will return home, and we put our efforts into rebuilding and reaching out to the disenfranchised. Bring the country back together as one nation sharing a common goal."

Claire stood and began to pace. "We've made mistakes. The government, I mean. There wouldn't have been so many people willing to follow this maniac if there weren't serious issues. Maybe it's time to look at where we are. Go through his manifesto to see if there's some truth mixed in with the madness." She stopped pacing and faced the group assembled around the table. "We can never condone his methods, but we'd better, by God, figure out how he got here, how to keep more from following his path. I try hard not to think of the work ahead. My God, so many dead, and no matter what we do, many more will die. We may never be the world power we once were. The scars will be physical for many years and psychological for lifetimes."

Ben had been confused about a lot of things today, but not about Claire Louise Young. His country had been very, very lucky that she had not been in Washington.

Larry and General Clifton burst back into the meeting. "I'm sorry to hold you up, Madam President," General Clifton blurted out.

"No problem, Terry. What's going on?"

Both men took their places at the table, and General Clifton said, "It appears we got lucky."

"In what way?"

The general opened the red file folder he'd brought with him. "His name is Stuart Williams. He escaped from the compound just before dawn this morning. Defected, I guess, would be a better word. He claims a woman close to Boyle in the camp is going to detonate the bomb. He doesn't know how she's going to do it but trusts her to get it done. He also has information on the bomb here, and *there is a bomb here*," Terry stressed, looking up from the file at the president and pausing.

"I never said there wasn't, General."

"Of course, Madam President. I'm sorry."

President Young nodded. "That's great news. How far do you need to pull back to be safe?"

"I'm hoping to be back at least fifty miles, but considering the terrain, twenty-five or thirty is probably fairly safe."

Sid leaned forward in his seat and removed his glasses. "Any chance this is a ploy to keep us busy and make some room for them to get out of the camp?"

"Good point, Sid." President Young added. "Well, General?"

"I can't rule it out. But my people on the scene are confident of his sincerity. They have a website, The Happy Gardener. We're checking on that now. He gave us the password. I just couldn't take the chance of leaving my men in harm's way, even if there's some doubt he's on the level. In a few hours, I'll know more—be able to check on more of the information. Until then, I've got to rely on my intelligence as well as my gut and intuition. I wish I had a better answer for you."

"We don't have much to lose by playing it safe for now," Larry added.

"I agree," President Young stated with finality. "Sid, can your people help in the intelligence gathering? The bombs and the website?"

"Sure thing. I'll make a few calls. General, can we spend a few minutes after we finish here?"

Clifton leaned back in his chair and spoke softly to an aide standing nearby. After he finished, he turned to Sid. "Give me about five or ten minutes, then, sure."

President Young said, "I want the bomb here to be a priority."

"Yes, Madam President. I already have two companies heading toward that location."

"It wouldn't have changed anything."

"Madam President?" the general asked cocking his head.

President Young stood and began to walk around the table as she spoke. "Knowing for sure that a bomb was in Denver. I wouldn't have left, regardless. You see, it's about standing tall, resisting the danger, and showing the American people that *we're* in control, not him. It wouldn't have changed a thing."

General Clifton smiled. "Yes, Madam President. I know that. But it's my job to play it safe with you. The country needs you alive, needs your strength and vision."

Ben was shocked at this exchange between these two apparent adversaries. Even Sid looked a bit taken aback.

President Young now stopped behind General Clifton's chair. "Thanks, Terry. You've done your job well. I look forward to working with you under much better circumstances." She gave his shoulder a squeeze, then turned and walked toward the rear doorway leading to her office. "Let's reconvene in an hour," she said as she left the room.

ARTICLE XXVI

Washington DC, January 21, 2001, 11:21 AM EST

"It's broken," Mike almost whispered to Sally. TJ and another Marine continued to remove debris from Sally's body. The false ceiling and lighting had crashed down on all of them, but Sally had evidently taken the worst of it.

"Are you sure?" Sally asked, nearly pleading with him to change his mind.

Mike looked her square in the eyes. "Yes, I'm sure. Now hold still. It's not going to be any fun when I splint it. TJ, please hand me those two metal rods over there." He pointed near Sally's legs.

"Here you go, Doc." TJ handed the two-foot rods to him. "You need anything else?"

Mike scanned the room. "Yes, the cleanest rag you can find and something to tie this off."

"How clean does the rag have to be?"

"The bone has gone through the skin, and I don't want it to get infected."

A few minutes later, TJ returned with a white washcloth and some lightweight rope.

"Okay, Sally, hang on. This is going to hurt like hell," Mike told her as he prepared to pull the bones back into place.

TJ and two of his men held Sally tightly while Mike tugged firmly on her wrist. The sound of grinding bone and Sally's screams echoed down the smoky hallway. Thankfully, after only moments Sally lost consciousness, and Mike finished placing her arm firmly between the two rods. He laid the clean cloth over the tear in her skin and tied the rope around the splint. "That should do it," Mike said after tying the last knot in the rope.

"Can I go check on your buddy now?" TJ asked.

Mike looked all around the office. "You mean Billy? Why did he leave?"

"Does that surprise you?"

"No, not really. The bastard doesn't care about anyone but himself."

TJ stood and headed down the hall. "I'll be back."

"Hang on a second, TJ. I'm done here," Mike said. "Okay, hon, don't move around too much. I'll be back in a few minutes. I want to make sure TJ doesn't kill Billy," he whispered to Sally.

When Mike and TJ arrived at the small room, Billy was hunched over the open safe. On the floor were bright red tape-sealed folders. Billy picked them up one by one and placed them into his pack.

"Find what you were looking for?" TJ asked from the doorway.

"Yes. Please stay back."

"Don't worry, hero. I don't want your little secrets," TJ shot back.

"Oh, and by the way, Sally will be okay," Mike added sarcastically.

Billy continued loading the folders. "I knew you would take care of her. Besides, she's pretty tough. It would take a lot to bring her down."

"What do you say we cut the bullshit?" TJ shot at him.

Billy zipped the backpack closed and turned to face him. "Meaning?"

"Meaning, we both know those files are all you care about."

"Okay. If you say so, tough guy."

"Yeah, I say so, and I also say we're headed back now." TJ pointed his weapon in Billy's general direction.

Billy straightened and took a step toward him. "Not yet. We aren't finished," he said through clenched teeth.

"Yes, we are. Sally's hurt, and one of his is dead," Mike interjected. "We're done. The plates will have to wait. Besides, we've gotten way too much radiation exposure already."

Billy squeezed past TJ and Mike, moving into the hall. "You two may be done, but I'm going on."

"Alone then," TJ stated.

"Nope, Mike and Sally are going with me," Billy informed TJ with his arms now cradling his weapon.

TJ stepped closer to Billy and shifted his rifle so that his finger was closer to the trigger.

"Sally's arm is broken badly," Mike said as he tried to maneuver himself between the two men. "I'm not even sure how we're going to get her up the shaft and to the surface. So, she damn sure isn't going anywhere with you."

Billy tried to appear calm. "Fine. Then TJ, you take her back. Mike and I will go get the plates."

"Not a chance," TJ answered flatly. "I would let my mother attend the KKK headquarters for lunch before I would let him go with you alone."

"Seems we're at an impasse." Billy looked TJ straight in the eyes.

The situation Mike feared most was unfolding, and he prayed he could head it off before it got worse. TJ apparently didn't share Mike's thoughts.

TJ moved Mike to the side and pointed the muzzle of his weapon directly at Billy. "That's where you're wrong, asshole. Put the gun down and move down the hall with the others."

"And if I don't?

TJ looked passed him for an instant. "Whisner. If this man does anything other than carefully and slowly place his weapon on the floor, shoot him in the fucking head."

"You've been watching too many movies, TJ."

"One way to find out."

The sound of an M-16 being cocked behind him wiped the smile from Billy's face. The soldier said, "You're messing with my sergeant. Do you have any idea what I would do for this man?"

TJ took one more step toward Billy, getting in his face. "This discussion is over. Do as you were told. Now."

Mike added his plea. "Come on, Billy. Is it worth getting shot?"

Billy released his grip on the weapon and let it slide to the floor.

"The forty-five, too," TJ said as he picked up the rifle and slung it over his shoulder.

Billy's eyes flared. "What if I need it? There are still assholes outside."

Whisner stepped close enough to Billy that he must have felt the man's breath on the back of his neck. "I would be more worried about the assholes here if I were you," he whispered.

TJ grinned. "Not to worry. Your files will make it back safely. If you don't, well, shit happens."

Shifting from one foot to the other, Billy looked over his shoulder at the Marine covering him, then back at TJ, and finally directly at Mike. Slowly he reached inside his coat and produced the 45 automatic. Holding it out for all to see, he lowered it to the floor. "Happy?"

"Almost," TJ quipped. "Knife."

"You should have kept it, because now you will have to get it back."

"Gladly." TJ placed the weapons on the ground and took a step toward Billy.

Mike's voice boomed through the hallway. "TJ, what the hell are you doing?"

"Billy and I can work this out," TJ replied.

"Billy, just give him the damn knife," Mike said firmly.

"Go to hell, Mike. I didn't start this. Talk Rambo down." Billy shot back.

"TJ?"

"The radiation levels are too high. Sally is hurt, and it's over for now. End of discussion."

"That makes sense to me, Billy," Mike said. "We can send another team back in for the plates."

"Those weren't my orders."

"Just exactly what were your orders?" Mike probed.

Pausing briefly, Billy spoke firmly. "Get the files, get the plates. At *any* cost."

Mike moved closer to him. "We did the best we could. You almost got all of us killed. The time has come to regroup, live to fight another day."

Billy hung his head. "I'm sorry, Mike. I can't do that."

Mike held out his hand. "Then give me the files and go get the damned plates. I'll see they get back."

Billy looked at Mike and then at TJ. "Alright. When we get up top, I'll entrust them only to you. Then I'll go for the plates alone."

Mike nodded. "Okay, Billy. I wish you would go back with us, but you have to do what's in your heart."

"I'll need my weapons back."

"When we get up top, a trade for the files," TJ stated flatly.

"Deal?" Mike asked Billy.

"Fine." Billy turned to move back down the hall.

"Good. Now let's get Sally up and out of here. She's in a great deal of pain and can't use one arm."

TJ held Mike's arm, keeping him from following Billy down the hall. "Watch him, Doc. I don't trust him. He still has his knife in his boot."

"He won't hurt me. Let's try to keep the conflict down until we get out of here, okay?"

"Fine by me. But watch him. He's a dangerous man right now," TJ added before following the group back down the hallway.

ARTICLE XXVII

Western Montana, January 21, 2001, 6:38 AM MST

"Dammit, is everyone trying to give me a heart attack today?" Jamie shot at the major still standing in the doorway.

"What the hell are you doing in here, Jamie?"

"Didn't the guard tell you? I have Harvey's permission to be here. I just wanted to look at it," Jamie said, trying to sound as nonchalant as possible.

"Could you give us a break and call him General like everyone else?"

Jamie pondered for a moment about how to respond. Was this the time to take advantage of her position with the general, or should she try to sweet-talk her way out of this? Or meet strength with strength, as Harvey had told her over and over.

"You had better get out of my face, Major. I'll call him whatever I want. If you have a problem with that, take it up with him. I'm sure he would be glad to discuss it with you."

Hollis looked around to see how close the sentry was and if he had overheard Jamie's comment. "There's no need to get snotty here. I'm still a major, *Private*," he snorted, moving inside the doorway and closing the heavy door behind him.

"Okay, so you saved face with the sentry. Now, what the hell is your problem?" Jamie asked him.

"You," Hollis said quietly. "The general is one of the brightest men I have ever known. Except when it comes to you, he makes bad choices, things that hurt morale. Everyone else here is supposed to focus on training and our objective. Then they see him playing house with you, letting you have the run of the camp, calling him *Harvey*. Christ, it makes him seem like a lovesick teenager. We all know you're playing him. You're young enough to be his daughter."

"Be careful here, Major." Jamie hoped she sounded more confident than she was.

"Save it. You don't scare me." He moved to stand within inches of her. "You see, I'm in this meeting, a very important meeting, mind you, when I get a message that the general's plaything is in with the bomb. Now I ask myself, 'What possible reason would Private Cupcake have to be in there?' When I ask the general if he knows you're here, he says in front of all the high-level staff, 'Sure, I let her go up. I think it made her wet between the legs to think about the power of the damned thing.' Then he chuckled like a little boy. You think that's the image of a man all these fine soldiers will follow to hell and back, Jamie?"

Terror struck Jamie. Would he dare talk to her like this if she was going to walk out of that door alive? "You're wound up too tight, Major. Seeing things that aren't there."

The veins on the major's head sprung to life as he seethed over her words. "Wound up too tight? Do you have any idea what happened yesterday? The largest superpower on earth was brought to it's knees by us. Do you think they're going to lie down and take it? Do you think my life, your life, or anyone's life will ever be the same? I need the general's head clear. I need him to think with his big head, not the little one. If we screw this up, we're all dead."

"Okay. So you've made your speech. What's the bottom line here?"

"You're leaving. I'll make sure the patrols don't bother you."

"I'm a redhead, not a blonde."

"Meaning?"

"Meaning, I take off through the woods, and someone is sure that I've gone to throw you all under the bus. Now I'm sure no one will know for sure who fired the shot that killed me, but someone will indeed fire it."

Jamie took a half step toward Hollis as she finished.

Hollis backed away from her a bit. "So, what do you suggest? How do we solve this?"

"Tell him where the bomb in Denver really is."

Hollis appeared stunned by her remark. "You don't think he knows?"

"We both know he doesn't."

"So where is it, Jamie?"

"In the prison boiler room, where my husband is."

Hollis' eyes narrowed. "And just how do you know that?"

Stuart told Jamie this morning that Hollis had made a mistake having the bomb placed there. He had lost his contact inside and now couldn't get to it. He had been afraid to tell the general the truth. "Doesn't much matter, does it?"

"No, I guess it doesn't. What good would it do to tell him, though?" Hollis asked, now pacing the small room.

Jamie straightened, now more confident of her circumstances. "Tell him the team screwed up. They thought the prison was the best place for the bomb. Their hearts were in the right place, you know. Blow up that drug-pushing bastard. But you didn't find out until today where it really was." Jamie paused for a long moment, letting Hollis soak it all up. "Now I'm the only one who can get to it. I can walk right in there. They wouldn't suspect me. You need to send me out to set the timer and then get out safely and back to him."

Hollis stopped pacing and stared intently at her. "And would you arm it?"

"No. I won't kill him or the thousands of others. However, I would be out of your hair, and he would hate me forever," Jamie said, studying Hollis's face for a reaction.

Hollis sat down hard on a box sitting in the corner near the door. "With what you know, how can I trust you?"

Jamie knelt in front of him. "Don't you think I'm up to my eyeballs in this? They would give me a cell right next to my husband and throw away the key. I'm screwed no matter who wins this thing. I plan on heading to Canada, crossing somewhere in the mountains. I'll change my name and try real damn hard to stay alive." Jamie could only pray she sounded convincing because, in large part, she believed what she was saying. It did sound good to run away and not look back.

Hollis lowered his head. "I don't think he'll let you go."

"You let me handle that. But you will have to sell it. Make it seem like it's the only way. Go through the whole scam. Have someone train me to arm the bomb. Give me the details of where it is. It has to be real, or he won't go for it."

Jamie suddenly wished the manual to the bomb wasn't inside her boxer shorts. The information Stuart had provided her before he slipped over the back gate about the Denver bomb had proved to be the key to the puzzle she needed.

Hollis stood and began pacing again. "I don't know. It's damn risky. He isn't stupid, you know? Not to mention I don't really trust you not to roll over on me. Christ, I should have just told him about the screw-up right away, but he was so angry."

"Major, we need to settle this. We have plans to work out and no time to do it."

"I know. I know. Who brings it up? Has to be me, right?"

Jamie placed her arm in front of him to stop him from continuing his relentless pacing. "Yes. He can't know we've talked about it. I'll act as surprised as possible. Tell him you don't know of any other way to get it done. The new president must be taken out or at least be in a position not to stop us."

Hollis looked Jamie in the eyes. "You seem pretty damn anxious to get out of here."

She lowered her head a bit. "I won't lie to you, Major. I'm in over my head with the general and this war. It's not that I don't believe in what we're doing. I do. But I just can't understand how he can be so callous about the innocent people he killed. Knowing about it changed me, but it didn't change him at all. Maybe soldiers are just used to death and have grown hardened toward human suffering. Hell, I don't know. Can you tell me it doesn't bother you? Is this the way you would have done it?"

Hollis looked away from her and said nothing for a long moment. "I'm a soldier. I follow orders. It doesn't pay to think too much when you've chosen this life. Would I have done it the same way? No. But that's why I'm not a general, and maybe that's why you have to leave." Hollis paused again and turned toward the door of the bunker. "My mother lived in Chicago. I tried so hard to make her move. I begged her to come out here. I'll leave God to sort that out. And I'll have to wait to see if it was in His plan to have her there with Him now. Maybe I was supposed to be the instrument that brought her home to the Father. In the meantime, sleep is not a pleasant experience for me."

It was obvious to Jamie that he was fighting back tears from the pain of his involvement in his mother's death. Would she soon be asking that question of herself about the major's death? She tried hard to remind herself how many more would die if she failed to act.

"Maybe this can somehow help you. Get me out of here and spare the millions in Denver that would die if you sent someone else." She was gambling that his guilt would overcome his duties as Boyle's second in command.

He turned from the door and made eye contact with her again. "Okay. Right after lunch, then. Be in the cabin with him, and I'll come to you. Now let's get the hell out of here."

Jamie struggled for an excuse to remain behind and return the manual to the desk. "I don't want the sentry to think you made me leave, okay? You go back, and I'll follow in a couple of minutes. The fewer people who see us together right now, the better."

Hollis studied her face. "Okay. Don't be long. I don't want the whole camp to know you got in here."

"I know. I'll be right behind you. Thanks, Major."

"Don't thank me just yet. There's no guarantee the general will go along." Hollis paused again at the door. "I don't think you know how much he loves you. What he would be willing to do to keep you with him."

"Well, we can hope that he does go along. I would hate to think what you might do to me if he doesn't."

The Major seemed to look right through her. "One way or the other, then," he said hollowly and stepped through the now-open door into the sunlight.

Jamie stood inside the small enclosure and began to sob. The roller coaster she had been riding for the last couple of days was exhausting. Now the dye had been cut. She would either kill everyone in the camp or be dead herself. Maybe both.

Through the tears in her eyes, she fumbled with the desk drawer and replaced the manual where she had found it.

ARTICLE XXVIII

Denver, Colorado, January 21, 2001, 11:19 AM MST

"I think about how life might have been going forward if you had gotten killed," Ashley said softly.

"I know, babe," Ben whispered back to her. "It was a dumb thing for me to do. I just had to know what Robbins knew and what, if anything, he could do to help us." He looked into her eyes. "I'm old now, but you would have had to live with losing me and the harm to your career for a long time. And for that, I am truly sorry."

"You're not old." Ashley wrinkled her forehead.

Ben chuckled. "Okay, well, in comparison to you, I'm old."

"Old-*er,* maybe. Old? No."

"Do you have any idea how old I'll be when you're my age?"

"Older than me," Ashley responded, now laughing.

Before Ben could respond, President Young entered the conference room, and they both rose to their feet. "Sit, sit. I'm a little early." She took her place at the head of the table. "Is anyone else as tired as I am?"

Ben offered her a warm smile. "You've been going at it hard, Madam President. I don't know how you do it."

President Young exhaled loudly. "*Whew.* Tell me about it. That last meeting with Dr. Dun was not only morose but maddening because of the language thing and close to three hours long."

"How is the relief effort going?"

President Young shook her head. "I wish I could tell you. As you might imagine, everyone is moving away from the blast areas. We can't seem to get much information in or out. I do know the devastation was everything that the original reports indicated and more. The flood of victims pouring from what's left of the cities is crushing."

Claire paused, rubbing her forehead for a few seconds before continuing. "To tell you the truth, it may be many days or even weeks before we actually get in to check things out. Far too late for most of them, I'm afraid. We're collecting supplies and food from all over the country to prepare for them. I've asked that all elective surgeries be postponed freeing up hospital beds. The Navy and Air Force are sending all the planes they can spare to transport the sick and injured. Many private companies and individuals have offered to help."

"That sounds encouraging," Ashley added.

President Young smiled briefly and then frowned. "I wonder why people are like that?"

"Like what?"

"Why they wait for the worst to bring out their best?" Ben asked softly.

"Exactly," President Young said, nodding in agreement. "They can walk down the street and step over someone sick or drugged out. However, someone a thousand miles away needs aid, and they drop everything to help. It doesn't make any sense. They fight with the neighbors about their dog. Then run through flames, risking their lives to save that same damned dog in a fire. All the ugliness surrounding war, and yet when the war is over, we rebuild the cities and start posturing to prepare for the next one. We can justify almost anything and never seem to learn. I mean, think about it. This madman in Montana really thinks he'll build a better world by blowing it up."

When she stopped to take a breath, Ben said, "You're right, Madam President."

She straightened in her chair. "Boy, I hope I don't fall off of this soapbox. I could be killed from the fall. That's it. I've become a raving lunatic."

Ben smiled. "With all due respect, you may be the sanest person to hold this office in a long time."

She returned his smile warmly. "I wish I could say I earned my way here."

Ashley said, "I think under the current circumstances, you've earned a lot more."

The president gave Ben a pointed look. "Well, I guess if there's anyone around to write it, we'll let history decide that."

Ben laughed. "If I have anything to say about it, and I usually do, it will be accurate and therefore flattering."

"Thank you, Ben." The president looked from Ben to Ashley. "How much did you pay him to say that?"

Ashley laughed and unconsciously reached out for Ben's hand. "Not enough, Madam President. Not enough."

President Young's grin widened. "Well, we won't go there, will we?"

Ben imagined his face was as red as Ashley's as she removed her hand from his. "No, ma'am, we sure won't," he added, trying hard not to appear amused.

Thankfully the door opened, and Larry, Sid and General Clifton strode into the room. They appeared to be even more upbeat than the last time Ben had seen them.

Ben spoke quickly before the meeting started. "Madam President, is there a chance I can make another call to my editor? I wanted to ask in front of everyone so that it wasn't a surprise."

"Well, gentlemen, what do you say?"

General Clifton glared at Ashley. "Have we added another set of ears to our meetings, Madam President?"

"Terry, please sit down and give me input on Ben's request," she said, not responding to the barb.

After a moment of silence, Sid offered, "If we can read it first, I think we have all come to trust him."

After not hearing anything to the contrary from the rest of the group, Claire looked at Ben. "You heard him. Get me the copy."

Ben thought he saw just a whisp of a smile on her face. The dynamics of the group had changed for the better in a short time. He nodded and looked back at his notes.

Larry broke the brief silence. "Madam President. I think we have some very good news for you."

"Great news, huh? I don't think anyone has used that phrase with me since I started steering this boat."

Unsure if it was intended as a joke, no one at the table, save for Ben, laughed. "Sorry, Madam President. I wasn't making light of the situation."

"Forget it, Ben. Most of my best lines are wasted on these guys." Ben was certain that her barb didn't amuse Larry, Sid or General Clifton, but they did smile, nonetheless. "So, what is this great news, Larry?"

"We just got off the horn with the commander of our forces in Montana. Using sound technique, I believe we can say definitively that there's a bomb located there. We have a solid positive lock on a radiation signature on a hill just outside the camp. In addition, they've continued their debriefing of this defector from the camp and feel confident he's telling the truth about this woman inside—Jamie, I think her name is—intending to try to detonate that bomb and take them all out."

"That is great news. But why would she do that?"

Ben was going to ask the exact same question and listened carefully for the answer.

Sid cocked his head and made a strange motion with his mouth. "Well, it's odd that I didn't think of that." An additional few seconds passed before he spoke again. "I was so happy to hear her plan, I didn't ask. I assure you I will find out and report back."

The president seemed to be as shocked as Ben by the admission from Sid. "Uh, okay. Please do." Looking over at Bobbie, then back at the table, Claire shuffled a few papers around before speaking again. "Sorry, Sid, I wasn't trying to deflate the balloon. Was there more information we needed to hear?"

It was an unusually awkward moment with the confident personalities in the room shifting around, trying to find the center again. Ben scribbled a dozen notes, most of which wouldn't be included in the news copy.

Larry smiled slyly and pulled the wireframe glasses from his face. "Let's try this again. Along with the great news from Montana, the National Guard in Alabama has pulled back and is no longer threatening our base there. Also, the Rangers in Texas have put down the uprising by the Free Texas group without any help from federal troops." Larry served up the words in a sanguine and polished voice like he had studied just the right inflection for days. He allowed his words to hang in the air for a brief moment before adding, "All in all, I would say we're more than halfway home to putting this thing down."

President Young hung her head. "Thank God." Following a short moment of silence, President Young asked Ashley to go and locate Bobbie.

Larry leaned close to Ben and whispered, "I have some news for you, too. Can we meet after this?"

Ben's heart jumped into his throat. He had tried hard not to overstep with Larry. He wanted to tell him that every minute that passed without him knowing what had happened to Chris aged him a year. Now he was close to an answer, and his spirit soared. "Absolutely. We can just stay here after the meeting."

Larry shifted in his chair, looking away briefly. "Uh... No, let's do it in my office right after this."

Ben's mind began to swim, now his stomach churned, and he thought he might get sick. Unable to speak, he simply nodded and placed his face in his hands. Ben had been around long enough to know that good news could be imparted anywhere, but bad news was done in private. His worst fears had been realized. Chris was dead.

"Ben, do you need a minute?" President Young asked, apparently having caught the exchange between them and Ben's reaction to it.

Still unable to form words, Ben simply shook his head and tried to compose himself. He was determined to finish what he had started here. Don would have finished, Chris would have finished, and dammit, he was going to finish. Under the table, Ashley gently squeezed his leg. Ben dug his fingernail into his own hand to help him refocus on the task at hand.

"Okay. Let me know if you do. So, gentlemen, what's next? Are we far enough away from the camp to be safe? Also, what kind of radiation cloud should we expect? Where will it go? Should we evacuate the population in its path?"

Sid leaned back in his chair. "We're working on all of those issues now."

General Clifton quickly added, "The troops have successfully pulled back and are at what we believe is a safe distance away."

Larry said, "We'll have answers to the rest of your questions in a few hours, Madam President."

"Do we have any clue as to when this might happen? The bomb, I mean. When it will go off?"

"No. I'm sorry to say we don't. The plan was not completely formulated when this young man left the camp. I would be guessing if I gave you a timetable."

"Take one," President Young said flatly.

Larry blinked and cocked his head. "Madam President?"

"A guess. Take one."

Larry shifted in his chair and glanced over at Sid and General Clifton. Unfortunately for him, neither of them volunteered any help. "Sometime today?"

"Good. Then tomorrow, at noon, we hold a press conference."

Larry leapt from his chair, nearly shouting, "But, Madam President—"

"Relax, Larry." She motioned for him to sit back down. "I won't say anything about the camp if it hasn't gone off. We'll cover the other items, the positives. Touch on the relief efforts and the cleanup. If, however, the camp has been dealt with, we'll announce that too."

Larry settled into his chair and appeared to gather his composure. "I can live with that."

President Young laughed softly. "I wasn't asking you for permission. Just wanted you to know."

"Of course. I just meant that sounded like a good strategy." Unlike General Clifton, Larry had always known how to avoid a confrontation when one wasn't called for.

The president closed her folder, rose and started toward her office. "Thank you, Larry, and the rest of you, too, for your hard work. If there isn't anything else, I need a power nap. For a change, I think maybe I might get a few hours without a nightmare. Wake me if anything happens before our five o'clock meeting."

The abrupt end to the meeting took Ben by surprise. He had hoped for a few minutes' warning so he could prepare for the news Larry was about to drop on him.

"You ready?" Larry asked Ben as he stood.

"No, but let's go, anyway." Ben plodded down the narrow hallway, following Larry to his office near the rear of the bunker. He tried not to think about what would be said or how he would react to it.

Larry reached the door and held it open as Ben entered. "Have a seat,

Ben." Larry made his way to a chair beside him. "We finally got some word on your son," Larry began slowly.

"So, he was killed in Chicago then?" Ben interjected before he could continue.

"No. Your son wasn't in Chicago."

Ben was perplexed but thrilled. "That—" He swallowed hard. "That's great. Oh my God, I can't believe it. I can't tell you how—"

"Wait, Ben." Larry held up a hand, cutting him off. "The only reason we know he wasn't in Chicago is that his name showed up as a last-minute addition to the list of press at the inauguration. I'm very sorry."

Ben sat staring across the room at the wall. What a cruel twist of fate it had been. Chris was out of town, just as he'd prayed would be the case. But he'd gone to where the damage was more severe. Slowly, almost imperceptibly, he began to tremble and then cry.

"I'll give you some time," Larry said as he rose to leave the room, stopping briefly to squeeze Ben's shoulder. "Let me know if there's anything I can do to help." He quietly left the room, closing the door behind him.

"Bring Chris back," Ben said to the empty room. "Bring back my son."

ARTICLE XXIX

Western Montana, January 21, 2001, 12:38 PM MST

"How did the meetings go?" Jamie asked General Boyle as he entered the cabin.

Boyle almost looked surprised to see Jamie in the cabin waiting for him. "Fine, I guess. Things aren't going as well as I would like. If I can't get this damn bomb in Denver to go off soon, they might get a bit dicey." He hung his coat on the massive oak hall tree near the door.

"What's the problem? Why can't they detonate it?" Jamie asked, probing to see if Hollis had started the plan yet.

Boyle plopped down in front of his desk. "That's a good question, sweetie. Hollis wants to meet me in private about it. He should be here soon. Can you go in the other room when he gets here, please?"

"Sure, no problem. Did you eat?"

"Yeah, we had sandwiches at the meeting. But thanks."

His endearing treatment of her was a bit unsettling. She had become accustomed to his brashness and mean tone. "You okay?"

He sat back with a sigh. "Even Christ had second thoughts."

Jamie moved closer to the desk where he'd begun shuffling papers. "Are *you* having second thoughts?"

"Doesn't matter." He waved his hand.

"Matters to me."

He stopped working and turned to face her. "Don't read too much into it. The news this morning wasn't good, and that always gives a commander pause. You start thinking about your plan, wondering if it was the right one. Could you have done anything differently? I don't doubt it was the right thing to do, just if it was the right time or the right way."

"And if it wasn't?"

Boyle turned and looked out the cabin's front window. "Then I'll go down in history as a madman. A killer, traitor, etc. It won't be true, but that's how they'll write it. The Father knows the truth, though. I'll sit at his side and watch the world continue to be overrun by Satan. Maybe one day He will even send me back—in some other body, of course—to finish the job."

"You really believe that, don't you?" Jamie asked, already knowing the answer.

"No, Jamie." He turned to face her again. "Believing and knowing are not equal. I believe you love me, but I *know* the Lord is my savior. I believe we'll win this war, but I *know* we were right to try. Can you understand that?"

Before Jamie could answer, a knock sounded on the front door. "Come in, Major," the general yelled. Jamie slowly rose from her chair and began to move toward the bedroom.

"Can you stay, please, Private?" Hollis asked as he entered.

"I thought you wanted privacy, Major?" the general said sourly. "I asked her to leave us alone."

Major Hollis didn't look at the general but kept his gaze on Jamie. "This involves her. I'd like her to hear it from the beginning."

"Is there something I should know, Jamie?" Boyle asked, searching her face.

Jamie took a few steps back toward the two men. "If there is, I don't know what."

"She doesn't know about it," Hollis stated.

Boyle motioned for Hollis to sit in the chair across from him. "Fine. Then let's hear it?"

"I've discovered what went wrong in Denver." Hollis sat down across from Boyle. "Robbins apparently started covering his ass months ago. He changed the placement location of the bomb."

"That son-of-a-bitch is dead," Boyle's spat out. "So, do we know where it is?"

"Yes. That's why I asked the Private to stay. It seems Robbins had someone he could trust inside the federal prison on the outskirts of Denver. He arranged to have the bomb placed in a boiler room off of the visitors' area." Hollis paused and appeared to be watching for Boyle's reaction. When he didn't say anything, Hollis went on.

"Once Robbins decided to chicken out, he called in a favor and had his contact transferred to the state prison in Canyon City. He was supposedly killed by a lifer the following week."

"So, you want her to go in and set it off?" Boyle asked, wildly pointing at Jamie.

"It's the only way, General. She could walk right in, go to the restroom, and crawl a short distance through a small duct to the boiler room. The timer is set four hours ahead. That's plenty of time for her to get clear before it goes. We can train her here using our bomb. Show her everything she needs to know. I think the risk will be minimal to her, or I wouldn't even suggest it."

Boyle rose to his feet and began to walk slowly around the room, his hands behind his back. Following his second circle, he stepped close to the major. Without warning, he swung full force with his open hand striking Hollis on the side of the head. Tumbling off the side of the chair, the major came to rest on the floor, glaring up at the general with disdain.

"That's for screwing this up in the first place," Boyle said through clenched teeth. A large rush of air and an agonizing grunt came from Hollis as the general kicked him hard in the ribs with his heavy boot. "And that's for making me place her life in peril." Boyle walked away calmly and sat back down hard in his chair. "Now get up off the floor."

Hollis struggled to his feet, a noticeable grimace on his face. After regaining his seat, he narrowed his eyes and stared right into the general's. "I take it that means we'll move forward with this plan. When do you want to start the training?"

"Aren't you forgetting something, Major?" Boyle asked.

"What's that, General?"

Boyle pointed at Jamie. "Asking her if she'll go."

Hollis paused briefly, undoubtedly wrestling with the correct answer and the one his pride so demanded he deliver. "Yes, sir. Of course." Looking at Jamie with more hatred than she thought possible, he asked, "Will you do it, Private?"

Jamie fought her first instinct and said nothing for a moment. "May I think about it for a little while and let you know, Major?"

Hollis slowly stood and walked toward the door. "Of course. You know where to find me."

"Thank you."

"Major," the General barked.

Hollis stopped with his hand now on the door handle. "Yes, General?"

"You're dismissed," Boyle said, his voice ugly with anger.

Without turning around, Hollis opened the heavy wooden door with a grunt. "Thank you, sir."

After the door closed behind Hollis, Jamie said, "I wish you hadn't hit him."

"I don't think clearly when it comes to you. A soldier would almost rather be shot than treated like that."

"It will blow over."

"Yeah, it will."

"I want to help. Do you think I can do it?" Apparently, not hearing or understanding, the general didn't respond to her question. "Harvey?"

"I heard you."

Jamie moved from her chair and stood across from him. "Well, what do you think?"

Boyle rose from his chair and moved to Jamie. Placing his arms around her waist, he pulled her close. "Don't ask me to decide this for you. You're far too important to me to make an impartial decision. You must go or stay based only on your gut. Trust yourself. I do."

He spoke in a warm tone Jamie hadn't ever heard from him before. She looked at this man she thought she had loved so much only a few days ago. His eyes were beginning to water, and his hands shook ever so slightly. Why had he chosen to be so evil? They might have lived a good life here, unhindered by the vile world out there. Now she must do something she hated him for, murder hundreds of people. Maybe in his mind, he could justify what he had done, much as she was doing now.

"Okay, I'll do it. For you," she finally said, knowing in her heart what she was really saying. *Okay, I will do it* to *you.*

Boyle kissed her lightly on the cheek. "Fine. I will send a message to Hollis. You should get started right away." He quickly released his grip on her, went back to his desk, picked up the radio, and began barking orders.

His behavior was strange, somehow, just different, and Jamie wondered if he hadn't hoped she would say no. That she would tell him he was too important for her to risk leaving and maybe never see him again. The longer she knew him, the less she understood him.

She turned to exit the room. Now finished on the radio, he shouted over his shoulder, "Meet them at the bomb in forty-five minutes. I need to run.

Catch you later."

Boyle retrieved his jacket and disappeared out the front door. Jamie guessed he was headed out into the woods to be alone until he had regained his composure.

She probably should use the time to pack for the trip, she thought and made her way to the bedroom. It saddened her when she realized that all her earthly possessions could be packed into such a small bag. A few changes of clothes, her wallet, and some pictures of her family were all she had left of her life. The house in Kansas City wasn't much, but it had been theirs. There was no way to keep up with the payments after Ken got arrested. So much money had gone to the lawyers, plus all the other bills and it wasn't long before the debt swamped her totally.

She remembered all too well the day the sheriff showed up to make her move out. The neighbors peering through their curtains at all their clothes and furniture sitting on the curb. She had cried for weeks. She lost the new Camaro too. Luckily, it had taken the repo man almost eight months to find the car in rural Colorado, but eventually, one morning, it was gone. She did have a few things still stored at her brother's house, but not much.

Sitting on the edge of the bed, Jamie leafed through the photographs, a few visiting the zoo with her mom and dad when she was seven or eight and several pictures of her and Ken on their honeymoon. She slid the pictures inside a small waterproof pouch and tucked them inside her bag.

The general hadn't returned yet, so she began the climb to the bomb building alone. Maybe it was her imagination running wild, but it seemed that everyone she passed knew where she was going and what had happened in the cabin with Major Hollis. Eyes that used to light up when they saw her now only stared back coldly. She hoped they would not have any time before the end to realize that she had been their undoing.

Lost in her morose thoughts, she didn't even slow down when the sentry stepped out and pointed his weapon at her.

"Oh, it's you," he said bluntly and moved back to let her pass. Jamie entered the code on the pad, and the door swung open. Three men she only casually knew were already inside, talking quietly. "Hi. Sorry, I think I'm a little early." She closed the door behind her.

"That's okay, Private," the closest man to her said. It was Lieutenant Bob Matthew, chief technician for the camp. "This is Corporal Dines and Corporal Drieth. They'll be assisting me in your training."

Jamie stepped forward and shook all three men's hands firmly. "Thank you, all. I hope I'm a quick study."

"It isn't that tough, Jamie," Bob responded. "I know that's a scary statement, but setting off one of these babies is the easy part. Getting your hands on one is the tricky part. Corporal Drieth, will you please show the private where to start?"

"Yes, sir. Step over here, please, Private."

Jamie placed herself directly in front of the bomb. "This key goes into the security lock set here." He slipped the small silver key into the lock. "We have keyed them all the same, so we didn't have to worry about losing keys or having spare ones floating around. This is the key you'll use to unlock the Denver bomb."

"Does it look the same as this one?"

"The key? It's the same. I just explained—"

"No, Corporal. I understand that. The bomb? Is it the same type?"

The Corporal smiled. "Sorry. I didn't mean to snap at you. Yes, it's exactly like this one."

"Thank you."

"No problem. Stop me anytime you have any questions. Now after I turn the key ninety degrees to the right, it will lock open. Use the key to pull the door open. Be careful not to twist or turn at this point. You might snap off the key. Pull straight up and open the lid."

"Okay," Jamie said, nodding. She was beginning to understand why the manual wasn't being used. The Corporal had committed it to memory. "Go on, please. I understand."

"Good. Now once you get the lid open, the timer and code pad are visible."

"Obviously."

"Is there something wrong, Private?" the younger corporal asked.

Jamie turned to look at him. "It's not that I'm ungrateful. I'm glad you're all helping me. But please stop treating me like I'm stupid. Concentrate on the tough stuff." The corporal looked over Jamie's shoulder at the lieutenant.

"Do as she asks, Corporal," he said, waving his hand.

"Yes, sir." The corporal turned back to the bomb. "The code pad is always locked. Two codes are needed to access the timer. The first set of codes is to unlock the pad. Press each key in order, making sure you hear a beep." The corporal turned to the other young man and took a sheet of plastic-covered paper from him. "These are the codes for all of the bombs." He stated without emotion.

"Okay."

"The first sequence is the keypad unlock."

Jamie pulled the sheet closer to her. "So, for this bomb which is it?"

"This bomb is number six, so at the bottom there," he said, pointing to the list.

"And mine?"

"Number four."

"Okay. So, I would enter this number first?" she asked, pointing to the first number of the Denver bomb.

"Yes, that's correct. Let's try this one for practice. Of course, we won't go all the way," he said with a nervous laugh.

Jamie chuckled. "No. That wouldn't be good."

The corporal moved to the side, making room for Jamie to step in. "Alright, let's unlock the pad."

Jamie turned to the bomb and the large keypad containing letters and numbers inside. Next to it, several LED lights and a red timer read *0 hours 00 Minutes 00 seconds*. Jamie read the code from the sheet aloud, not only trying to do it correctly but also memorizing it for later. "F12J987BW AS3288" Slowly, she pressed each one in sequence. Following the final number, the LED lights all flickered once, and the green *Unlocked* light stayed on.

"Whew, that was interesting," she said.

The corporal chuckled. "Not to worry. We aren't even armed yet. Now the second code—"

"What if I mess up?"

"No problem. Just press the orange reset button here," the lieutenant interjected.

"Well, twice anyway," the corporal added. "Three resets and the keypad will go dead for forty-eight hours. It's an anti-tamper safeguard. If memory serves me correctly, it will take something like nine thousand years to randomly try all of the possible combos with that in place."

"Okay, but I'll never remember all these numbers," she said, trying to sound helpless. Once again, the corporal looked back at his superior.

"She can study them here, but they don't leave the camp," he interjected with finality.

"Good," Jamie said, feeling as relieved as she sounded. "ZA3DT9JJ7. Wow, that one is shorter." She entered the code. When she finished the final number, the timer suddenly switched to read: 0 Hours 10 Minutes 00 Seconds. The red LED under *Armed* now burned brightly. "Oh, the timer is on!"

"Yes, it is. Only one more step and the bomb would be set to detonate," the corporal said calmly.

"How do I change the amount of time?" Jamie asked.

"You don't."

"But ten minutes? I can't get clear in ten minutes."

"Relax, Private. Each bomb has been preset with a detonation time. Yours will have four hours. Plenty of time to get out."

"Why is this one so short?" Jamie asked, trying to hide her fear and disappointment.

The lieutenant answered, "The general wanted to make sure that whoever lit this candle was willing to die to do it. Kind of a failsafe."

Jamie faked a smile. "Oh, yeah. That is a good idea." Her stomach turned, and she was close to getting sick all over the device. "So, what's the last step?"

"You enter the first code again," the corporal replied, "except you go in reverse order. That locks the keys again, and the timer will start. Then close the lid, lock it, and get the hell out of town. Any questions?"

Jamie fought with her insides but managed a joking tone when she said, "Yes. How do I turn this damn thing off?" All three men laughed.

"Good question." Still chuckling, the corporal said, "Enter the arming code again, which will deactivate the bomb. Then the key lock code in the right order will lock it again."

"Thanks," Jamie said with a smile. "I appreciate the help. Really I do."

"We appreciate what you're doing too."

"Thanks. May I take the codes and study them?" she asked the lieutenant.

He stood looking at her for a moment. "Only to the cabin. Thirty minutes max and no one sees them. We clear?"

"Very clear, Lieutenant. Thank you." With that, Jamie slid the paper inside her shirt, crisply saluted the three men, and left the room. She barely glanced at the sentry as she quickly made her way back to the cabin.

Her initial reaction over the diminutive number of minutes on the timer had passed, and she felt more peaceful than she had since all of this started. Maybe it was only right that she perished with them. After all, she, too, had been part of the whole thing for a long time. This was repayment time for them and her.

Opening the back door to the cabin, she was relieved to see that Harvey wasn't back yet. Locking herself in the bathroom, Jamie began to memorize the numbers she would need. Suddenly she realized how stupid it was to attempt to remember the codes. Frantic now, she searched for something to write with. In the back of the medicine cabinet, she found one of her old eyebrow pencils. Quickly she pulled down her pants and sat on the stool. Carefully she started to write the codes on her thigh. Barely halfway through the first code, she heard the front door open and close.

"Jamie? Jamie, are you here?"

"Back here, Harvey. In the bathroom. I'll be right out." She continued to copy the numbers onto her bare leg with the crude pencil. Then jumped and let out a small scream when the general rapped loudly on the door.

Laughing, he said. "I love doing that."

"Funny, Harvey. Very funny." He attempted to open the door, and she froze as she watched the knob turn around and around.

"It's locked. Let me in."

"No. Go away. I'm trying to study," she said, trying hard to finish writing.

"I'll help. Let me in."

"No," Jamie said with finality.

There was a brief pause. "Fine. I'll get the key."

She knew it would be only seconds before he gained access. Quickly she scratched out the last of the code just as he returned and slipped the key into the lock. A split second later, the door flung open, and Jamie leaped to her feet, pulling up her pants as she went. Boyle looked pleased and then suddenly quite perplexed. In terror, she followed his eyes down to the floor as the eyebrow pencil rolled slowly across the tile floor, coming to rest against the toe of his boot.

"What in the hell are you doing in here?"

"What in the hell do you think I'm doing?" Turning her back to him, she quickly flushed the toilet. "I got my period, if you must know. You want to see?"

"No, of course not. That's gross. What's with the pencil?"

"It's an eyebrow pencil. Just something I forgot when I packed earlier."

He placed his boot over the pencil and began grinding it into the floor. "Planning on making yourself up like a whore for him?" he asked through clenched teeth.

She turned to the sink and began washing her hands. "For who? Oh, you mean my husband. Christ no. I just thought I should look more like a harmless little woman than a soldier when I go in." Lying to him was becoming easier each time she did it.

"Maybe I should send someone else."

"You'll do whatever you want, I'm sure. I didn't fucking ask to go." She whirled around to face him. "However, it is strange that you can trust me to blow him up but not to see him through a window."

Boyle stepped back to allow her to pass by him into the bedroom. "Here, let me have that. I'll get it back in the lockbox," Harvey said, taking the codes from Jamie's hand as she passed. "I'm sorry. I don't want to fight.

Really, I don't," he said to her back.

"Me either."

"I want you before you go."

Jamie's mind flashed to the writing on her leg. "Oh, Harvey, I told you I got my period."

He moved up behind her. "It doesn't matter, babe. We'll put down a towel."

Jamie was desperate and determined not to have her plan go south when she was so close. Turning to face him, she said in her sexiest voice, "Isn't there something else I can do just for you?"

"You would do that?" he asked in amazement.

He had asked her many times for that special favor, but she had always held that as something she only did with her husband. What did it matter now? She would be dead before the day was out.

"It would be my pleasure," Jamie said as she began to lower herself to her knees.

The general cooed and reached past her to slam the bedroom door shut.

ARTICLE XXX

Washington DC, January 21, 2001, 3:02 PM EST

"There is no way I can climb that rope, Mike. No way," Sally groaned.

Mike stepped out onto the roof of the elevator and looked up into the dark shaft. "Any ideas, TJ?"

"I'll send up two men. We can tie her off and pull her up."

Mike walked back into the hallway where Sally sat. "Does that sound okay? You think you can make it?"

"Do I have any options? I can't fly and sure as hell don't want to stay down here."

Sally's pain was obviously intense, and Mike cursed himself for not bringing any painkillers with him. "Does it hurt a lot?"

Her eyes flared. "What the hell do you think? It's killing me, and I'm sick to my stomach to boot." Lowering her head, she spoke quietly. "Sorry. I know this isn't your fault. I can't begin to explain how much I hate you having to take care of me. Please just get me out of here."

"I didn't take it personally. We'll get you out, don't worry."

"I'll go up first," Billy said, walking toward the dangling rope.

TJ held his arm out and placed it against Billy's chest. "No, hero, you go up last. You go up first, and no one will see you again."

Billy got in TJ's face by shoving his chest into TJ's arm. "You really think I would leave them down here?" Billy asked, pointing at Mike and Sally.

"I think you would leave your mother down here if it served your mission. Now, back off."

His stare fixed on TJ, Billy turned and walked away. TJ barked,

"Whisner, Meach, up the rope. Take a second to make sure it's secure up there, and then prepare to pull her up. Got it?"

"Got it, Sarge," both men shot back in unison.

With the ease of mountain climbers, the two men scampered up the two floors inside the shaft. After a few moments, one of the men leaned into the shaft, gave a quick whistle, and a thumbs-up. TJ nodded at Mike.

"Okay, Sally, let's get you out of here," Mike said, grasping her good arm to help her up off the floor.

"Be easy, please."

"We will. I promise."

TJ wove the rope around her waist and through her legs, creating a saddle of sorts. "Does that feel okay?" he asked, checking the ropes to ensure the knots would hold.

"Yeah, it's alright. Don't drop me."

"My guys are the best," TJ said with a wink.

She smiled. "Good. Let's do it."

"You got it. Now, keep your legs on the wall, and use your good hand to steady yourself and protect your arm." TJ pulled firmly on the rope twice. "Slowly," he shouted up the shaft, and Mike watched as Sally began the journey moving six or eight inches with each tug on the rope.

Suddenly, with Sally only a few feet from the top, gunshots rang out. The sound echoed down the shaft, followed closely by the falling body of one of TJ's men. Narrowly missing Mike, he hit with a sickening thud on top of the elevator car. Mike glanced up in time to see Sally slide back down the shaft six or seven feet stopping with a jerk. More shots rang out from above, these sounding as though they came from the one remaining Marine TJ sent up. Then silence, deafening silence.

Mike strained to see through the smoke now hanging in the shaft. "Sally?

Sally, can you hear me? Are you okay?" There was only silence.

TJ kept his weapon pointed at the opening above while he leaned down and checked the young Marine for a pulse. "I think he's had it," he said sadly. "Doc, please double-check for me. Meach, you okay?"

"Yeah, Sarge, I'm here. I got him. Is Gary okay?"

TJ looked down at Mike, who was checking on Whisner. Mike just shook his head. "No, sorry, Soldier. He's gone."

"Damn idiot getting himself shot," Meach said flatly. "I'm in a bit of a jam up here, too, Sarge," he said after a short pause.

"You hit?" TJ asked.

"No, the rope was wrapped around my arm. When it caught, I think it broke my wrist. Hurts like hell."

TJ placed his M-16 on the body lying beside him and put on his gloves. "I'm coming up. Can you see Sally? Is she alive?" he asked as he spit on the dry leather gloves.

"Can't tell, Sarge. Got my weight away from the door and my foot against the jam so she doesn't pull me in. I can't feel any movement on the rope, though."

Mike stayed quiet and tried not to panic. He glanced over at Billy, who stood with his weight against a wall, his face expressionless. Mike wanted badly to hit him. The whole reason for his mission wasn't making any sense. What was driving Billy to be so callous? Mike was determined to find out. Perhaps TJ could beat it out of him.

TJ wrapped his legs around the cables running down the center of the shaft and began pulling himself up. After only a few seconds, he reached the area where Sally dangled. Reaching out with one hand, he checked for a pulse. "She's alive, Doc. Got caught on a piece of steel. I think that's what actually stopped her from falling. She does have a pretty ugly cut on her leg from it, though."

A few drops of blood fell, striking Mike in the cheek as he looked up. Mike blinked, wiped away the blood, and quickly moved a bit to the left. Even more panicked now, he hurriedly asked, "How bad, TJ?"

"Can't tell. I'm going on to the top. Should I lower her back down there or bring her up?" he asked between grunts.

Mike rubbed his head, pondering the best course. "Take her up if it's safe. Then get me the rope quick. Put some pressure on the cut as soon as you can, okay?"

"Got it, Doc. I'm up now, so hang on a minute."

Mike glanced down at the area where he stood. A small pool of blood had begun to form from the steady drip of Sally's life force. "Hurry, TJ. There's no time to be gentle. She's out of it anyway."

About ten long seconds later, TJ finally spoke. "I got her, Doc. Here comes the rope."

Mike grabbed the rope as it dropped. Absent his usual hesitation, he started the climb, finding footholds along the wall. Suddenly, his grip on the rope slipped. The blood from Sally's leg had soaked it completely, making it difficult to hang on to, and he struggled to keep from falling. Using every ounce of his strength, Mike tightened his grip, found a better foothold, and pulled himself up. At last, his hand reached the edge of the floor above. Sighing audibly, he made one final pull and crawled out of the shaft.

Talk about the world not making any sense. Sally, one of the best FBI field agents in the country, had been kidnapped, beaten, crushed and now cut. And soft, desk jockey Mike, not a scratch so far. Who the hell was in charge of this insane event. Mike scrambled to where TJ hovered over Sally a few feet away. "Thanks, I got her, TJ."

Mike was relieved to see that Sally's eyes were open. A tear slowly made its way down her cheek. "It's going to be okay, babe. I'm here now," he whispered and replaced TJ's hand over the cut in her leg with his.

TJ stood and placed a hand on Mike's shoulder. "I'll get the rest of them up. I need to get the body up, too. I'm not leaving him here to rot. You alright?"

"Yeah, thanks. Seems like every fifteen minutes, I owe you another one."

TJ just smiled back. "We all owe something, Doc. So far, I owe God two Marines. That's my job," he said as he turned and walked away.

Mike lifted his now bloody hand from the cut on her leg. A deep, three-inch gash on her outer thigh still oozed a good deal of blood, but it wasn't an artery, something Mike had feared. She was going to be alright and would live to snap at him another day.

He turned back toward TJ and the others. "As soon as my bag makes it up, I need it, okay?"

"She going to make it?" TJ asked softly. Mike was so full of emotion that he didn't attempt to speak, so he winked and gave TJ a thumbs-up. TJ returned his smile and turned back to the shaft. A few minutes later, Billy, the remaining Marine, Whisner's body, and their gear had been hoisted to the top floor. Mike firmly bandaged Sally's wound and helped her sit upright.

"What happened?" she asked, her voice weak. "Who did the shooting?"

Mike had been so involved with her that he hadn't asked or noticed what else was going on around them. "Not sure yet. TJ, do we know who was shooting?"

TJ moved closer to them and lowered his voice. "Yeah. Just one man. At least this time, it appears to be one of the bad guys. He's not security or regulation army. He was wearing a homemade uniform and using a cheap semi-auto. He's either ARA or an opportunist looking for money or guns."

Mike shook his head. "The world goes from strange to more bizarre with each passing hour."

"Right you are. So, what do you say we get the hell out of here before it gets dark?"

"Couldn't be too soon for me," Sally said, smiling.

Before leaving, Mike took a minute to look at Meach's wrist. Luckily it wasn't broken. Mike wrapped it tight with an ace bandage to hold down the swelling. "You good to go?" he asked the young soldier.

Meach popped to his feet. "Won't slow me down a bit."

TJ broke into a large grin. "Move out," he snapped.

Mike helped Sally to her feet, and they made their way slowly back to the half-track. Once there, the Marines began loading their gear in the back, and Mike asked Sally to sit facing out on the back seat so he could check on her leg.

Without warning, from behind the open door, Billy grabbed Mike around the shoulders and head, placing his knife against his exposed throat. Maneuvering Mike around to place his body between himself and the Marines, Billy shouted, "Sergeant. We need to talk. Now."

"Billy, what the hell are you doing? Mike asked, trying not to move as he spoke.

"Shut up, Mike. This is between him and me."

TJ now stood a few feet away. "Well, if it's between you and me, why is the doc the one with a knife to his throat?"

"All I want is to go after the plates. Oh, and by the way, the files stay with me."

"Out of the question. What is your obsession with the files?" TJ glared at Billy. "There's something fishy with you, boy. What's in those files, Billy?"

"That's not your concern. Do you want him to die?" Billy said, increasing the pressure on the knife blade, causing Mike to wince.

"That stupid act would be followed promptly by your own slow and painful death," TJ shot back.

Billy pulled Mike's head back even harder. "You dumb bastard. I'm not afraid to die."

"That's good," Sally said just before pulling the trigger on the Glock placed against the back of Billy's head.

ARTICLE XXXI

Denver, Colorado, January 21, 2001, 2:03 PM MST

It was so quiet that even the gentle knock on his door startled him. "May I come in, Ben?" President Young asked.

Straightening his clothes, Ben rose from his chair. "Of course, Madam President."

"Relax, and sit down, please. This isn't an official visit. I just came by to let you know how saddened I was to hear about your son."

"Thank you. That means a great deal." He returned to his seat. "I think I've known since I first heard about the explosions, but I kept holding out some hope."

"Hope is all we have now." She sat down on the small bed. "I'll tell you something no one else knows. Needless to say, I would trust that it never goes any further."

"If it's of a personal nature, it won't."

Staring at the wall behind him, she began, "His name was Gary, actually Gerald Wayne Atkinson, Assistant Field Director at HUD. We had to keep it quiet with him working in my agency and all. I didn't even tell my family or friends. Never wanted to place them in a position of having to lie for me. But, next week, after my term had ended and his move to the Department of Transportation had been approved, we were going to announce our engagement," she whispered, fighting back tears.

"I had just spoken to Gary yesterday morning. His voice was so full of love and joy. Said he missed me and couldn't wait to hold me again. Wanted to walk down the street holding my hand and scream from the top of the Washington Monument that I was his lady. His seats for the inauguration were in the front row." No longer able to hold back her emotion, she broke down and cried quietly.

Ben got up and sat beside her on the bed, unsure what to say to her. "I'm very sorry, Claire. I know from my own experience there isn't anything I can say to ease the pain. No words can do that, not for me anyway."

Battling to regain her composure, she wiped her eyes and looked up at him. "We aren't alone in this, you know. Nearly everyone lost someone they knew or loved. Regenerating the bricks and steel will be the easy part. Rebuilding our lives and the country's soul... That will be the challenge."

Unable to speak, Ben simply nodded.

After a long pause, Claire added, "Maybe it's better that we know the pain firsthand. We might not be as likely to forget how they feel or lose sight of the personal side of destruction. I know I talk a good game, always pretending to be tough and in control. I'm scared they'll see it on my face, see how afraid I really am."

Following another brief silence between them, Claire said, "At first, I thought, we can't possibly survive this. There isn't anything I can do to make this better. Then I thought of Europe after the war. Their countries had been bombed beyond recognition. They had no infrastructure, no economy, millions dead, wounded, and homeless. They did what they had to do. It wasn't easy, and it didn't happen overnight, but it can be done. We'll do it too. From the time our country was founded more than two hundred years ago, we've rebuilt dozens of destroyed countries around the world. Now it's time to rebuild ours."

Ben wasn't sure if she was talking to him or at him, but it certainly had changed her mood. Emerging from her own anguish, President Young once again shouldered the country's collective sorrow.

Now standing, she looked him directly in the eyes. "We will make it through this. I promise you that."

"I know we will. Thank you for taking the time to stop by."

"We all need friends, Ben. I hope I can always count you as one of mine."

Ben chuckled. "We might have to change our professions for that to happen. A bit like the spider and the fly hanging out together."

She nodded and returned the smile. "I know, I know, and I'm the spider, but I'll try hard to have the most open and honest government possible. Part of this mess can be blamed on how we've handled things over the last twenty years or so. Not excused," she added when Ben looked up at her with a raised brow. "Never excused. What Boyle has done is pure evil. But guys like Terry and Sid created the atmosphere for him to flourish and convince others to follow him. If you think my relationship with them is rocky now, wait until I start changing the way they do business."

"I would like to be a fly on the wall for that."

"Maybe you will be. Maybe you will be." She rose and started toward the door. "I need to go now. I have a lot to do before the five o'clock. Are you coming to that?" she asked, opening the door.

"Of course, Madam President. I'll be there." Ben hadn't ever really believed in fate or, for that matter, God. But the greatness of this woman and the fortune of the country to have her now, could it really be all luck?

ARTICLE XXXII

Washington DC, January 21, 2001, 3:25 PM EST

Silence hung in the air following the click of the hammer from Sally's weapon as it struck home. "That was to let you know that I will do it," Sally said as she pulled the slide back, cranking a live round into the chamber. "This one is for real."

Billy drew in a deep breath. "Come on, Sally. It's me."

"I know. That's why I have to be the one to stop you. I'm responsible for you being on this mission, and I talked Mike into it under false pretenses. Right now, his life means more to me than yours, or mine for that matter. His motives for being here are the only ones that are truly pure. If it means that you die and I go to jail for him to live, then so be it. Now drop the knife, or I will drop you."

"You would do it, wouldn't you?"

"You know I will."

Billy slowly released his grip on Mike's neck as he reached over his shoulder and handed Sally the knife. "There. Now, aren't we just one big happy family again?"

Mike grabbed Billy's arm, ripping it from around him. "Take your fucking hands off me."

Sally moved directly in front of Billy. "TJ is on to something. All of this just doesn't make sense. What's in those files, Billy?"

Billy slumped against the wall, his legs no longer supporting his weight. Mike could see the turmoil on his face. After looking at the ground for what seemed like an eternity, he finally spoke in a strange low tone. "Things. Dangerous Things. Things you don't want to know about. Things about doing the hard work of keeping us safe. Things people will kill you for knowing. Things I will take to my grave."

"It doesn't have to be like that now," Mike said. "Most of those people are gone. Let's start fresh."

Billy looked up at Mike and shook his head. "You stupid bastard, I am one of those people. Many of the things in there, I did."

TJ took a step closer to Billy. "Okay, enough of this crap. We can get the gory details later. Meach front and center. Escort this piece of shit to the back and put him inside. If he doesn't do everything you say, shoot him."

"Yes, sir," the Marine answered, already moving up to cover Billy.

"Any questions, hero?" TJ asked.

"You be the boss, Sarge."

TJ turned and started toward the other side of the vehicle. "Good. Then let's load up and move out."

Mike rubbed his neck where the knife blade had been. "He's crazy, you know? Sally, please tell me you weren't in on any of this shit."

Sally reached out to touch Mike's arm. "I'm sorry, Mike, really I am. You know I wasn't. Since he appears to be one of them, I doubt if the boys in charge will do anything to him, but I intend to write it up. Believe me."

"Even the last part?" Mike asked.

"Just like it happened."

"Let's go, Doc," TJ shouted from inside the vehicle.

Mike got in and slammed the heavy steel door. "Mind a suggestion?" he asked TJ.

"What's on your mind?"

"The chopper," Mike said, watching TJ's eyes.

TJ took his hands off the wheel. "What about it?"

Mike shifted around in the seat, partially facing him. "I was just thinking that by the time we get back to the base, it'll be well after dark. The trip up here wasn't all that much fun in the daylight. But we could have the chopper pick us up at four thirty without any problem. It's only a few miles to the west, and we'd have an hour to get there."

TJ sat looking out the front window, tapping his finger on the steering wheel. "What about the half-track? I wouldn't want them to get their hands on it."

"We disable it," Sally said from the back seat.

TJ began to nod slowly. "Okay. It makes sense. Let's give it a try." He started the noisy diesel engine and placed it in gear.

"TJ, wait a second," Mike shouted over the roar.

"What is it now?"

Mike broke into a large grin. "Just wanted to put my seat belt on," he said, snapping himself tightly in.

"Smart ass," TJ shot back, trying hard not to smile.

Moving further from the center of the city, the rubble became less of an obstacle to travel, and they made considerably better time than they had anticipated, even driving on the street some of the time. A scant forty minutes later, they approached the area where the chopper was scheduled to meet Billy.

"This is close enough," TJ said, shutting off the ignition switch. "It should be that empty field over there."

Mike groaned softly as he released the catch on the seat belt. "They sure don't build these things for comfort, do they?"

"Try it with your leg half ripped off and a broken arm," Sally said only half-jokingly.

Mike hopped out and opened her door. "Sorry. Let me have a look at that." He reached inside for her leg.

"Stop poking at me," she demanded. "The bleeding has stopped, and it only hurts when you mess with it. My arm, however, is killing me. If you even think of touching that, I'll shoot you in the head."

Mike smiled broadly. "I can always tell when you're feeling better. You change from a really bad patient to the bitch I know and love."

"Doc!" TJ yelled from the other side of the vehicle. "Over here."

Mike hustled around the hood and stood next to TJ. "What is it?"

"Hush up, be quiet and listen."

Standing as still as possible, Mike strained to detect what TJ had heard. The voice was so soft it was barely audible, but Mike heard it. "Help. Please help me."

"Where's it coming from?" Mike whispered.

"That car over there just off the road. Down in that small ravine." TJ pointed to a car that had evidently struck the corner of a building, then fell into a large drainage area.

Mike began to move toward the car, but TJ grabbed him by the shoulder, pulling him back. "Wait." TJ turned and tapped on the half-track. A few seconds later, Meach emerged. Using hand signals, he motioned him to circle around behind the suspect car while TJ approached from this side. Carefully the two men crept toward the abandoned car. Several times Mike heard the diminutive cry for help. Close enough to nearly touch the car, both men sprung upright, pointing their weapons inside. Seconds later, TJ lowered his rifle and motioned for Mike to proceed.

"What do we have?" Mike asked, striding quickly up to the door.

"Just somebody hurt. Fricking miracle he's still alive."

"God, am I happy to see you," the young man said, his voice weak.

Mike strained hard to pry open the passenger door. "Where are you hurt?" he asked as he crawled inside the small car.

"My leg. It's pinned against the other door." Mike began checking him over. He was young, maybe in his twenties. I few facial cuts from the flying glass made for ugly-looking wounds, but they weren't life-threatening.

"You have any pain in your neck or back?" Mike asked as he felt up and down the young man's spine. "No, I think that's all okay, and I never lost consciousness."

"Good. That's good. Can you feel or move your leg?"

"Wish I couldn't. Hurts to beat hell."

"Okay. All we need to do is get you out of here." Turning to TJ, Mike said, "So how in the world are we going to do that? We could sure use the Jaws of Life right now."

TJ leaned inside the car behind Mike. "The winch on the half-track might do it."

Mike perked up. "Great idea. Let's move it over on the other side, pull from there."

"You got it."

TJ jogged away, and Mike returned his attention to the injured young man. "Alright, I think we have a pretty good plan to get you out. I need you to relax. Okay?"

"Thanks, Doctor. Hey, what's your name? Doctor, what?"

"Mike Jenkins, just Mike to you. What's yours?" Mike asked, stretching to shake the young man's hand.

"Chris Bleser. I'm from Chicago."

"Work here?" Mike asked.

Chris chuckled and then winced in pain. "No. In fact, this is my first visit to DC, and I can't say as I care much for it to tell you the truth."

Mike smiled back. "Know what you mean, Chris. I didn't like it much when it was in one piece."

TJ positioned the half-track so it was pointed directly at the crushed car, and Meach tried to stretch the now slack cable. However, his wrist wasn't strong enough to get it down to the car. TJ jumped out and finished wrapping it several times around the doorframe. After he had tied it off securely, he nodded to Mike.

"You ready to try this, Chris?" Mike asked him.

"I've got nothing to lose. Sure don't want to stay here."

Mike motioned for TJ to begin drawing the cable back toward him. "This might hurt a bit. Let me know if it gets too bad." Chris nodded, closed his eyes, and squeezed Mike's hand a little harder.

Mike decided to try to talk to him and keep his mind off the pain. "How did it happen?"

Chris opened his eyes and looked a bit surprised by Mike's question. "If you mean the explosion, I haven't got a clue. But if you mean, how did I get down here. It was luck and reflex, I guess. The trip was last minute, so I had to rent a car. Stupid thing broke down two nights ago in Claysville, P.A. Long story short, I was running late for the inauguration, hauling ass into the city, and suddenly I catch this flash of light out of the corner of my eye." Chris stopped briefly, wincing as the sound of tearing metal creaked.

"And?" Mike prodded.

Focusing again, Chris continued. "I hit the brakes and turned the wheel, just reflex, you know? Ended up slamming into that damn wall. But I guess it saved my ass by sending me into this hole. When the blast came through. Most of it went over me. It was still enough to take out the side window and burn me a bit."

"You work for the government?" Mike asked.

"Worse. I'm a reporter," Chris said with a groan.

Mike laughed just as the door flew open with a loud snap. "You okay?"

"Yes. What a relief it is to have that off," Chris said, placing his head down on the seat.

"Great. Hang on. I'm going to go around to the other side to look at that leg before we try to move you. Okay?"

"Yes, of course. But, if it isn't there or just hanging by a thread, I don't want to know about it."

Mike trotted to the opposite side of the car, squeezing past Meach, who was carefully untying the cable from the door. The leg was bruised and swollen but didn't appear to be broken or badly cut. "It looks pretty good, Chris. Do you want to try and walk on it?"

Chris began to shift his weight toward the door and reached for Mike's arms. "Let's give it a shot."

Unsteadily at first and then with more strength, Chris stood and began placing weight on his leg. "How does that feel? Is there any sharp pain?" Mike asked, still concerned about a broken bone.

Chris winced slightly as he took a step, using Mike to keep him balanced. "Dull pain. Doesn't feel like it's broken. Sore as hell, but I expected that."

"Cool. Now let's get you over to the truck." Mike steered him toward the half-track, continuing to take some of Chris's weight as they traversed the ten or fifteen yards. "Sit down in here," he said, opening the driver's side rear door.

"Welcome to the cripple section," Sally said as he entered.

"Don't mind her. She's in a bit of a bad mood," Mike said, grinning at Chris. "But then again, she's been in a bad mood since 1988."

"You're hysterical," Sally said in her best sarcastic voice and turned to look out the window.

Mike winked and shrugged at Chris as he finished getting him settled. "I'll get you some radiation pills from my pack, Chris. You were lucky but still likely got a pretty heavy dose."

"Don't get too comfortable, Doc," TJ barked. "I hear the chopper. Meach, lay down some white smoke and let them know we're here."

Meach jogged to the edge of the field, drew a small canister from his pocket, used his good hand to pull the top, and heaved it into the grass. A cloud of thick white smoke soon began to billow into the twilight sky.

"TJ, if you can help Chris, I'll get Sally," Mike shouted.

"Okay, Doc. Meach, get the hero out of the back," TJ commanded as he reached in and snatched Chris from the seat.

A few yards from the edge of the field, Mike caught sight of the helicopter flying low toward them. The crackle of small arms fire echoed from a few blocks away, and Mike froze in his tracks. "Are they shooting at the chopper?" he yelled to TJ.

"Don't think so. It's coming from the other direction." TJ turned back to look for Meach.

Meach had just started toward them but didn't have Billy with him. "Where's the hero?" TJ shouted, trying to be heard over the ever-increasing noise from the helicopter.

"Gone, Sarge. Sorry. Must have slipped out while we were opening the car door."

"Dumb, bastard. Well, there isn't any time to look for him. He's on his own now."

Mike nodded in agreement as he stared into the darkness. Thinking to himself, *What a waste no part of his stupid secret mission was accomplished. It was all for nothing.*

TJ turned to Meach and shouted as loud as he could, "Stand by the half-track and drop a grenade in it when I give you the signal." Moving closer to Mike so they could hear, he said, "I don't want to blow it until they've landed. They might think it's an attack, or we might need it in case something happens to the bird before it gets down."

Mike nodded and gave TJ a thumbs-up.

The army helicopter landed gently in front of them. Mike and TJ fought the wind from the blades as they helped Sally and Chris inside.

Once Chris was in, TJ stuck his head into the front door. "My man is going to blow the track, so don't get excited, okay?" The pilot nodded in acknowledgment. TJ signaled Meach and jumped in the chopper. Dropping the grenade in the front seat, Meach ran full speed toward them, diving inside just seconds after the fireball engulfed the vehicle. "Hit it," TJ yelled to the pilot after they were all safely inside.

Mike began to relax a bit as they rose gradually from the ground. Shortly after takeoff, the chopper started pitching its nose forward as the pilot headed for home. This angle provided Mike an excellent view of the ground below. About a block from the landing site, he noticed several figures moving below them.

"TJ, look over there," he said, pointing. TJ tapped the pilot on the shoulder and pointed to the men below. Taking a wide turn, the pilot brought them back over the spot and hovered.

"It's Billy," Mike yelled, seeing him crouched behind a concrete block of rubble. Mike had just gotten the words out of his mouth when another man stepped from behind a nearby wall and began emptying his automatic weapon into Billy. Dust flew from his clothing, and his body jerked violently as the bullets ripped through him. His body left behind a gruesome trail of blood as it slid down the side of the block, then fell slowly face-first into the dirt.

"Bastards," Mike said softly.

TJ shook his head. "Captain, have you got any rockets?" he yelled to the pilot.

"Full load, Sergeant. Where do you want them?"

"Right on top of them," TJ yelled.

"You got it." She maneuvered the ship into firing position. The chopper rocked back slightly as four or five hissing rockets launched from underneath. Several large explosions lit up the darkening sky in front of them as the fireballs rose from the ground.

TJ patted the pilot on the shoulder. "Nice shooting, Captain. Now, let's go home." Returning the smile, the pilot headed the ship back to the safety of the base. TJ leaned close to Mike's ear. "I guess he got what he wanted."

"Yeah, I guess so. But, after all that crap, we don't even have the damn files."

TJ grinned widely. "Yes, we do. They're right here in my pack," he said, patting the green sack on his lap.

Mike smiled. "You want to come over for dinner tomorrow?"

"I'd love to. I'll even bring the beer."

ARTICLE XXXIII

Western Montana, January 21, 2001, 4:00 PM MST

"I need to go over to the main building and get the rest of my briefing for the mission," Jamie said as she made her way toward the door.

General Boyle stopped pouring his coffee. "You'll come back before you leave, won't you?"

Knowing this would be the last time she ever saw him, she looked him straight in the eyes. "Of course."

"Okay. See you in a bit."

"Goodbye, Harvey."

Jamie made her way slowly up the hill, taking time to breathe the air, enjoy the view, and soak up as much of the last few minutes of her life that she could. How strange it was to be relieved about one's own death. She had always imagined the day Ken would be released, meeting him at the gate, wrapping him in her arms, and kissing him for hours. Right now, he would be sitting in his cell, unaware of what she was about to do. Maybe he would never know that she had done the right thing, never find out about her sacrifice. But she would know, wherever it was she was going, she would know.

Her heart beat a bit faster as the small building came into sight. The sentry stepped from behind a tree and blocked her path. "What are you doing up here again?"

"That's none of your business."

"Look, I know who and what you are, but don't use that tone with me. Understand?"

Jamie decided to take a different track with him this time around. She needed quick access without raising his suspicions. "You saw me up here with the technical team this afternoon?"

"Yeah."

"And you know what they're trained to do?"

"I do."

"There's a bomb out there," she said, pointing away from the camp. "In a city that I can't talk about. I'm going out to set it off. I won't say any more than that."

"That explains a lot. I had no idea." He finally said, "Go ahead on in. Oh and Jamie."

"Yes?"

"Good luck," the sentry said as he gave her a quick informal salute.

"Thank you." She nodded and quickly made her way past him. Closing the heavy door, she fell hard against it and let out a massive sigh. Thankfully, someone had left the light on, and she wouldn't have to search for the pull string.

Mustering every ounce of her strength, she walked over to the bomb. Reaching into her pocket, she extracted the silver key and opened the lid covering the keypad. "Breathe, Jamie," she reminded herself as she lowered her pants to read the codes she had written there earlier. It turned out to be a good plan since Harvey snatched the codes away from her at the cabin.

"F-1-2-J-9-8-7-B-W-A-S-3-2-8-8 to unlock," she said aloud. "And to arm, Z-A-3-D-T-9-J-J and J-J— Oh shit," she exclaimed. She was unable to read the last character in the code. Boyle's interruption had caused her to write quickly and, unfortunately, illegibly.

"Come on, Jamie. Try harder." She sucked in a breath and exhaled slowly. "Okay, it's a one, maybe, or a Z, perhaps even a seven." Jamie swore again silently. She would have to try them all until one worked. Then the Corporal's words played in her head. *Three resets and the keypad will go dead for forty-eight hours."*

She had better be right by the third time. That much was for sure. Trembling slightly, she entered the first code. The keypad flickered, and the green *Unlocked* LED burned brightly. Slowly she began to attempt the arming code, Z-A-3-D-T-9-J J. "Now for the last..."

But which one should she try first? Saying a quick prayer, Jamie pushed the letter Z as the last of the sequence.

The timer remained dark.

Disappointed, she pressed the reset button and began again, this time finishing with a one. Once again, the timer failed to light. Jamie slumped. How much of this could she take? One more wrong code and it would be over. She'll have failed everyone counting on her.

Drawing in another deep breath, she reset the pad and tried again. Her finger shook so badly it nearly slipped off the seven key when she pushed it. What must have been only a fraction of a second seemed like an eternity as the timer came to life.

00 Hours 10 Minutes 00 Seconds

"Thank God."

After taking a moment to compose herself, she entered the correct code in reverse order. Following a distinctive click, the timer began its deliberate journey toward zero. Completing the sequence, Jamie re-locked the keypad. Glancing at the timer one more time, she pulled the lid closed.

00 Hours 09 Minutes 06 Seconds

Locking the lid, she tossed the key on the ground behind the bomb, turned around and sank into the chair. Certainly, she could only get a mile or so from the camp before the explosion, so why bother? She would stay here. It would be sudden, painless, and soon.

00 Hours 08 Minutes 35 Seconds

***

"She left here thirty minutes ago," the general told Hollis. "Said she was going to the main building."

"I just left there, sir. She never showed up."

"So, where the hell did she go?"

Hollis shifted from one foot to the other. "I have a report that she was headed up the hill toward the bomb."

"Be careful, Major."

"I'm not trying to imply anything, General. Just passing along the information I received."

"So, what do you suggest?" Boyle asked, lifting his eyes to stare straight at Hollis.

Hollis shifted to his other foot and cleared his throat. "I was hoping you might go up and see if she's okay."

Boyle narrowed his eyes and furrowed his brow. "Fine. I'll go get her and bring her to you."

"Thank—

"Dismissed," the general said, cutting him off in mid-sentence. Hollis turned and left the general standing in the cabin.

Snatching his coat off the rack, the general stepped outside and lit one of his cigars. "Damn that woman. What the hell is wrong with her?" He blew a smoke ring into the crisp air. After a few more long draws on his stogie to calm himself, he dropped it on the ground and marched quickly up the rocky path.

"Is she in there?" he asked the sentry.

The sentry snapped to attention. "Yes, sir."

"Thank you, Soldier. At ease," Boyle said as he began to enter the code needed to open the door.

***

00 Hours 01 Minutes 02 Seconds

Jamie jumped to her feet as the creaking door swung open. "Harvey! What the hell are you doing up here?"

"I came to get you. You're late."

"Oh yeah. Right. Let's go then." She moved quickly toward the door, but Boyle held his hand up to stop her from advancing.

"What have you been doing up here?" he asked, slightly cocking his head and peering hard into her eyes.

"Nothing. Just thinking. I uh…needed to be alone."

Glancing at the bomb, the general saw the light indicating it was activated.

00 Hours 00 Minutes 48 Seconds

"My God. What have you done?" he asked with terror in his eyes.

No longer afraid of him, she answered calmly, "What I had to do."

"Disarm it," he shouted, pulling his sidearm out of its holster.

She backed toward the desk "I can't do that.".

"Then I will."

"I won't give you the codes," Jamie fired back in defiance.

00 Hours 00 Minutes 23 Seconds

The deafening roar of the gun echoed in the small room. The bullet struck Jamie in the shoulder, throwing her on top of the desk and splattering blood on the wall behind her.

"I don't need your help. I have a key and the codes," Boyle roared, his eyes now narrowed and angry. "Don't make me shoot you again," he added as he moved across the room to the bomb.

00 Hours 00 Minutes 13 Seconds

Boyle fumbled for his key, finally inserting it into the lock and opening the lid. His eyes widened, and his shoulders fell as he read the timer.

00 Hours 00 Minutes 05 Seconds

Turning to Jamie, he raised the gun and pointed it at her head. "You stupid bitch."

Jamie smiled. "See you in hell, Harvey."

00 Hours 00 Minutes 00 Seconds

***

A thousand miles away, in the monitoring room of the National Earthquake Center, Boulder, Colorado, an intern muted the pinging alarm.

"What is it?" the assistant director asked, entering the small room and sliding his reading glasses down to the end of his nose.

"A pretty good shaker. Up north, somewhere near Western Montana, maybe. A four-point-nine, perhaps five-point-oh," the young woman responded as she examined the readout.

"Hmm. Western Montana, huh? Well, at least there isn't anyone out there."

Smiling, the woman nodded. "Anyone you want me to call?"

Sliding his glasses into place, he turned and began walking back to his office. "Nope. Everybody has enough on their plate right now. It can wait until morning."

ARTICLE XXXIV

Denver, Colorado, January 21, 2001, 4:41 PM MST

Ben sat down at the table for what he knew may be the last time. He had heard the news. It was wonderful, it was horrific, it was more death. It ended just as it began, in a blinding flash and people dying.

The rest of the group finished filing in, and the president finally spoke. "So, it's over then," she said, bowing her head.

"For the most part, yes," Larry replied. "We have a few mop-up issues, but the last bomb has been recaptured. With Boyle out of the way, the remaining scattered resistance should fold quickly."

"I thought I would be happier," she said aloud. There was a brief pause as everyone at the table tried to digest their own feelings. "Sorry about that," President Young said finally. "We stopped them, and that's what counts in the end. He started it. We finished it."

"Everyone did what they had to do, Madam President," General Clifton said in a low reflective tone.

"Yes, they did. I'd like to thank all of you here for your hard work and loyalty. Now it's time to get ready for the rest of it, the rebuilding and cleanup. I'll need a few things for the press conference tomorrow from you, gentlemen."

"Of course, Madam President. Name it," Larry said.

"First, the complete report on who, where, and how the weapons were obtained."

"Not for the press conference, Madam President?" General Clifton exclaimed.

"Yes, for the press conference, General."

"I can never agree to the release of that information to the public."

"It's not your decision."

"I would have to side with the general here," Sid interjected. "This could be damaging to national security."

President Young swung her gaze to Sid. "Not your call either, Sid."

"But," Larry began, "Madam President—"

"Stop. Stop right there, all of you," President Young shouted. "I'm thankful you all agreed to come out of retirement to help, and if you choose not to remain with me, I'll understand. But this is my government, and things are going to change. The old rules don't apply any longer. Things have been so damn secret that I don't think anyone actually knows what's going on. Somehow in this great secret vacuum, Boyle got his hands on seven warheads, transported them all over the country and damn near destroyed our way of life." She paused briefly and rose to her feet. "Now we are going to try it my way. Christ, we share more secrets with the Russians than we do the American people," she said, pounding her fist on the table.

"Consider this my formal resignation," General Clifton said defiantly.

"Accepted," President Young snapped. "Larry? Sid? What's it going to be?"

Larry looked up at her and smiled. "I think I'll stay awhile."

"Me too," Sid added.

"Good." Claire visibly relaxed a little and let out a breath. "Thank you. General, unless you want to reconsider, you may leave."

Terry rose from his chair. "Thank you, Madam President. I'll leave the formal papers on my desk."

"You're welcome, General. And if you don't mind, I'd like a recommendation for your replacement."

General Clifton nodded as he shook hands with both Larry and Sid. Reaching the door, he paused, turned, and saluted her crisply before leaving.

"That report will be on my desk by morning then, Larry?" the president asked, retaking her seat.

"Yes, of course."

"Thank you. There are a few other items of note. The acting governor has agreed to give us some office space in the Capitol Building. I'll move over there in the morning. You're all free to move out of this bunker whenever you like. Just so you're aware, I sent out an announcement proclaiming Denver as the temporary United States Capital."

Surprised, Ben looked up from his notes. He felt a guilty pride. He loved Denver. It was his home. So many mixed emotions circled his brain. Why had they been spared? Chris taken? Maybe after some time to grieve, he could figure it out.

Claire threw a telling glance at Ben. "It's nice to know that some things never change. Within two hours of its release, I heard from eight governors and four mayors lobbying for the permanent dedication." Everyone at the table chuckled with her. "Okay, I think that's it for the moment unless any of you have anything?" she asked, looking around the table. When no one spoke, she stood and began to shake hands with each of them.

"You owe Ashley dinner, you know?" President Young said, grasping Ben's hand.

"Yes, Madam President. I believe you're right. I owe you much more," Ben said, covering her hand with his.

Smiling broadly, she said, "I'll collect on that someday, Ben. Keep in touch. You'll always have access to me."

"Until then, be careful." He turned and headed to his room.

"You need a lift?" Ashley asked Ben as he strolled toward the elevator.

"As a matter of fact, I do, Agent Prescott."

"Ben," Larry yelled from the other end of the hall. "Hold up a minute, Ben."

Larry half ran down the hallway until he reached them.

"What is it, Larry?"

"Call this number in an hour. Someone wants to talk to you." He thrust a small piece of paper into Ben's hand.

"Who?" Ben asked, fully confused.

"Claims to be your son." Larry grinned widely as he raised both eyebrows.

Ben nearly fell to his knees. "My son? How?"

"I don't have all the details, but it seems we had a team in DC. They found him injured on the outskirts of the city just before they were extracted. I can't tell you how happy it makes me to give you good news for a change."

"Thank you, Larry." Ben wiped the tears from his eye. Ashley took his hand, squeezing it softly while Ben shook Larry's hand with his other. "Let's get out of here," he said to Ashley.

A few minutes later, Ashley and Ben sat in her car before starting the trip back outside. Wrapping a hand around the back of her neck, Ben pulled her close and kissed her hard. "Is it too soon to say I love you?"

"I was going to give you a couple more hours and then shoot you if you hadn't by then."

"What's with you always threatening to shoot me?" Ben asked, a deep belly laugh boiling up inside him. "Get me the hell out of this hole, Agent Prescott."

Outside, Ben reached over and tuned the radio to the small AM station in Deer Path. The man who escaped the compound had told Ben about it when he interviewed him last night. It was apparently where many of Boyle's crazies got their information. The reception was scratchy, but the words were clear enough.

> *"Well, the deceit continues, folks," the announcer said sarcastically. "Our new, improved government is telling us that one of the ARA members detonated the bomb in Montana. Don't you believe it. I've had several reports from people seeing a stealth bomber headed to that location just before the explosion. In addition, my sources high up in the military tell me they know it was the Air Force that dropped the New York bomb and the bomb on LA. Just another example of how they lie. They will never tell you the truth. The only good news I have for you is that we're still here to make sure you get the truth. Stay tuned.*

Ben reached over and turned the radio off. After a few minutes of quiet, Ashley asked him. "What are you thinking?"

"Just something I learned a long time ago in civics class."

"What's that?"

Ben recited in a rhythmic tone:

> "'We the People of the United States, in order to form a more perfect union, establish justice, insure domestic tranquility, provide for the common

defense, promote the general welfare, and secure the blessings of liberty to ourselves and our posterity, do ordain and establish this Constitution for the United States of America.'"